Acclaim for *Bill War...*
Last Chanc...

"[A] moving tale."   ...ople

"*Bill Warrington's Last Chance* is full of fascinating things to talk about—like the coming-of-age of a young girl juxtaposed with an old man's search for redemption, not to mention the touching but unsentimental way they grow to care for each other. . . . Perhaps one of the best things you can say about a novel is that the story lingers after you finish it. I have gone on thinking about this one without trying."   —Sue Monk Kidd, author of *The Secret Life of Bees*

"Funny and warm and touching . . . If you think there are lots more than two sides to any story, you should enjoy the expansive view of family life presented in [this] new novel."
                                       —Joe Meyers, *Connecticut Post*

"A fascinating novel of family dynamics that will resonate with readers on many levels."   —Holly Scudero, *Sacramento Book Review*

"[An] enjoyable first novel."   —*Publishers Weekly*

"*Bill Warrington's Last Chance* turns out to be quite a ride for all the characters involved—and it proves that taking a chance may not turn out exactly as you had planned, but it's darn worth a try."
                                       —Dee Ann Grand, *BookPage*

James King lives in Wilton, Connecticut, with his wife and two children. This is his first novel.

BILL WARRINGTON'S LAST CHANCE

JAMES KING

Penguin Books

PENGUIN BOOKS
Published by the Penguin Group
Penguin Group (USA) Inc., 375 Hudson Street, New York, New York 10014, U.S.A. • Penguin Group
(Canada), 90 Eglinton Avenue East, Suite 700, Toronto, Ontario, Canada M4P 2Y3 (a division of
Pearson Penguin Canada Inc.) • Penguin Books Ltd, 80 Strand, London WC2R 0RL, England • Penguin
Ireland, 25 St. Stephen's Green, Dublin 2, Ireland (a division of Penguin Books Ltd) • Penguin Books
Australia Ltd, 250 Camberwell Road, Camberwell, Victoria 3124, Australia (a division of Pearson
Australia Group Pty Ltd) • Penguin Books India Pvt Ltd, 11 Community Centre, Panchsheel Park, New
Delhi – 110 017, India • Penguin Group (NZ), 67 Apollo Drive, Rosedale, Auckland 0632, New Zealand
(a division of Pearson New Zealand Ltd) • Penguin Books (South Africa) (Pty) Ltd, 24 Sturdee Avenue,
Rosebank, Johannesburg 2196, South Africa

Penguin Books Ltd, Registered Offices:
80 Strand, London WC2R 0RL, England

First published in the United States of America by Viking Penguin,
a member of Penguin Group (USA) Inc. 2010
Published in Penguin Books 2011

3 5 7 9 10 8 6 4 2

Publisher's Note
This is a work of fiction. Names, characters, places, and incidents either are the product of the author's
imagination or are used fictitiously, and any resemblance to actual persons, living or dead, business
establishments, events, or locales is entirely coincidental.

THE LIBRARY OF CONGRESS HAS CATALOGED THE HARDCOVER EDITION AS FOLLOWS:
King, James, 1955–
Bill Warrington's last chance : a novel / James King.
p. cm.
ISBN 978-0-670-02161-1 (hc.)
ISBN 978-0-14-311944-9 (pbk.)
1. Alzheimer's disease—Fiction. 2. Grandfathers—Fiction. 3. Granddaughters—Fiction.
4. Parent and adult child—Fiction. 5. Psychological fiction. I. Title.
PS3611.I5777B55 2010
813'.6—dc22   2010004251

Printed in the United States of America
Set in Celeste with BradloSlab
Designed by Daniel Lagin

To Joanne, my inspiration,

and Katie and Daniel, my motivation

BILL WARRINGTON'S LAST CHANCE

CHAPTER ONE

Bill Warrington listened to the final huffs and pings of the engine and the crackle of the vinyl settling about him as he removed the key from the ignition and let his arms drop into his lap. He sat quietly for a few moments, staring at but not really seeing the rack of garden tools hanging on the wall in front of him. Discipline was needed, a little self-control. He leaned his head back and closed his eyes.

It had been a good decision, he thought now, to attach the garage. He had considered building a separate one, similar to the one he had played in as a boy, sneaking into his father's DeSoto coupe and grabbing on to the thick steering wheel and pretending to drive out of the musty garage and onto the broad streets, waving at the awestruck neighbors as he made his way out of Woodlake, maybe even out of Ohio altogether. He had envisioned a son, maybe a couple of them, who would spend hours, as he had, dreaming up the kind of car *they* would drive someday, the places *they* would visit.

But the drywall installer had told Bill he'd be making a mistake. His future wife would complain about having to haul in groceries from an unattached garage, especially in foul weather. "That's all they do after you marry them," he'd said. "Complain."

The guy had been wrong about Clare. And he, Bill, had been wrong about the boys. Mike never took much of an interest in cars when he was young, and Nick was convinced that the garage housed not only cars, but also boy-eating monsters.

Bill opened his eyes. He was wasting time, sitting there like that.

He got out of the car and went into the kitchen, directly to the counter drawer where he kept the address book—the same pocket-sized, vinyl-covered directory with his name embossed along the bottom in gold letters that he'd gotten some thirty or forty years ago as a holiday gift from a supplier. He fished around, wondering if he'd left it someplace else.

Bill studied the open drawer. Nothing to worry about, he told himself. This sort of thing happens all the time, no matter how old you are and no matter what any smart-ass doctor says.

He yanked the drawer out, emptied it onto the counter, and sifted through the items: a slim Woodlake telephone directory, several years old; a black umbrella cover; a sports watch with a broken band; the smiley IsoFlex ball Clare had used to take her mind off the pain; the Phillips screwdriver he'd spent an hour looking for in the garage last week; a pad of yellow notes stuck to the inside of a Tupperware lid; a Greetings from Grand Canyon key chain.

But no address book.

Bill picked up the ball, turned, and leaned against the counter. If he could remember the last time he'd had it, he knew everything would come flooding back. He squeezed the ball gently, then turned it over in his hand to smooth out the bulges. He may have done this a number of times without realizing it, for he gradually became aware of a chime. It took him a moment to recognize it as the front doorbell.

Who the hell?

Bill guessed the boy to be twelve or thirteen. He was wearing a black T-shirt and jeans, with a chain of some sort running through his belt loops and into one of his front pockets. Bill squinted. Was this kid wearing eye makeup?

"Mr. Warrington?"

The kid looked eager to get out of there, but apparently had the stones to stick around long enough to say whatever he'd come to say.

"I know you?" Bill asked.

The boy nodded. "Blaine Rogers? From down the street? My dad told me to ask you if you need help with the leaves."

Bill looked over the kid's shoulder. The trees had somehow gone bare without his noticing. The front lawn was a rumpled blanket of fading red, orange, and yellow.

"We have a blower," Blaine said. He fiddled the chain around his pencil-thin waist. "Wouldn't take long. I won't charge you or anything. My dad said you might want to take care of them in time for the pickup."

A glance at the brown piles that lined the curbs told Bill that almost all his neighbors were ready for the giant vacuum truck the city sent out to collect the leaves. The oblong mounds looked like freshly covered graves. Why hadn't he noticed them? And why hadn't he realized it was time? Raking leaves was one of the few chores he'd always loved—especially before they outlawed burning them. The boys would stand by the fire on the side of the street, waving their arms back and forth while chanting incantations they'd made up or heard in a cartoon. Later, over Clare's pot roast, mashed potatoes with thick gravy, and tall glasses of ice-cold milk, they'd argue about who the smoke had obeyed more. Clare would laugh.

"Mr. Warrington?"

"What?"

"You want me to blow your leaves, or what?"

Bill looked at him. "Your old man the one with that ridiculous yellow Hummer?"

Blaine shifted his weight.

"A Hummer. Yeah."

"There a war around here I don't know about?" Bill asked.

Now the boy appeared confused.

"Listen—tell your dad thanks for volunteering you, but I'm not crippled yet. Do I look crippled to you?"

"No, sir."

The "sir" surprised Bill. He smiled.

"All right, then. Anything else I can do for you? Like maybe lend you a real belt?"

Blaine looked down, then back up at Bill. He offered a half smile before turning and walking across the front lawn. Bill was tempted to call out to him that front walks were made for a reason, but he stopped when he noticed that his was almost completely covered by leaves.

Bill closed the door and turned back toward the kitchen, hesitating for a moment before remembering what he'd been looking for. He then decided to check the dining room. Last time she was here, Marcy had been in there, cleaning—

Marcy! Of course!

He walked back into the kitchen and to the wall phone that she had brought him last year. She'd made a big deal out of the speed-dialing feature, pointing to the column of black buttons and reading what she'd written on the tiny white directory next to them, as if he couldn't read the names of his own children. The only other entry was 911.

"You apparently don't know this, Billy Boy," Marcy had said, "but you can actually place calls and not just receive them. So, every now and then, pick up the goddamn thing and punch one of these buttons. That's how we'll know it's not time to collect our inheritance."

Bill smiled at the memory. His daughter was a smart-ass, for sure, with the mouth of a drill sergeant, but she always could make him laugh. And she was the most likely of the three to help him. She might even come over and clean the place up. It'd been a while. He never asked, but she always ended up doing some housework during her visits. A female thing, he supposed.

He tilted his head back, straining to read the names next to the buttons. Why in the hell hadn't she written them bigger? He gave up and punched the third one from the top, assuming they were set up according to birth order. First there'd be Mike, then Nick, then Marcy.

The call was answered on the fourth ring, but the voice was deep and low. That sour feeling flared up. "Who's this?" he demanded.

"Dad?"

A geyser made it halfway up Bill's throat. This jackass had refused to call him Dad when he was married to Marcy, so why now? And what was he doing at Marcy's anyway?

"I thought you were long gone, you shiftless—"

"Dad!"

Wait: that voice. *Damn!* He was talking to one of his sons. But which one?

"Guess you dialed the wrong number."

It was Mike. Wouldn't have been his first choice, or even his second, now that he realized this call was long distance, but there you go.

"Marcy got me this new phone," Bill said. "Programmed all these damned buttons. I guess dialing is too much work these days."

Mike didn't laugh. He seemed to be waiting for Bill to continue.

But Bill found that he couldn't think of a thing to say, or to explain why he had even picked up the phone in the first place.

"Well, I'll let you call whoever you meant to call."

"Wait!" Bill heard himself saying, although he'd be damned if he could imagine what for. "What's the big hurry?"

"No hurry."

"Everything okay there?" Bill asked, and then shook his head the way he used to when Clare was listening and he knew he'd just said something stupid—usually to one of his bosses.

"Look, Dad," Mike said, and now Bill heard the impatience. "You obviously didn't mean to call me. So why don't we just—?"

"Oh, come on. Don't tell me I've hurt your *feelings.*"

Bill bit his lip. This was not the way you wanted a conversation to go with someone you haven't talked to since . . . when?

"Well, that didn't take long, did it?" Mike sounded relieved—triumphant, even.

"I want to ask you something," Bill said, trying another tack, but the silence that followed scattered his thoughts, like the leaves that rose up and flitted about in the wake of the neighbor kid's shuffle across his front yard.

"Okay," Mike said after another annoying pause, as if he had made a momentous decision regarding the value of responding at all. "Ask away."

Why was this so difficult? When Bill decided to call Marcy, he didn't bother thinking about what he would say; he could just tell her he wanted to see her and she'd be over in no time, her face lined with concern and a pail filled with bottles of Ajax and Windex at her side. He'd be able to make his request then. But he couldn't make that same request, in the same way, now. Not with Mike. Especially not with Mike.

"They close the roads out there in Chicago? Shut down the airport?"

"Huh?"

"A man should know his grandkids."

Mike exhaled. Bill wondered when he had become so deliberate. Growing up, Mike had had a hair-trigger temper that convinced Clare of an "imbalance" of some sort. She'd wanted him to see a shrink.

Bill assured her that Mike would grow out of it. And he had. But he'd gone from a hot poker to an ice cube. He was so careful about what he said. It was like talking to a goddamned politician.

"From what I understand," he said slowly, "you hardly know the one who lives in your backyard, practically."

"What are you talking about?" Bill heard his voice rising, helpless to stop it. "Who?"

"I rest my case," Mike said. "Dad, you can see your grandchildren whenever you want, but you're going to have to come here. And before you do, you'd better check their schedules. Those grandkids you suddenly want to see so badly are in high school now. Your grandson is probably taller than you. Captain of the lacrosse team."

"I know that," Bill said, the back of his neck suddenly itchy. He managed to resist asking what the hell lacrosse was. "I know that."

"Fine." It was the calling-your-bluff tone Bill himself had long ago mastered. "When do you want to come?"

"Actually, I was thinking we could *all* get together. Here at home. The four of us. You know, you, me, Mike—I mean, you, me, Nick, and Marcy."

"So you don't want to see the grandchildren, after all."

"Of course I want to see them." Bill swallowed hard to stop himself from yelling. He didn't succeed. "But I want to see my own kids, too, goddamn it. Why do you always have to twist my words around?"

"I gotta pack for a trip, Dad, so I'll just cut to the chase, if you don't mind."

Bill minded but kept his mouth shut. *For once,* Clare might have said.

"Home for me and my family is Schaumburg, not Woodlake. If you want to see Clare or Tyler or Colleen—that's my wife, in case you've forgotten—you're going to have to make the effort to come here. We're not going to Ohio."

Bill thought he might lose his balance trying to figure out how to straighten the words and logic his oldest son was twisting into incomprehensibility.

"Don't beat around the bush, do you?" Bill said.

"At the feet of the master, as they say. You sure everything's okay?"

"Of course everything's okay. I told you that already."

"All right, then. Call if and when you book a flight."

The line went dead.

Bill made an effort not to slam the receiver back into its cradle. What had he said that was so awful? That he wanted to see his sons and daughter? What had he *ever* done to deserve that kind of crap? He picked up the phone again. He had to stay focused. Marcy could help. He needed to call her. Get back on track, back on the horse.

He stared at the speed-dial panel.

Which button had he just pushed?

CHAPTER TWO

April focused on her lyrics so she wouldn't have to look at her mother's tongue, the tip of which was sticking out of the corner of her mouth as she switched gears and checked her mirrors a few thousand times. Parking a car, apparently, required superhuman focus and attention. April was pretty sure she could do a better job of it, and she was a year away from her first driving lesson. Maybe her mother was just whacked about the visit she obviously, for some reason, didn't want to make alone.

Whatever. That tongue was embarrassing. And gross.

April cranked up her iPod, closed her notepad, and looked at her grandfather's house. It had been a while since she'd been here—six months? more?—and it looked a little tired. Leaves covered half the roof and were spilling out of the gutters. Part of a downspout had broken away from its bracket and pulled away from the house like it was trying to escape.

April could relate.

She'd been able to get out of the last several visits by lying about homework or cramps or something, but this time her mother had insisted.

"He's never asked me to come over before," her mother said. "I think he's lonely. And I'm sure he'd love to see his granddaughter."

Never did before, April wanted to say. On the other visits, she usually just watched TV while her mother cleaned and talked the old guy's ear off in the kitchen. In fact, now that she thought about it, April didn't think her grandfather had ever been especially interested, one way or the other, in seeing anyone—even his own daughter.

She felt a sharp jab on her thigh.

"Jesus!" April yanked the white earbuds out of her ears and glared at her mother. "What was that for?"

"Don't 'Jesus' me. I'm trying to ask you a question. And if you couldn't hear me, you've got that damned thing cranked up too high. You want to be wearing hearing aids when you're thirty?"

"I hope I'm not alive when I'm that old," April said. She continued to rub her leg. "What did you do that for, anyway?"

"I don't want to scrape the tires. Am I getting too close?"

April exhaled and shifted in her seat, slowly, to take a look. "No," she said.

Her mother put the car in park and the two of them got out. April put her notebook in her pocket and waited. Sometimes it took longer to actually get out of the car than to park it.

"Hey!" Her mother was pointing to the space between the car and curb. "It's at least a foot and a half away."

April shrugged. "You asked if you were too close," she said slowly, happily selecting the condescending tone that she knew drove the woman bonkers. "I said you weren't. And you aren't."

Her mother climbed back into the car, slammed the door behind her as if it were April's fault her parking skills sucked, and made a few dozen more attempts to get closer to the curb. April almost burst out laughing at the back-and-forth lurching of the car and the frequent, not-so-muffled cussing emanating from within.

"You want some clown to come along and scrape it?" her mother demanded as she emerged from the car, pushing back her hair and, in so doing, revealing a most unattractive moon of underarm perspiration.

"Our thirdhand Camry?" April said, looking away. "How tragic would *that* be."

"Secondhand, barely, and I need that car for my clients, Miss Wisebutt. That car helps put bread on our table."

April stuffed her iPod into the front pocket of her jeans, looking down for a covert roll of the eyes.

"And don't forget," her mother said in the suddenly lighter tone that April recognized as the to-keep-the-peace-I'm-going-to-ignore-that-one voice, "you'll be driving that thirdhand Camry in a year."

April shrugged. "Then I hope someone totals it. Maybe we'll get a car built in this century." She put the earbuds in her other pocket, with the notebook. "Can we just get this over with? Grandpa's watching us from the window. It's creeping me out."

April couldn't actually tell if her grandfather was looking at them or just staring off into the distance. He was framed in the middle of the pane, dressed in a red and green flannel shirt and jeans. He looked shorter and a little skinnier than she remembered. Maybe it had been longer than six months since she'd seen him. She had always thought of him, whenever she thought of him, which was pretty much next to never, as being bigger and gruffer-looking. From here, he just looked old.

Her mother waved, but her grandfather didn't respond. Her mother waved again.

"Wouldn't it be easier to just go ring the doorbell like normal people?" April asked. "We're standing here waving at him like a couple of dorks."

As they made their way to the front door, April noticed other things about the house that you couldn't see from the street. More of the gutter at the front of the house hung away from the roofline, and patches of peeling paint were visible around the front picture window and door.

"You didn't tell me Grandpa's gone ghetto," April said.

She saw that her mother was looking at the gutter. "You probably won't believe this, but this place was once immaculate. Did I ever tell you that your grandfather actually built this house for your grandmother?"

"Right after he got back from Korea and then proposed to Grandma Clare in the front yard the day he finished it and Grandma Clare said no at first as a joke? No, Mom, you never told me."

"It's starting to look like what we'd call a fixer-upper."

The "we," April knew, had to mean Hank Johnson, her mother's creepy new boss at the realty office. An unpleasant memory of Hank's hearty hi-how-are-ya handshake and let-me-sell-you-something smile when he picked her mother up for an open house made April cringe. How could her mother not see that Hank was a complete phony and most likely a letch?

Since Hank was on the brain, April thought at first that the voice calling out to her and her mother now was somehow his. But it was her grandfather's. He was holding the front door open.

"Don't own the stock, you know. Move it or lose it."

He closed the door and walked away.

"That was random," April said. They started up the front steps, which were covered, like the front walk, in leaves. "What's he talking about?"

"Stock in the electric company," her mother answered. "He always said it when one of your uncles left a door open or if it took us more than half a second to get something out of the refrigerator. Been a while since I've heard that one."

Her mother pushed the front door open.

"Hey, Billy Boy," she called out, "you'd better clear those leaves off the walk or someone's going to trip and sue your bony little—"

She stopped so suddenly that April bumped into her. Newspapers were strewn all over the floor, the couch, the piano bench, on top of the television—everywhere, it seemed, except on the faded brown recliner in front of the television. April saw that her grandfather had returned to the spot by the front window. The newspapers under his heavy work boots crinkled as he turned.

"What?" he asked.

Her mother was looking at the mess, and then at the old man, and then back again. April figured she'd better do something before her mother got whiplash. She stepped up next to her mother and gave her grandfather a small wave.

"Hi, Grandpa."

Her grandfather stared at her.

Excuse me for being polite, April thought.

"Hi, April. Hi, Marcy," her mother said, a statue no more. "How nice of you two to come so soon after I called."

He broke his death-ray stare on April and turned to his daughter. There was a trace of the start of a small smile. "Still the smart-ass, I see," he said.

Her mother put her hands on her hips. "Falling behind on your housework?"

April's grandfather looked around as if he didn't see anything out of place in covering your living room with yellowing newspaper. She was dying to break the silence with a nice long *Okaaaaay.*

"Let me put some coffee on," her mother said, finally. "Then we can talk." She walked toward the kitchen without another look.

April realized she had never seen the two of them hug or kiss. Her grandfather, meanwhile, refocused his death-ray gaze on her. Was he trying to freak her out? She noticed black and gray hairs sticking out of his ears.

"How have you been, Grandpa?"

He kept up the eye-lock for another moment.

"Haven't seen you in a while," he said.

Looks like you haven't seen anyone in a while. Or a razor and comb, for that matter.

"Yeah, well," April said.

"Startin' to develop, I see."

April felt the blush rush up from her neck to her face. What was she supposed to say to *that*?

"You look just like she did at your age," he said.

April frowned. "You mean, my mom?"

"Who do you think I mean? Jayne Mansfield?"

"Who's Jayne Mansfield?"

Her grandfather cocked his head. "You're kidding me."

They both jumped when they heard the shout, but April was the first to rush through the dining room to the kitchen, where her mother stood in the doorway. A sharp rustle of newspapers and footsteps followed behind, and a moment later April heard—and felt, thank you very much—the wheezy breathing of her grandfather on the back of her neck.

"Jesus," April said as she looked over her mother's shoulder.

Dirty dishes filled the sink and lined the adjacent counter space. The cupboards were open and empty, save for a mug and a couple of plates. One of the drawers was upside down on top of another counter, the contents scattered beneath and around it. On the small kitchen table was a teetering mountain of aluminum TV-dinner trays reaching halfway to the ceiling, encrusted with the dried remains of whatever entrée each had held.

Her mother turned. "What in holy hell is going on here?"

April's grandfather sidled past them to the counter.

"I was looking for something," he said. He angled the drawer back into its groove. "Haven't had a chance to put everything back." He swept some of the stuff on the counter back into the drawer.

"I'm not talking about that." Her mother's voice was rising in that way April knew could lead, if left unchecked, to wall-shaking decibels. "At least that mess doesn't attract flies!" She pointed at the stack of TV-dinner trays. "*That* goddamned mess does!"

"Mom," April said quietly, warning.

"You're going to attract mice. Rats, even! How can you live like this?"

Her grandfather continued putting the items back in the drawer. "Just haven't gotten to it yet," he said. "Don't worry. I'll take care of it." He closed the drawer and turned. "That and the leaves. No sweat. I can handle it."

He winked, then started toward the sink.

For the record-setting second time in a single day, her mother seemed uncertain of what to say or do. She stared at his back as he turned on the faucet. But then she rallied. "Hold on, old man." She turned to April. "You go straighten up the living room. Put the papers in piles. I'll start on the dishes."

April nodded but didn't move. She fought the temptation to click her heels and yell, *Jawohl, Herr Kommandant!*

Her mother shut off the water and pointed at her grandfather. "You—get a big garbage bag and start clearing the table of those disgusting trays. When this place is halfway cleaned up, you can tell me why you wanted to have a little chat."

"You mean those black garbage bags, like for trash cans?" he asked.

"Yeah, those." April was embarrassed by the way her mother stuck her butt out as she hunched over to open the cabinet, stretching her pants for the world to see every line of her mom-style underwear.

"Don't think I have any," her grandfather said.

"What a surprise. Where do you keep your cleanser?"

"Should be there."

Her mother shook her head. "Where else might you keep it? And some plastic gloves?"

"You usually have that stuff in your car, don't you?"

"Why would I? Clients would think I'm a cleaning woman."

"What clients?"

Her mother straightened and turned. "I told you. I'm a real estate agent now. Don't you remember?"

"Of course I remember," he said, after a moment. "I just thought you might have—"

"You old bastard."

"What?"

"So that's the reason you called? The important reason you wanted to see me? You need someone to do your goddamn housework!"

Her father put his hand up. "Hold on, Marcy. Not true."

"I've told you several times I've been studying for my real estate exam and I might not be able to make it over as often. Not that you ever seemed to care one way or the other. But now you do, apparently, now that the house is so filthy you can't take it anymore." Her mother pushed one of the chairs up against the table, nearly upsetting the tray tower. "This is unbelievable. Even for you."

"I just wanted to talk with you, Marcy." His voice sounded suddenly strained, almost feeble. "That's all. I have a favor to ask. And it isn't this." He waved his arm to indicate the dirty dishes, the TV-dinner trays, the house. "Please."

"No more bull," Marcy said to her father. "Every other time I come here I end up cleaning, so I know you were hoping I'd do exactly that today. Deny it and I'm out of here."

He raised both hands this time, surrendering, and with that her mother faced the sink and began to fill one of the filthy pots with hot water. Without turning, she called out, "April, isn't there something you need to do?"

Now April did click her heels, but since she was wearing sneakers, there was no sound.

She went to the living room and began picking up the newspapers, starting with a pile near the small brick fireplace. All the papers were the *Ledger,* as if there were any news to report from Woodlake. After she had created four neat stacks, she stopped to check out the row of photographs on the fireplace mantel. Three of them were high school graduation pictures of her uncle Nick, her uncle Mike, and her mother, all of them sporting the Big Hair look. Jesus, what were they thinking?

The rest of the pictures were of Grandma Clare. Most of them were informal: one standing beside a Christmas tree; another with Grandpa at a restaurant. The next one was one that April knew well. Her mother had a copy of it on a bookshelf in their living room. Grandma Clare was standing outside the front door of the house, teenaged Nick and Mike on either side, with her arms draped around her daughter's shoulder, pulling her close. April guessed her mother was about ten years old at the time. She'd never really paid attention to it before, but now April recognized in the picture the familiar shape of her mother's smile. It'd been a while since she'd seen that smile so wide and—April searched for the word—*free?*

Another picture was one she was sure she'd never seen before: her grandmother in a more formal, studio-style pose. April was struck at how young she looked. In all the photographs she'd ever seen—in her mother's photo album, on the mantel here at her grandfather's house—Grandma Clare looked, well, grandmotherly. Not here.

She picked the picture up by its frame to examine it more closely. Black dress—or maybe not, since it was a black-and-white picture— and a simple, single string of pearls. Pretty, shoulder-length hair. Could have been a model. Or the subject of a song. She pulled her notepad out of her pocket, sat in her grandfather's chair, and started writing.

Betcha didn't think
When you had your picture took

Someday you'd be a grandma
Married to a . . . kook?

She returned to the mantel to look at the picture again. Like the others, it was covered by a thin layer of dust. But unlike the others, this one had a large thumbprint in the lower corners of the frame. Her grandfather's, she realized. She imagined him standing by the fireplace, holding the picture in his hand, staring at it for a while before replacing it, as April did now.

She'd have to find a word to replace "kook," she decided.

The only papers left were strewn around the easy chair, so April started gathering those up. As she did, she uncovered a huge over-flowing ashtray on the floor and a pipe next to it. April picked up the pipe. It was old-fashioned, one you might see a dad on Nick at Nite smoking at the dinner table, dispensing wisdom to his attentive and appreciative children. April picked up the ashtray and pipe and took them to the kitchen, where her grandfather was now sitting at the table.

"Not a good idea to keep a pipe and ashtray under newspapers, Grandpa. Might start a fire."

He looked at her for a long second. "You must be in those ad-vanced classes."

"Since when did you start smoking a pipe?" her mother asked without so much as a glance at them. Her grandfather took the pipe from April and turned it over in his hand. April thought he looked younger now.

"Used to smoke it before you kids came along," he said. "Your mother made me stop, though, when Mike was born. She was way ahead of all these secondhand-smoke crackpots today. I used to enjoy it, so I thought I'd take it up again."

"You used to enjoy drinking, too, but that doesn't mean it's a good idea to take it up again."

"I haven't had a drop in—"

"I'm only saying about bad habits."

He snorted. "Bad habits? Hell, wish I'd had more. Give me more stuff to think about, since my kids don't seem to want to visit."

Her mother turned off the water and turned to face him. "You're kidding, right? About not having enough bad habits? And do you really want me to tell you why your children—your other children, at least—don't visit?"

He stared out the window. April was beginning to wonder if his sudden silent staring poses were some sort of defense posture, like what those ugly possums do on the nature channel.

"I didn't think so." Marcy turned back to her scrubbing.

"I don't think I've seen anyone smoke a pipe except in old movies," April said. "I thought that kind of went out, like . . . in the Stone Age?"

There was that twinkle again. "Funny you should say that. Because pipes were pretty popular not all that long ago. Like when your mom was your age."

Marcy shut off the water. "That's enough," she said.

April's eyes went wide. "Are you saying—?"

"April, go finish cleaning up," Marcy said.

"Why?"

"Go finish," her mother repeated.

"I *am* finished. Nice, neat piles, as you commanded."

"Then take them out to the garage. I want to talk to your grandfather."

April stomped back into the living room, picked up one of the stacks she'd formed, and started toward the garage door. To get there, she had to cross through the kitchen. Her mother had joined her grandfather at the table. Her grandfather had lit his pipe. Her mother seemed about to say something, waiting until April went through the door.

It wasn't until after she'd dropped the newspapers by the trash cans that she noticed the car. It wasn't quite as boring as a Camry, but it wasn't exactly what you'd call a sports car, either. It might have been cool a long time ago. But now it was just, like her grandfather, old.

"Quite a ride you've got there, Grandpa," she said when she went back into the kitchen.

Her grandfather, his head in a swirl of smoke from the pipe, looked at her quizzically.

"Your car. Might be the only one in existence more ancient than ours."

Her grandfather nodded.

"That, young lady, is a 1982 Chevy Impala SS," he said. "Best car I've ever had, and still has a lot of life in her." He patted his pants pocket and looked at April. "Want to take her for a spin?"

"No," her mother said immediately. "God almighty, old man. She's only fourteen."

Her father swatted at his pockets again, apparently looking for his keys. "All right, then, just up and down the drive."

"No!"

April looked at her grandfather looking at her mother.

"Why not?" he asked. "I used to let you do it. If memory serves, you were thirteen."

April smiled triumphantly, until a glance at Fun-Sucker Supreme told her that it wasn't going to happen.

"Go watch TV while your grandfather and I talk," her mother said.

"Come on, Mom."

"Go!"

"*Sieg Heil,*" April muttered.

But she did as she was told.

CHAPTER THREE

Marcy Warrington Shea tried to concentrate on the road, but she kept thinking about Hummels.

She supposed it was because they were her mother's and as old as any memory she could call up that she'd never thought of the tiny figures as tacky—in other homes, sure, but not there, not in that dining room, and not on that particular hutch. During most of her visits to her father, she eventually found herself picking up and replacing the boys and girls in lederhosen holding hands, waving hello or good-bye, or playing with the tiny brown dog. Doing so still gave her a feeling she couldn't name, even after all these years. She would have done the same earlier if she hadn't been in a state of shock at the septic shambles that had once been her home.

She was glad Hank hadn't been there. How would he have reacted? Would his opinion of her change, as if she were somehow responsible for her father's living conditions? No, Hank wouldn't have gone there. Instead, he would have encouraged her to think opportunity, to search for that diamond in the rough, to make lemonade from lemons. Marcy smiled. Hank was a walking gold mine of selling clichés and strategies. He'd probably suggest she make a features/benefits list, which is exactly what she'd found herself doing as she touched the figurines. Nice yard, good neighborhood, excellent location. The house was in desperate need of repair, but of course she wouldn't actually say that. She'd say it was waiting for some tender loving care, a great opportunity to give it one's own personal touch, make it a home of one's own.

A good realtor needs an objective eye, Marcy reminded herself. So she decided that if there were to be an open house, the Hummels would have to go.

She punched the horn when it became clear the driver in front of her was oblivious to the fact that the light had changed. April, scribbling away in her notebook with her earbuds firmly in place, looked up. Marcy considered an apologetic wave to set a good example, but then the driver ahead accelerated slowly, extended his arm out the window, and offered Marcy his middle finger. April didn't even attempt to suppress her laugh.

You have to pick your battles, her brother Nick liked to say, as if that were some sort of one-stop solution to every new problem that cropped up—like her daughter's increasingly frequent threats to run away from their crappy little house and its "gestapo bitch" to find her father. Marcy could deal with the insults and name-calling, but the thought of April running away from home terrified her. And the idea that April wanted to have anything to do with the man who had abandoned her, abandoned *them,* always enraged her. How did that bastard get canonized in her daughter's eyes ahead of the person busting ass to give her a normal life?

Marcy wondered if she'd been so incredibly disdainful at that age herself. Definitely not. By the time she was fourteen, her own mother had been dead for two years and her father—well, no one would have argued her right to give *him* a little lip now and then.

Another red light, another lagger. This time, a tiny woman in a huge SUV, gabbing away on her cell. Marcy resisted the urge to honk, feeling her daughter's watchful eye despite the feigned indifference. As she accelerated, she assured herself that April would just have to deal with the kind of parent who didn't go along with the idea of a fourteen-year-old girl who'd never driven before driving her grandfather's car up and down his driveway.

It wasn't easy to hold her ground, especially with someone as pigheaded as April, but she could handle it.

She grimaced when she thought of those words. They were the same ones her father had used a little while ago, when he was putting the stuff back in the kitchen drawer. With his back turned, slightly hunched over, he'd looked like a kid being forced to put his socks away. *Just haven't gotten to it yet. Don't worry. I'll take care of it. That and the leaves. I can handle it.*

And then that goddamned wink. It sent Marcy back some thirty years, lurking behind the kitchen door on her hands and knees, preparing to surprise her daddy, who had just gotten home from work. But something in the tone of his voice—and her mother's—had stopped her. She'd tried to listen, but they were keeping their voices low. She peered through the crack in the door and saw her father, leaning against the counter the way he had earlier today. He looked very tired. "Why did you have to say that?" she heard her mother ask.

"The guy was a jerk. Wasn't happy ordering everyone around—he had to insult them, too. I only said what everyone else wanted to say. Lucky I didn't deck him."

"But how will we manage, Bill?"

"Don't worry," her father had said, moving away from the counter and straightening up as he faced his wife. "There's always a sales job out there for someone with brains and some get-up-and-go. I can handle it."

Marcy made a left on Grandview—a little too sharply, apparently, because April shot her a dirty look before quickly turning away to avoid further eye contact.

"A smile would come in handy right about now," Marcy said, but April didn't respond. The only sounds in the car now were the tinny, rhythmic noises that were busily ensuring that her daughter would one day be deaf to her for good.

Gotta pick your battles.

When they got home, April made a beeline for her room. Marcy threw her keys on the kitchen table and plopped onto one of the chairs. She was debating whether to cook something, order a pizza, or suggest to April that they go to the diner when the phone rang.

"Hello, beautiful."

It was corny, but Marcy was grateful. "Hello, Hank."

"You sound tired. Feel like talking about it? Say, over some nice veal marsala and a bottle of red?"

"Actually, I think the talk I need to have tonight is with my daughter."

"Ah, the joy of the teen years. Say no more," Hank said. "Rain check?"

Marcy smiled. "Rain check."

She hung up and thought of the woman who had "warned" her about Hank. It was during Marcy's first office meeting with all the associates. Hank was making a presentation on the importance of always "talking benefits" when describing the features of a house. Marcy listened carefully. After all, the man drove a Lexus and mentioned, none too subtly, that he lived in a 3,600-square-foot condo at the marina. "Hankering Hank," he called himself, attributing his success to a never-ending hankering for sales. The woman sitting next to her—Marcy couldn't remember her name—who'd leave the agency just a day or two later, leaned over and whispered that Hank's biggest hankering was for other realtors. *Female* realtors. Marcy was startled to see Hank, at that moment, wink at her. Her immediate inclination was to flip him off. But this job was too good an opportunity to piss off a heavy hitter—at least right off the bat. Besides, maybe he hadn't winked at her. Maybe it was a wink at the audience, a little public-speaking technique to show how comfortable he was in front of groups. She forced herself to listen to his message: Think buyer perspective. Think sales. Think commissions.

She did so now, even though she felt guilty about it. But what was the point of ignoring the inevitable? She guessed that she could get her father a 150K, maybe 200K for his house. With a 2.5 percent commission, that would mean . . . Oh, hell, she'd figure it out later. The more immediate challenge would be to convince him to move into an assisted-living facility before it was too late and the only option would be a nursing home. His mind was still sharp, but he was obviously losing the ability to take care of the place. Assisted-living feature: no lawn. Benefit: no worries about mowing and raking and shoveling. Feature: smaller living area. Benefit: less to keep clean. Feature: communal dining room. Benefit: healthy eating, no TV-dinner crap.

Sad, she thought. He used to yell at me if I didn't hang up my jacket within thirty seconds of walking in the house. And god forbid it should fall off the hanger and onto the closet floor.

Marcy got up and opened the refrigerator. Something smelled, but a quick check of the meat drawer—chicken cutlets thawing for the dinner that she now couldn't muster the energy to cook—revealed that the source was somewhere else. She closed the fridge and checked the garbage, which she should have known would be the culprit. Emptying the trash was about the only thing she asked April to do every day—and every day, it seemed, she needed reminding. Marcy considered calling up to her to come and empty it, but the thought of even the smallest argument threatened to drain her completely. She pulled the garbage bag out of the wastebasket, tied it, and put a new liner in the trash can.

Feeling the heat from the still-warm Camry engine as she squeezed her way to the trash cans in the garage, she tried to see the car through April's eyes. Was it really that awful, that uncool? Tough. When she was April's age, she wouldn't have dreamed about being so picky about what she drove—or was going to drive. Good thing, too, since she ended up behind the wheel of the family's Dodge station wagon throughout her teen years. April, of course, wasn't interested in hearing about that. She wasn't interested in hearing much of anything that didn't have to do with her.

Back in the kitchen, clearing and setting the table was not an appealing thought. She'd been balancing the checkbook earlier, and bills and receipts were spread across its surface. She'd also been reviewing some listings and collating materials for an upcoming open house. Sprinkled in the mess were a dozen or so grocery coupons she had clipped that morning.

Ironic, Marcy thought. Less than an hour earlier, she'd been sitting at a table with a different kind of mess. And *she's* the one expected to clean it up. Why was *she* the one the old man called? It seemed that during her visits, if and when he'd decide to string more than a sentence or two together and actually converse, it was always Mike this or Nick that.

But it was always she who ended up tending to him, as she did tonight, listening to his harebrained request for a family reunion, blinking away the smoke in her eyes, ignoring his cranky insults and her own daughter's Nazi cracks.

Her illustrious older brothers? Nowhere.

Marcy looked out the window. All that was needed to complete this happy moment, she thought, flipping through the mail she'd brought in that morning, was another missing child support payment from the man April so adored.

Which reminded her. She checked her pocketbook to see if she had enough cash for dinner out.

CHAPTER FOUR

April pressed the lock button on her bedroom door as gently as she could, hoping the telltale click wouldn't echo in the hallway like a cannon and alert her mother to come running up the stairs and start pounding on the door, asking why this door was locked and saying, *We don't lock doors in this house* and *People who don't have anything to hide don't lock their doors* and *What are you doing in there, young lady?* and on and on. And on. Living in this house meant having your every move monitored, like on reality TV—only instead of a bunch of cute guys, there was only her mother.

She opened her laptop and keyed in her password to access her list files, which she kept in her algebra folder in case unwelcome visitors—such as her math-averse mother—nosed around. April used to think there was such a thing as privacy, certain rules you just didn't violate. But then one day she came home from school and found her mother waiting for her in the family room, holding a joint in one hand and, in the other, the sock she'd found the joint in. How lame was that? Not just snooping in a sock drawer, but actually examining each pair. Lame *and* creepy.

April began reviewing her lists. TITS (Things I Think Suck) included such things as cramps, zits, and boys who lie their asses off and still have girls chasing after them. All the items here had first put in time on PU (Patently Unfair), which at the moment included the fact that boys could pee whenever they had to no matter where they were, the age requirement for driving, paying premium dollar for crappy weed, and ridiculously early curfews. She also maintained a SOO (So Obviously Orgasmic) list of her favorite musicians, songs, and television shows, as well as SOIL (Signs Of Intelligent Life), currently empty.

The file she worked on the most, the one she clicked now, was PITS (People I Think Suck). Time for some hard-core prioritizing: Heather Rosen needed to be added.

Heather had been texting her all afternoon, begging her to call. It was so obvious that the only reason Heather wanted to talk was to tell lies about the party last night and the probably no more than seven seconds she spent within a hundred feet of Keith Spinelli. The messages had started coming in when April was tying up the newspapers at her grandfather's. *Call me. KS is 2 hot. Wher r u? U won't bleve.* Heather's texting was so pathetically full of it since Keith Spinelli, April was sure, wouldn't have anything to do with Heather Rosen, much less actually *do* anything with her. No way.

So April had some choices to make. First, how high on the PITS list should she put Heather? Definitely in the top five, given that Heather knew, she *had* to know—despite the fact that April never actually said anything—that April kind of liked Keith Spinelli. That alone should justify the highest ranking. But putting Heather in the top spot was not a decision to be taken lightly, especially since the current titleholder—April's mother—had been number one for sixteen straight weeks.

April double-clicked on the Word icon and created a two-column table. At the top of the left column, she typed in her mom's name; in the right, Heather's. Her father had once told her, when she was try-ing to make up her mind about something—it was so long ago she had forgotten exactly what—to do a pros and cons list. The column with the most entries would win, although April soon discovered that sometimes one item in a column could easily outweigh all the entries in the other. Still, she felt duty-bound to justify any action she might take on this high a PITS ranking. She started on the left column. Beneath her mother's name she wrote:

- Nags the crap out of me. Constantly.
- Calls my clothes slutty. Sometimes.
- Won't let me practice driving. Ever.
- Checks with other moms for sleepovers. Always. And always embarrassing.
- Wears clothes that emphasize her lard-butt. Often.
- Suddenly starts crying but won't talk about it. Ever.
- Acts like talking to a guy will impregnate me. First time.
- Doesn't think I do enough homework even though I get straight A's. Always.
- Trashes Dad constantly but denies doing so. Always.

April stopped typing. There was no point in continuing, as there was no way that Heather—no matter how many obnoxious lies she told—could unseat her mother.

An instant-message bubble popped up on her screen. Heather, of course: *R U there?!?!?!*

April checked to see if anyone else, like Keith, was online. Of course he wasn't—anyone with half a life was out doing something interesting. Heather, case in point, obviously had nothing better to do than lie about her pitiful sex life. And thanks to her mom's insistence on visiting her grandfather for the first time in several centuries, April didn't have anything interesting going on, either.

April flopped on her bed and lay there, hands behind her head, staring at the ceiling and at her Don't Care poster—another sore subject with her mom, who wanted it taken down. She was constantly threatening to take it down herself, saying it was "inappropriate" to be lying in bed and staring up at a guy—"especially *that* creepy-looking guy." But as usual, her mother was totally clueless. April wasn't interested in Ian Max, the skinny cokehead with the trying-too-hard body art and piercings and the totally obvious and gross way he played the guitar between his legs. She concentrated on Roxie Reece, DC's lead singer and current holder of the number one position on her SOO list.

Her mom said that Roxie's name made her sound like a pole dancer. April didn't care. She loved the way Roxie sang without looking at Ian. Some groups make a big deal out of looking at each other and screaming in each others' faces while they play and sing. *Look, everybody! We rock gods are having all kinds of fun up here while you peons down there worship us.* That wasn't Roxie's style. From the expression on her face, it's obvious she is just into the music, into her song, and she doesn't give a crap about the audience or how she looks or even about the no-talent guitar player standing next to her.

April learned from an MTV special that Roxie came from a broken home in California, hung around some part of San Francisco called North Beach, and basically pestered the local bands to let her sing. Somehow, she hooked up with Ian Max and they got the group going. There was talk about Roxie and Ian, but April knew that Roxie couldn't care less about that dickhead. Roxie, not Ian, had written their best song. Roxie was the one, according to *Rolling Stone,* who handled the money and bailed Ian out of jail whenever he trashed a hotel room or got caught with some sixteen-year-old. What did Roxie need Ian for? She didn't. It was the one thing April didn't understand about her. Why didn't Roxie dump the loser?

April jumped at the sudden turn of the doorknob, which was followed by an impatient knock and her mother's fingers-on-chalkboard voice.

"April, why is this door locked?"

"Because I'm dropping acid."

"That's not funny. Open up."

"I'm changing!" April yelled from the bed, not moving. "God!"

"What are you changing for?" Her mother's voice was only slightly muffled by the door. April thought of a new song title: "Door Voices." No, people would think it was some sort of Jim Morrison cover. "Doors and Voices." Better. "Voices through Doors." Yeah.

"Where are you going? You didn't tell me you were going out. And who said you *could* go out?"

"I'm not going out, so don't worry about me having any fun," April said. She bit her lip. Her answer had been totally reflexive—a habit of saying the first thing that contradicted whatever her mother had just said. Even though this time it was the truth—she wasn't going out—she didn't want her mom to know that. She had been thinking about calling Megan or Erica, but they'd probably all immediately ask where Heather was, and she didn't feel like making something up. So what she had just told her mom was, sadly, true. The best April could hope for was that her mother would go shopping or to the grocery store alone so that she, April, could have some time to herself, maybe crank up DC full blast, fill the house with sound.

"Then why are you changing?"

April had forgotten her mother was there.

"Because the clothes I wore to Grandpa's are gross," she yelled. *Fast thinking, eh, Rox?* "I can still smell the smoke from his pipe."

"Ugh, I know what you mean," her mother said. "I have no idea why he's taken that up. It makes absolutely no sense."

April went on high alert at the sudden, friendly change of tone.

"You want to go to the diner for dinner?"

There it was: the ultimate trap—stuck in a diner with your mother on a Saturday night. It would be like putting a sign over the booth: "Loser with No Friends Having Dinner with Mommy. Feel Free to Ridicule."

"No, thanks," she called out. "I want to get a head start on my English paper."

April held her breath. What would come next? The disbelieving *On a Saturday night?* The commanding *You'll have plenty of time afterward?* Or the pouty and sarcastic and guilt-trippy *I've had a really rough day and wanted to go out but I guess I'll cook dinner so that you aren't in any way inconvenienced?*

"Okay. Then I guess I'll start dinner." April heard her mother start to walk away. "And unlock this door."

April looked in her closet for other clothes to change into. She congratulated herself again on her quick thinking about her grandfather's pipe. Then she started thinking about her grandmother's picture. Her mother didn't talk much about her, but when she did, she usually said something like, "Things just weren't the same after she died. Your grandmother was the glue. She knew how to handle your grandfather . . . and your uncles."

Her uncles as kids was a hard concept for April to get her brain around. She had trouble thinking of them as anything but too old and too boring to get into any sort of trouble. Not that she knew them all that well. She saw Uncle Nick occasionally; Uncle Mike and his family, never. She had met her cousins only once, when she was around six, and she often wondered if, meeting Clare somewhere and not knowing it was her cousin, they'd each think the other was cool. April hoped so, but with the cast of characters in her family—highly doubtful.

Her grandfather, though, had potential. April liked the way he traded insults with her mother, something not too many people even attempted. She especially liked the way he was all set to toss her the keys to his car, until her mother lived up to her billing as Primo Party Pooper.

Old guy . . . living like a pig . . . three kids but none of them see him that much. April closed the closet door, rushed to her desk, and pulled her notepad out of her pocket. She was glad she always kept it on her, especially when sweet moments like these popped up, when words seemed to barge their way into her brain, impatient as hell, begging to be written down.

What you thinkin' 'bout, Mr. Ear Hair
Sittin' alone in your newspaper chair?
Watchin' tube, collectin' dust
While your joints and memories
Turn to rust.

Something about TV-dinner trays would have to be worked into the lyrics. That could be a song, couldn't it? The kind Roxie might sing? The kind she, April Shea herself, could sing . . . after she changed her name and got into a band of her own?

April stared at the words for a while before closing the notepad and putting it back in her pocket. She began rummaging through her drawer for a top.

The only way she was going to escape this ridiculous life of hers was to get as far away from it as possible. But she'd need a car to do that, and she'd have to wait more than a year—two, if they passed that stupid law raising the driving age—before she could even get her learner's permit.

Unless her mother had a sudden and completely out-of-character change of mind and agreed to teach her.

Or unless *someone else* was willing to teach her.

What you thinkin' 'bout, Mr. Ear Hair?

April opened her bedroom door.

"Mom, we can still go to the diner, if you want," she called out. "I kind of have an idea for my paper I want to ask you about."

CHAPTER FIVE

Nick Warrington slowed. He wanted to be careful. He was surprised—"amazed" might be a better word—that he was with this woman.

"Keep going?" he asked.

Peggy Gallagher looked up at him, a shiny line of perspiration clinging to her upper lip.

"What are you, a machine?" she asked. She waved her hand in front of her face, soap opera style. "What will people say when I'm walking funny tomorrow?"

Nick blushed. Less than an hour together and she felt comfortable enough for a double entendre. But maybe that wasn't her intent at all. He told himself not to make assumptions.

The Woodlake High School track was filling up with walkers, some carrying pink banners. Many wore casual street clothes and sneakers, but most were dressed in running outfits. A lot of the women sported matching nylon pants and jackets. As far as Nick was concerned, none looked as athletically slim as Peggy did.

"As cochair, it might look bad if I sit down now," he said. "But that doesn't mean *you* can't take a break."

Peggy nodded. "Tell me again—how many laps are in a set?"

"Four. Each set confirms a pledge."

"And how many have we done?"

"Sets? Or laps?"

"Sets, silly."

Nick wished he didn't blush so easily. Her "silly" was an endearment, a caress.

"Well, together, we've done three-quarters of one. But I walked three sets before you got here." He hoped that didn't sound like he was annoyed. She had been more than an hour late, but he hadn't been irritated so much as . . . expectant? "I committed to five, so I had to get here early," he said quickly. "I got someone to handle cleanup so we can leave when I finish." Nick bit his lip. *My god, I'm acting like I run Exxon.* "We could grab a bite somewhere. Maybe the Filling Station."

"You like the Filling Station?" Peggy asked.

Had his choice of diners said something about him? He and Marilyn used to go to the Filling Station frequently. They switched to the Parthenon when the Filling Station's Greek omelets started getting too runny and too stingy with the black olives. Marilyn had to have her Greek omelets. Nick hadn't been to the Parthenon since the last time he and Marilyn ate there. He had no plans to return and wasn't about to suggest it as an alternative.

"Anywhere works for me," he said. "I just figured that since we'd be wearing our running stuff, we probably wouldn't want any place too fancy."

"Then the Filling Station is perfect."

Peggy waved at someone on the side of the track. Nick saw Peter Jackson, standing next to the "Walk for a Cure" banner, wave back.

"You know him?" Nick asked, immediately regretting the question. Obviously, she knew him.

"My ex and I were friends with him and his ex," Peggy answered. "She moved away with her new husband. Pete's still a friend."

A friend, she had said, as in *No big deal.* And it wasn't, as far as Nick was concerned. After all, he had plenty of friends who were women. Well, he *could* have plenty of female friends, if he put his mind to it.

"Why don't we do one more lap together before I take a break," Peggy suggested.

Something about the way she said "together" made the other walkers disappear for a moment. A cool breeze ruffled through his T-shirt.

"Sure," he said.

Peggy removed a pair of sunglasses from her pocket. "Getting too bright out here." She adjusted her baseball cap and tugged gently on the blond ponytail that stuck out of the opening in back. Nick wondered how such simple actions could look so . . . *feminine.*

She unzipped her running jacket. Underneath, she was wearing a pink tennis shirt. Marilyn had not been a tennis player. Her sports were running and swimming. They had, in fact, met at a Bowling Green State University swim meet. Nick was covering it for the *BG News,* the campus newspaper. The women had just won a division title and Nick needed a quote from the team's captain. Marilyn answered all his questions without making him feel like a nerd, and Nick would forever remember being distracted by the smell of chlorine in her hair, her slightly bloodshot eyes, the closeness of her near-naked body, and most of all the reddish brown freckles that, sprinkled lightly across her forehead and cheekbones, formed a snowy pattern that forced your eyes down her neck to the rounded smoothness of her shoulders and the soft valley formed by the ridges of her collarbone. He ended the interview by asking her out. She declined. But he had been a persistent nerd, and eventually he would spend countless hours running his fingers over her skin, over the freckles he was not allowed to call "cute," marveling at the patterns, exploring the places they led him.

"So, how did you get involved in the charity? Son or daughter?" Peggy asked.

Nick frowned. Was she asking if he'd lost a son or daughter?

"My son picked this charity for his community project," Peggy continued before he could respond. "Bobby Gallagher? On the lacrosse team? Maybe your son or daughter knows him."

"Oh, I see. Actually, I don't have any kids. We just never . . ." *Answer the question, idiot.* "I actually got involved in this through my wife."

"You mean your ex-wife, unless you were at the Suddenly Single meeting under false pretenses, naughty boy." She chuckled.

Nick felt a drop of sweat run down his back.

"Actually, not my ex-wife. My wife. She, um . . . Well, we got involved in this when she was diagnosed."

"Oh my god." Peggy leaned forward and placed her hand just below her throat, as if the surprise had knocked the breath out of her. "I am so sorry! Here I assumed you were like everyone else around here—divorced, and glad of it."

Nick laughed. "No, no," he said. "We'd been married for fifteen years. Hardly ever fought. But when we did, we made up quickly. Always followed that saying about never going to bed—".

Nick stopped. He was speaking about Marilyn to another woman. He had said the word "bed."

"I'm sorry. I shouldn't talk like this."

"No, no. That's all right. How long has it been since she died?"

"Three years." It was, more accurately, three years and two months. He was learning to not be so specific, so absurdly aware of exactly how long he'd been without her, just as he was learning not to cringe every time someone said "died" when talking about Marilyn. That morning, while lacing up his running shoes, he stared at Marilyn's Reeboks, which he hadn't yet donated. He had vowed not to even think about Marilyn for at least the rest of the day.

"Three years," Peggy said. "You must be getting sick of the dating scene by now."

"I don't exactly—"

"I've only been divorced nine months and, frankly, the whole thing is worse than high school," Peggy continued. She pointed an accusatory finger at Nick. "You guys never change. You want one thing and one thing only, and you just can't take no for an answer."

Next to the small brick concession stand, a young couple was stretching. The woman sat with her legs straight in front of her, holding on to her toes. The man was bent over at the waist, fingers grasping at his feet. He looked at her and said something. Nick saw her laugh. He smiled.

"Actually," he said, "you're my first."

Peggy stopped. She was nearly rear-ended by the walker behind her, a hefty woman wearing a dozen or so pink ribbons on her chest. The woman scowled, stepped to her right, and lumbered past.

"No way! This is your first date in three years?"

Nick nodded, the shame weakening his knees. He knew the picture he was painting: the dead wife, the long grieving period, the continued involvement in the charity for the disease that killed her. *Upbeat, man,* he told himself. *Don't be a drag.*

"C'mon," he said, forcing energy into this voice and his step. "Just a half lap to go." He strained to think of a different subject.

"Wow, three years," Peggy said. "That's admirable, I guess." She picked up the pace slightly. "So what made you finally decide to get back in the game?"

Was that what this was, a game? Nick didn't like to think of it that way, but he supposed Peggy was right. After all, convincing Marilyn to go out with him had been a game of sorts, with all its feints and dodges, its timing of certain maneuvers, the planning for the move after the next move, the constant pursuit. Peggy was right to call it a game. She was being straightforward. An admirable characteristic. One to be emulated.

"I saw you at the Suddenly Single meeting, and then the next night at the steering committee meeting for this. Sorry how this might sound, but I took it as kind of a sign. You're . . . very attractive." Nick waited. Had she heard him?

"Steering committee? Oh, yeah. I had to drag Bobby there. I keep telling him that he has to show up at more than just one event if he wants to put this charity on his application. What if an admissions officer asks about involvement? But he was too busy, of course, with his new girlfriend. So I helped him out a little by going, you know, as kind of his proxy or whatever." She shook her head. "Like I said—one thing on the brain."

"Well, not mine," Nick said. "I mean, that's not why I asked you out." He didn't bother trying to stop. He'd just told a woman not his wife that he found her attractive. There was nothing left to lose. "I mean, you're extremely attractive, like I said. But that's not why I asked you out. I mean, not the main reason. The main reason is I figured you were the kind of person who gets involved, who believes in giving back. I admire that. That's the main reason I asked."

"So, you would have asked me out even if I looked like a line-backer?" Peggy smiled.

"Well, no, of course not." Nick paused. "I don't mean that the way it sounded. It's just . . ." He forced a laugh. "Marilyn used to say that my mouth sometimes runs faster than my brain. She had me pegged pretty well. Fortunately, we could be together for hours and not say anything, and it was all right. Anyway, I guess I'm a little out of practice. Sorry."

"Don't worry so much," Peggy said.

Nick appreciated that. He was beginning to think that Peggy Gallagher, in addition to being pretty, was someone who didn't care a lot about small talk or choosing words carefully. She seemed nice. And he wondered if, all things considered, Marilyn would like her.

"But as a woman and a friend," she said, "let me offer some advice. You might want to watch how much you talk about your wife. It doesn't bother *me*. In fact, I think it's sweet. But other women might not want to hear about this perfect woman. Which no woman is, by the way."

Nick felt his face redden yet again. "You're right," he said. "Sorry."

"So here's a question."

"Okay." Nick liked Peggy's breezy way of moving on to a new topic.

"When you asked me out, of course I had to check you out. So I asked Peter about you. Maybe he's the one that told me you're divorced. Anyway, he said you're an editor of some kind? That you work for one of the major magazines?"

Not exactly correct, but not entirely wrong, either, now that he was doing more freelance editorial work for the magazine that used to employ him full-time. But now was not the time to get into the differences between freelance and full-time. There would be opportunities later, he hoped, to correct the perception about his work that she apparently held—and admired.

"Right," he said. "I do a bit of writing, too."

"That must be so *interesting*."

Nick attempted what he hoped was a modest shrug of the shoulders. "It's not as glamorous as a lot of people think," he said. "But, yeah. I've enjoyed it. And thank god for that. I kind of threw myself into it after Marilyn died." His stomach dropped. *Enough about your dead wife.*

"I have an idea . . . a kind of favor, actually, for our next date," Peggy said.

He wouldn't have blamed her if she'd said, "How about letting

your wife rest in peace," but instead she had said "next date," an in-
dication that he hadn't completely turned her off yet. And was it his
imagination, or had she moved closer to him?

"When you come over to pick me up, maybe you could spend a
few minutes with Bobby?"

"Bobby?"

"My son—remember, silly?" Now she *definitely* moved closer.
"He's getting nowhere with his college essay. Maybe you could help
him? He won't listen to any of my suggestions, of course. What do I
know? I'm just the woman who made sure he did his homework and
drove him all over the blasted state for his lacrosse games."

Nick tried to picture him. The name conjured up a little boy. But
Bobby was a jock applying for college. He had to be seventeen or
eighteen and probably bigger than Nick himself.

"Of course, I'm not asking you to write the essay for him," Peggy
continued. "I would never do that. Just give him a few ideas, from
your perspective as a professional, on what a good essay looks like.
Maybe an outline or something. He's a smart kid. Once you give him
an idea—maybe even a really, really rough draft—he can take it from
there. Although it would be wonderful if you wouldn't mind taking
a look at it when he's done. Then we'll go on our date."

Our date, Marilyn used to say that to him. *What shall we do on
our date? Dinner? Movie? Stay home and . . . relax?*

"That sounds good, Marilyn."

Peggy looked at him sharply, then—with what he could see was
a conscious effort—softened her expression. Nick wondered if a jump
from the top of the nearby grandstands would be enough to kill him.

"Great," Peggy said. "It's a date."

They walked the rest of the lap in silence. Nick kept his mouth
shut for fear that he'd mention Marilyn again, or perhaps even en-
tertain her with a little story about his dead mother and how she got
that way. Or how his father hardly ever acknowledged the fact that

Marilyn had died, as if the death of his own wife were somehow a more significant loss than Nick's. Not that Nick had given his father a chance lately. It must have been a year since he even spoke with him. But he just couldn't take his father's impatience whenever he tried to talk about Marilyn to the one person who might be able to empathize. "You're a young man," his father would say. "Get out there and find someone else."

Someone else. As if Marilyn were something replaceable.

"Well, that's a lap," Peggy said when they reached the starting line. "I think I'll sit for a while. You go on without me."

Nick tried not to watch her as she walked to the sideline. *A date.* She had said it at least twice. The word sounded different coming from her than it had from Marilyn, but it still sounded wonderful. Nick picked up the pace. One more set.

His cell phone rang. When he read the caller ID, he almost decided against answering.

"We have to talk. Where can we meet?"

"Hello, little sister. Nice to hear the dulcet tones."

"Sorry. I'm a little scattered at the moment. But we really do have to talk."

Nick glanced over to the side of the track. Peter handed Peggy a bottle of water. It seemed to Nick that he was standing closer to her than necessary for that particular task.

"What is it now, Marcy?"

"What is that supposed to mean—what is it *now*?"

"Sorry," Nick said quickly, hoping to cut Marcy off before she really got going. "I didn't mean how that sounded. It's just that I'm a little busy right now."

One of the things he had promised her whenever he helped—especially with money—was that she'd never have to worry about his acting like their father had whenever he granted them a favor: the great man stooping down to help some unworthy.

"I'll kick your ass later," Marcy said. "But we have to talk."

"About?"

"I was at Dad's yesterday."

"And?"

"And we have to talk, damn it. I'm not going to tell you this stuff over the phone. Where do you want to meet?"

"When?"

"Are you on some sort of one-word diet? Today! Now, if you can."

"I told you I'm busy."

"I hear wind. What are you doing, raking leaves?"

"I'm at the track."

"You always carry your cell phone when you jog?"

"I'm at the walkathon. I think I sent you a flyer about it."

Marcy took a moment before replying. "Was that supposed to make me feel guilty?"

"You asked." Nick looked to the sidelines. He didn't see Peggy.

"When's it end?" Marcy asked.

"Well, I'm almost done here. But I have plans. Kind of a date."

Nick cringed. He hadn't had time to suppress the urge to tell someone, and it was too late for the undo button.

"Hey, Nick, that is so great." Her entire tone had changed, as he knew it would. "I think that's really great. If you don't mind my saying so, it's about time. Really. I'm sure Marilyn would want—"

"Enough."

"Sorry. Who's the lucky woman? Anyone I know?"

"No. Her name's Peggy Gallagher."

Marcy hmm'd. "Blond, right? About five-five. Thin. Probably hasn't eaten a doughnut in, like, ten years?"

"How do you know her?"

"You've got your track shoes on, right? Run like hell, Nick."

Here she goes, he thought. Knows what's best for everyone else. "She's nice," he said.

"Listen—this is me talking to you. Wasn't I the one who warned you about Betsy Haffner—Betsy Blue Balls? I was right, wasn't I?"

"Jesus, Marcy. Can we please graduate from high school?"

"I'm not saying you're going to have that particular problem. But I know Peggy Gallagher from one of the school committees. Her kid's a couple years older than April. Anyway, she ran the committee like she was secretary of state. She got all Stalin if people argued with her. I learned real quick not to mess."

"She's nothing like that."

"Wait a minute! I think her kid is on one of the sports teams. People said she was messing around with the—"

Nick turned his cell off entirely. Once Marcy felt threatened in any way, she lied. And in this case Marcy felt threatened for Marilyn. Marcy had loved Marilyn. Who didn't?

But it was time for him to move on with his life.

At the far turn of the track, he could check out the sidelines without being obvious. Peggy was sitting next to Peter Jackson. They were laughing. Nick imagined that Peter was planning his strategy. *Go ahead, Big Pete. Fantasize. But she's leaving with me.*

A flock of ravens from the field inside the track rose suddenly, wings flapping as they zigzagged overhead before diving back down to earth.

CHAPTER SIX

He scanned the clues. Eighty-seven across: *Rings of plumerias, e.g.* One hundred twenty-three across: *What barotrauma affects.* Fifty-nine down: *First name in comedy.*

Who knew these ridiculous things?

He focused. It can be done. Just break it down. Get all the ones you know and build from there. He revisited one across: *Treat for a dog,* five letters. Bones? No, the clue was *Treat.* Singular. Bill jotted in "bones" anyway, lightly, to check it against the words going down. One down: *Modern workout system.* If the word started with a "B," it would be . . . He moved to two down: *Bring home?* Three down: *Make a delivery.*

Damn! "Bones" was wrong. Bill stared at it. Five-letter word. *Treat for a dog.*

The squares danced before him. They called out to him, a playground taunt: *Na na na na na. Can't get even the first clue.*

He threw his pen across the room and then tossed the newspaper after it. It jerked up as if pulled by a string, pages crackling, and fluttered to the floor. Next he grabbed the pipe from the ashtray on the table next to him and tamped tobacco into the bowl. "Do crossword puzzles," Bill said aloud, mimicking his doctor. "Learn a new language. Play a musical instrument." Mind exercises! *Quack quack quack.*

But after he'd lit his pipe and took a few puffs, the smoke calmed him as it rose, thinned, and disappeared. He saw the outline of a stick figure, strands of hair, and, after a while, outstretched hands with long, skinny fingers. So crosswords weren't his thing. Big deal. Maybe he'd try a foreign language. Get some of those repeat-after-me tapes from the library. Visit Paris. Sit in one of those smoky cafes. He'd never been to Paris. He'd heard the women there were good-looking. Pretty liberal over there, too. Women didn't care if their husbands took mistresses. In that regard, Clare was definitely not French.

"Right, Clare?" Bill called out, as if she were in the kitchen, the way he used to call out to her when he saw something funny or ridiculous on the tube. "*You* would have cared. Cared? Hell, you would have castrated me."

He laughed. The newspaper he had thrown a few moments earlier made a soft rasp, still settling.

The mistress thing had never been Bill's fantasy. Even before they were married, right before he shipped out, he promised Clare he wouldn't do anything over there that he'd have to apologize for. They both knew what he was talking about. So while his buddies were obsessed with chasing poontang whenever they were on R&R, Bill occupied himself with the GI's second-favorite pastime: boozing. This led to a surprising discovery one night when Sammy Lefkowitz put his hand on a local fanny and one of the local men felt bound to defend her honor. Bill had just downed his third shot of bad Korean whiskey when he saw a screaming slope charging him, waving an empty bottle over his head. That's when Bill experienced the unique pleasure of simplicity: in this case, a simple punch in the nose. Most underrated punch of all. Hit the right spot and eyes watered, the face swelled up, and reaction time slowed enough for a knockout punch.

From then on, he joined Sammy Lefkowitz on R&R whenever he
could. Bill didn't know why he liked simplicity. He didn't know why
he had so enjoyed getting in fights. But he was glad he did. Gave him
something to think about as he sat in his chair staring at smoke from
his pipe.

"Never touched the women, though, Clare."

One of the few promises you kept, William Warrington.

Bill heard the words as if Clare were sitting in the room with
him—or, more likely, bending over to pick up something that one
of the kids had left on the floor. She had always been in motion, carrying laundry baskets, folding clothes, emptying, refilling, wiping
something down, mopping up. Bill felt the heat from the bowl of his
pipe.

He'd kept plenty of promises. It was just easier to bring to mind
the ones he hadn't. Like some of the jobs that didn't pan out because he refused to kiss up to his bosses the way she wanted him to.
Being civil, she'd called it. Or his assurances that he wouldn't have
one drink too many when they went out to dinner with friends, although it wasn't his drinking that often led to a loud argument with
whoever was stupid enough to bring up politics or religion. And he
supposed he could have been around a little more often when the
kids were small, but he usually had some sale cooking and needed
to seal the deal whenever a customer was ready to move forward.
Sometimes the commission checks were huge; other times he wasn't
sure how he would feed the family. *Hang on,* he'd tell Clare when she
started worrying about the bank balances. *The next check's going to
be huge.* Sometimes it was and sometimes it wasn't, but over the long
run things worked out just fine. Nice home. Good schools. Family
vacations.

"Made things interesting, didn't I?" Bill said, calling out again.
"Never bored you, did I?"

He'd started talking aloud to Clare about six months ago. He liked it. He figured it might be good for him, too. Exercise the vocal cords. He could go for days without saying a word to anyone—except maybe when he hurled a curse word at Dr. Phil or offered a compliment to that queen of ballbusters, Judge Judy.

He laughed as a ring of smoke encircled his head.

He saw something move on his left.

"Jesus Marie!" he yelled at the figure standing outside his window. It took a second to see it was a kid. She had a small backpack slung over one shoulder, probably filled with Girl Scout cookies or magazines to sell or some such baloney. He stood to get a better look—and glare, maybe scare the kid away.

But he saw that, no, it was not a kid, or just any kid. It was his kid's kid. Marcy's. Here just a few days ago.

"You always sneak up on people?" he asked when he opened the door.

"I wasn't sneaking," April said, taking a step back. "I was gonna knock."

"Well, if you're *gonna* to do something, do it. Worse thing in life is talking about things you were *gonna* do."

Bill watched for his granddaughter's reaction. She was holding her backpack with both hands, her right arm across her chest to keep the pack from slipping off her shoulder. Why didn't she wear the thing the way it was supposed to be worn? For that very reason, he supposed. She was squinting up at him, and Bill was reminded of Marcy—not so much by the physical resemblance, which unfortunately the poor thing shared with her good-for-nothing father, but by the way she stood her ground, not stepping back, not breaking eye contact.

"Fine," she said. "Life lesson number one. Do you want to close the door so I can knock, or can I just come in?"

Bill snorted and stepped aside, holding the door open for her. "Just like your mother," he growled as she walked past him. He caught a whiff of some sickly sweet gum. Or was it a perfume? Whatever it was, it made his teeth hurt.

April sat on the couch and took a spiral notebook from her backpack. "This place is already a mess again, Grandpa. How many newspapers can you read?"

"It's important to keep up with what's going on in the world," Bill said as he sat in his chair. "And I'm not talking about these knucklehead celebrities the media is obsessed with."

"The media wouldn't be obsessed with knucklehead celebrities if people didn't want news about knucklehead celebrities," April said.

Bill fiddled with his pipe, noting the tone of youthful conviction . . . and scorn.

"You in the debating club?" he asked.

"Those nerds? No way."

"So you're just naturally argumentative." He looked around for matches, checking his pockets and between the cushions of his chair before finding them where he'd left them: next to the ashtray, in plain sight. What had he done with them?

April shrugged. "Least I don't talk to myself," she mumbled.

Bill paused just before relighting. He took a few puffs, watching April carefully. She avoided his gaze, writing something in the notebook she had just removed from her backpack.

"So that's how it's going to be, eh?" he said. "Okay. It's a deal."

April looked up at him. "What's a deal?" she asked.

"Complete honesty. Straight from the shoulder. No baloney. You and me. That's our deal."

April shrugged. "Whatever."

"So I'll start. What's your name?"

April looked up again. "Huh?"

"I know your mother named you after someone famous or a day of the week or some ice cream topping. I'm sorry, young lady, but I have a temporary mind freeze. I think that's what some nitwit on TV called it. Brain freeze. So remind me."

"April."

"Ah, yes, April. I hated that name when your mom told me."

April looked up, lip curled.

"Our deal, remember?" He checked to see if his pipe was still lit. "But it's kind of grown on me, your name. I like it now."

"I don't," April said. "Besides, you couldn't even remember it. How could it have grown on you?"

"What name would you rather have?"

April shrugged.

"You shrug too much. Makes you look weak. Just speak your mind."

"Life lesson number two," April said, scribbling in her notebook. She finished and returned her gaze to him, meeting his eye. He knew in that moment that she wasn't like other kids her age—not that he knew any. But he could tell she had a mind of her own. She didn't wait for some idiotic TV talk show host to tell her how she felt. And, unlike her mother at that age, she wasn't afraid of him. Bill shifted in his chair at the thought—there was no denying it now, no point at all in denying it—that his own daughter had once been afraid of him.

"What's all this about life lessons?" he asked.

April rolled her eyes.

"The reason I'm here?" she said. "School paper? Life lessons from a mentor? Remember I called the other night and told you about this stupid assignment for school and then my mom talked to you and told you she'd drop me off for an hour or so while she showed a client a house and I could, you know, like, interview you?"

Sometimes, the memory of something half forgotten washed over Bill as quickly as April's words were falling out of her mouth now. And as Bill remembered the conversation with April, the conversation with Marcy, he felt a warm wave pass from the top of his head to his stomach.

"So you consider me a mentor?"

April looked up at Bill. "No. But you're the oldest person I know."

Bill remained silent.

"Our deal," April said.

Bill smiled. He couldn't help it. "Sure. Sounds like a good assignment. Better than an essay on how to have safe sex or something, which I understand is what they're teaching you kids these days."

"Grandpa, please. Disgusting."

"Sex is disgusting?"

"Old people talking about it is."

"I see."

Bill remembered the conversation with April on the phone. He remembered the last time she was here. He remembered the white earbuds and the way she complained and how she tied up the papers and her questions about his car and how excited she got at the thought of driving it up and down the driveway—until her mother threw a cold blanket on the idea. It was good to remember things—and not just the things from twenty or thirty years ago. Remembering these things made him want to dance.

"What class?" he asked.

"Huh?"

"What class is this life lessons essay for?"

"English, of course," April answered, but Bill caught the hesitation.

He wanted to hug her. "Forgetting our deal already?" he asked.

April stared at him.

"You don't really have an essay assignment, do you?"

Her face reddened.

Bill laughed. "Your mother was a lousy liar, too. But she wasn't as creative. Not nearly."

He dug into his pocket for his car keys and dangled them in front of him.

"Ready for life lesson number three?" he asked.

The sun streaming through the front window caught one of the keys, sending sparks to the walls, to the ceiling, to April's widened hazel eyes.

CHAPTER SEVEN

It took the sight of bare branches reaching up to the sky, like the naked limbs of skinny old men, to remind Mike Warrington of the surprising number of trees that lined the main street of Cranston, Illinois. Cranston had always been small, but through the eighties it had been a moderately thriving hub of machine-tooling companies that supplied parts for every major industry in America. Now it was home to just two major employers. Mike could see one of them from his booth at the Waffle House: a call center for an insurance conglomerate headquartered on the East Coast. It was located in a strip mall in what used to be a discount electronics warehouse. Rumor along the Waffle House counter was that the 250 jobs—held primarily by locals with, at most, a high school diploma—would soon be outsourced somewhere, probably India.

The other business, and one of two reasons Mike made the seventy-mile trip down from Schaumburg, was ten miles outside of Cranston. Power Industrial Supplies used to be one of the biggest buyers of the precision metal-cutting tools and drills manufactured by Transcon Tooling, the company Mike represented as a regional sales director. Power-I, as they had branded themselves, didn't seem to be faring much better than the call center. Two of their major customers had gone belly-up over the past six months, and the industry itself was trying to extricate itself from a two-year slump. Consequently, Power-I was buying less and less product from Transcon.

Still, Transcon's account manager for Power-I, Stephanie Kraus—the other primary reason Mike traveled to Cranston—was starting to turn things around. Stephanie was one of the few women in the business and the only female sales rep who reported to Mike. Still, he knew that once the novelty of buying from a woman wore off, sales would slide again. It might take a while, since Power-I's buyer, Frank Chadwick, acted as if a thirtyish redhead with an athletic build, an MBA, and a boatload of ambition didn't notice the gut hanging over his belt, the bad comb-over, or his sophomoric attempts at humor. When Frank revealed, between not-so-discreet glances at Stephanie's chest during dinner the previous night, that Power-I had entered into an exclusive agreement for milling inserts with one of Transcon's major competitors, Mike finalized his decision. He kept the decision to himself, though. He didn't interfere when Stephanie set up a meeting with Frank for this morning.

"Just you today, honey, or will your wife be joining you again?"

The waitress was about his age, Mike guessed. Tight uniform, unaware or unconcerned about the bulges it revealed. Mike pushed his coffee cup toward her for a refill.

"Or is she your daughter?" she asked as she poured. No smile. Eyebrows raised ever so slightly.

"My colleague," Mike said evenly. Screw these small-town snoops. "She should be here in a few minutes."

"Sorry. *Colleague,*" the waitress said, nodding her head, her lips slightly pursed. "Y'all want menus?"

"No, thanks. We'll probably just have coffee."

The waitress offered a small, flat smile as she walked away.

Mike was a little ashamed of himself. He'd been in this restaurant at least a dozen times and always pretended it was the first time he'd laid eyes on the waitress. A good salesperson would have chatted her up. Salespeople were friendly, genuinely interested in other people. And for years Mike had played the part, psyching himself up to ask about the kids, the latest scores, the goddamned weather. He knew how to play the game. He'd learned it from his father years ago. Wherever he went with his dad, people called out to talk with him, be with him, get the surefire flattery they knew was coming their way. Everyone in the goddamned state of Ohio, it seemed, loved Bill Warrington. But they didn't know, *really know,* Bill Warrington.

Mike was much more comfortable in his current managerial role than with selling. He knew what had to be done. He could tell others what had to be done and how to do it. But he didn't actually have to do it himself—at least, not as often as he used to. And he didn't have to kiss ass.

Unless he wanted to.

Mike's back was to the door, but he knew Stephanie had arrived by the soft, fragrant cloud that seemed to surround her at all times.

She slid into the booth, pulling her briefcase in with her. She glanced around. Mike thought she was about to lean over the table and try to kiss him.

He took a sip of his coffee. "Did you check out?" he asked.

"Mmm hmm," Stephanie said, arranging herself.

"Receipt?" he asked, checking the inside breast pocket of his jacket for his own.

"God, you're paranoid. Have I forgotten before? Besides, do you really think some dweeb in accounting is going to compare expense reports and make sure we had separate rooms? He'd probably recommend you for a promotion for cutting expenses."

Mike offered a tepid smile.

"Would you like a menu, miss?"

Stephanie looked up at the waitress, who had picked up some dirty plates from the next booth.

"Just coffee, please," Stephanie said.

"Surprise, surprise," the waitress muttered as she started to walk away.

"Um, just a second," Stephanie said. "You know, I should have asked months ago, but I don't know your name."

"My name?"

Stephanie nodded. "You always give such great service, and you're the reason I keep coming back here. I should at least know your name."

Mike could see that the battle-ax wasn't buying it. "Edna," she said, voice as flat as the syrup-stained table that Stephanie now had her elbows on.

"Get out of town! That's my younger sister's name."

"Nobody names their kid Edna."

"Oh, I know!" Stephanie said, turning toward her. "And, no offense, my sister hates the name. But my mom had an aunt Edna who took care of her after my grandma died when my mom was a little girl. Auntie Ed, as my mother called her, was a saint."

Edna's face softened. "What's your sister call herself?"

"Edie," Stephanie said without hesitation.

"Me, too." The waitress was smiling now.

"How about that? Well, Edie, it's so nice to know you."

"I'll be right back with your coffee."

And she was, placing it down carefully and with a smile for Stephanie but not so much as a glance at Mike. Stephanie winked at him as she took her first sip.

"I didn't know you had a sister," Mike said.

"I don't. I just didn't want that judgmental old biddy spitting in my coffee." She was wearing a cream-colored top that revealed nothing unless she leaned forward, as she did now. "You seem preoccupied this morning. You were preoccupied last night. What's up?"

Mike took another sip of his coffee to avoid looking at her. He never was good at this part, and he hadn't expected things would get to this point so quickly. Or maybe he was just getting impatient with the age difference. Let's face it—it wasn't particularly arousing when he mentioned an event or something that had happened to him as an adult, only to realize that she hadn't yet been born. Maybe he was crazy to even consider doing what he was about to do. Any guy who looked at Stephanie, and almost every one she walked by did, would think so.

"Hey!"

Mike jerked from both Stephanie's voice and her foot, which was in his crotch. "Stephanie," he said, in a low voice.

Stephanie slowly removed her foot. "Somebody's a little sleepy this morning," she said. "Or doesn't want to talk with me. Which is it, Michael?"

She sometimes acted young enough to be his daughter; other times, old enough to be his mother.

"No meeting," he said.

Stephanie frowned. "Canceled? Why? He didn't call me. How do you—?"

"He didn't cancel."

"What do you mean?" She was sitting straight up now, her head cocked. "What's going on?"

Mike took a deep breath. He'd made a mistake. He had thought a public place would be safest. But this was Stephanie. Had he really thought a crappy little breakfast joint filled with truckers and retirees would stop her from saying what was on her mind?

"I'll handle the call," he said. "We're cutting Power-I loose, Stef."

Stephanie didn't react.

"Purely a bottom-line decision," Mike continued. "The margins aren't good enough to justify an account manager. We'll shift them over to our telesales group."

Stephanie remained quiet for another second. She looked Mike straight in the eye. "Sales are up 10 percent over the same date last year," she said, her voice even. "They're picking up new customers. Two big ones in Asia. And your margin argument is bullshit."

"Stephanie."

"That's my bread-and-butter account, Michael, and you know it. You cut them loose and I'm—" She stopped. Her eyes narrowed. She sat back in the booth. "I see," she said.

"It's not what you think," Michael said, careful to maintain eye contact now. "It's just one of those things. You just need to find prospects with a stronger need for some of our bigger tickets. And I've been telling you for some time now the importance of keeping your pipeline filled."

"Yeah," Stephanie said, no slouch in the eye contact department. "The pipeline."

Mike looked at his coffee cup. "I have no doubt you'll pull in some big orders soon. You've got the brains, the motivation, the—"

"Don't," Stephanie said, her eyes wide now, warning. "I'm in no mood for some bullshit sales pep talk. Maybe instead you can tell me how I'm going to pay the rent now that 90 percent of my income has just disappeared."

Mike nodded, trying to appear sympathetic but firm. "You knew this was a commission-based job when you took it, Stef. Shouldn't put all your eggs in one basket."

"Is that your secret to success, Michael? Lots of baskets to put your eggs in?"

Mike resisted the urge to glance behind him. He felt the waitress's eyes on the back of his head, like infrared targets. "You might want to keep your voice down, Stef."

"Might I?"

He waited. She usually calmed down quickly, but this was new territory. He was tempted to look at his watch. The meeting with Power-I was in fifteen minutes. He'd pick up the PO for the order Stephanie sold last night, then explain how Transcon's "Customer First" telephone representatives would take care of all of Power-I's future needs. The horny old bastard there wouldn't like it, especially when he realized he'd seen the last of Stephanie's boobs, but his business still needed several of Transcon's lines. Mike's numbers wouldn't take a complete hit.

"Look," Mike said. He reached across the table and took her hand. She didn't pull away, as he feared she might. "Line up some solid prospects, and I'll make some joint calls with you next time I'm down."

"Yeah? When will that be?"

"Whenever you say. You know that, Stef." Mike squeezed her hand. "Let's not mix up the business thing with us."

Stephanie inhaled deeply, and then covered Mike's hand with her own. "I should tell you to go fuck yourself."

Mike smiled. Crisis averted. For now. "But you won't?" he asked, dropping a twenty on the table with his free hand.

"I won't," Stephanie said. "But you'd better not be bullshitting me. Things would get ugly. Fast."

Mike had no doubt. "I think you know me better than that," he said, standing.

As he pulled out of the parking lot, he saw in his rearview mirror that Edna was at Stephanie's booth. She was holding the coffeepot and talking to Stephanie, whose head was bowed, as if examining something on the table.

Mike glanced at his watch. He'd be a few minutes late for his meeting, but he wouldn't rush. He would enjoy his last drive through Cranston.

CHAPTER EIGHT

As he waited for her in a booth at the Filling Station, sipping on his second cup of coffee and watching the incoming customers pull their jackets and Windbreakers a little more tightly around themselves, Nick realized that he no longer wanted to love his sister.

There were plenty of reasons a rational person wouldn't. She was embarrassingly loud. She still swore as much as she did as a teenager—a vice for which, admittedly, he and Mike would have to accept some measure of responsibility. It had been eight years since Patrick Shea took off and she still acted as if she were the first and only woman ever to be duped by a nice-looking guy. It wouldn't surprise him if April were grown with kids of her own before Marcy stopped talking about the challenge of raising a girl alone, as a single parent, a single woman, in today's ridiculously permissive society.

And now, as usual, she was late.

Try as he might, Nick was incapable of being late. Even when he left at a time he was certain would make him run late, the traffic cleared, lights turned green, he made all the correct turns, and he was always, invariably, maddeningly early. He was early for meetings, early for social events—even those he had no desire to attend. Marilyn had tended toward the fashionably late side of the equation, and it was one of the few things about her that irritated him. Nick would maintain a stony silence as they drove to whatever they were late for. Marilyn would ignore his anger and sit quietly, watching the passing landscape, maybe even humming softly. She might lean over to change the radio station, and Nick would catch a hint of her perfume. By the time they got to wherever they were going, he usually wished they could just go back home to be alone together.

Nick opened the menu for the third time since he'd arrived. Should have brought a book, he thought. That would be a good strategy for any time he and Marcy agreed to meet.

He wanted to not love his sister, but every time he resolved not to he was defeated by memories of when they were younger and in it together, she and he, against their father's drinking, against their mother's cancer, even against their brother's sudden interest in girls that put an end to the sorts of antics—the faces at the dinner table, the obscene gestures when their father's back was turned—that made all three of them laugh.

And so Nick agreed to meet Marcy despite his fears that her negative energy might bring him down after he'd been feeling pretty good. Thanks to Peggy, he saw a sliver a hope, like hallway light pulling itself through the bottom gap of a closed door, that just maybe he didn't have to be so stunningly alone for the rest of his life. Nick's inability to not love his sister, in fact, made him willing to enter into a conversation with her about a topic guaranteed to throw a black cloud over his recent high spirits. No good would come of this meeting, Nick decided, unless the news was that the old man had won the lottery or someone had been prescient and taken out long-term health care for him or—Nick closed the menu—the old man was dead.

Nick was composing the eulogy in his head—or, rather, the awe-

struck congratulations people would offer him after he delivered it—
when Marcy finally arrived.

"Nothing like November in friggin' Ohio," she said as she threw
her purse in ahead of her and slid into the booth. While shucking
off her coat and apparently not even thinking of apologizing for
being late, she said, "First things first. How is Peggy Gallagher in the
sack?"

Nick signaled for another coffee.

"Come on, don't be like that. You love talking about that stuff.
Remember your big night with Cindy Oxford, your first trip to second
base? You described it like a tour guide. No detail too insignificant:
the challenge of the buttons, the complexity of the back clasp—"

"We were kids, for god's sake," Nick said, looking around. "I used
to think a fart in church was funny, too."

"Tell me you still don't."

Marcy was desperate to get a smile. Nick knew it.

"What, exactly, can I do for you, Marcy?"

The sentence was out of his mouth before he realized the impact
it would have on Marcy. He had said those words once before, just
before lending her money for the third or maybe it was the fourth
time after she'd been fired from a job because she hadn't yet figured
out—as if *he* would ever be able to—how to juggle day care and
after-school care with a full-time job. The two seconds it had taken
to ask the question, using those words, changed their relationship
irrevocably. *You have no idea,* she'd sobbed. *And just who the fuck
are you, anyway?* Marcy never again asked him for money, and
Nick had not since been able to answer her question to his own
satisfaction.

"When's the last time I asked you to do anything for me, pencil
dick?" she asked now.

Nick nodded. "That was patronizing," he said. "Sorry."

Marcy turned to stare out the window. The sun caught her eye, and he saw that she was welling up. She fought it with a butt-and-sleeves adjustment and a push of some stray strands of hair to behind her ear. Maybe it was because he didn't see her that often now, but Nick thought that she was starting to look older.

"But pencil dick is Mike's line," he said.

Marcy laughed. "Definitely," she said.

And it was—most definitely had been—Mike's line once upon a time, when it seemed that Mike was always talking about penises. Nick wondered if that was the case with all brothers. Their beds had been separated by a tiny nightstand with a lampshade that Nick remembered glowed in the dark a few seconds after the lamp was turned off. Mike and Nick would lie in their beds and listen to the muffled conversations of their parents in the kitchen directly beneath their room. Their voices, low and high, created a kind of lullaby, accompanied by the clinking of the spoon as their father stirred sugar into his instant coffee. Mike liked to provide a running commentary.

"They're talking about you," he'd whisper. "They're worried that your dick is so small." Nick would hit Mike with his pillow and Mike would retaliate and it wasn't long before they heard their father bellow, "Knock it off up there, you two. You don't want me coming up there."

They'd settle and watch the lights from the cars passing on the street crash into the ceiling. Nick would start to nod off, and suddenly Mike would lean over and whisper loudly into his ear.

They're making a baby now!

They're doing it on the kitchen table.

Pack your bags, pal. They're signing the adoption papers.

By this time, Nick usually just rolled over and went to sleep. But one night Mike leaned over and said, "Mom's giving Dad a blow job." Nick jumped up and, to the surprise of them both, swung at—

and connected with—the side of Mike's head. The punch didn't do much damage. Mike's counterpunch did. Nick's nose exploded, he screamed like a girl (as Mike described it later), the room suddenly flooded with light, and Nick saw the crimson on his T-shirt before he realized what it was. When Mike jumped up and out of bed, saying, "He started it, he punched me first," his father backhanded him, knocking Mike against the wall.

"Bill!"

Their mother, who Nick hadn't realized had also come up the stairs, rushed by him in a dark flash, pulling the air after her. She grabbed at her husband's arms. While his father later claimed his elbow accidentally caught his mother on the chin when he turned, Nick had never been able to rid himself of the certainty that he had seen a split-second look between his father and mother before the arm snapped back and his mother was suddenly on her back between the beds, holding her head.

His father froze. Nick and his brother froze. The air froze.

She let out a short, soft moan. "Oh!" She sounded more surprised than hurt, as if she'd woken up from a nap she didn't mean to take. Her feet were flat on the floor and knees bent as if she were about to do some sit-ups. She didn't notice or care that in this position her skirt wasn't doing its job. Nick could not stop staring. He'd rarely seen his mother in her nightgown, much less in this pitifully exposed state. It made his father's "accident" all the more heinous—and his own staring all the more despicable. Mike noticed that he was staring and glared at him ferociously, demanding Nick's eyes while they waited for whatever was to come next. But Nick could not look away until his father moved. He started toward his wife, who suddenly held up her hand, fingers spread. Nick wondered how, still on her back and face covered with her hands, his mother knew that his father had stepped toward her. But that hand, thrust into the air from between the beds, seemed to control all that was going to happen in that room and all that would be afterward. His father turned and walked to the bedroom door. The light from the hall turned him into a silhouette, so Nick could not see who his father was looking at when he turned and said, "You little prick."

Mike flipped the bird at the now empty doorway and turned to his mother. Nick watched him approach her slowly. He bent over her, reaching down as if to adjust her skirt, his long arms sticking out of the pajama top he was growing out of. He hesitated, clearly uncertain how to go about such a mysterious task. He finally just touched her knee.

"Mom?"

She sat up with a small groan and, after a moment, adjusted her skirt. She stayed that way for a few moments, lightly touching her jaw, kind of the way Nick had seen her use a powder puff when she was getting ready to go out to dinner with their father. Finally, using Mike's bed as a brace, she started to get up.

"Thank you, dear," she said to Mike when he tried to help her up. She told them both to get into bed and said something about stopping all the silly arguing and fighting. Nick watched from his bed as she leaned over Mike and stroked his cheek.

"Are you okay, Michael?" she asked. Mike nodded, bobbing his head like an idiot, Nick knew, to ward off the tears. His mother leaned over and kissed him on the forehead. Nick decided he hated him.

"He's never hit you before, has he," she said. A statement, not a question. Mike, still fighting tears, shook his head vigorously. "And I know, without even talking to him about it, that he never will again. Do you understand what I'm saying, honey?"

More tearful nodding.

"It's important for you to remember that."

Even back then, Nick thought it was a strange thing for his mother to say. But he was too worried about being left out of his mother's sphere of interest to give it much thought. He wouldn't even remember those words until too few years later, after she was gone.

"What about you?" Nick called out, more to get his mother's attention than out of any fully realized concern.

His mother looked over and—finally!—saw Nick's bloody nose and soiled shirt.

"Oh my god!" she said. "Let's get you cleaned up."

Nick would never have trouble recalling the feel of the warm washcloth and the heat of the steam rising from the sink. He watched his mother's profile in the mirror over the sink, finding comfort in the way the lines around her eyes deepened and her lips tightened as she tried to dislodge the slightly congealed blood from his upper lip and nose. He felt a strange gratitude to his father for bringing all this about. His mother helped him out of his dirty T-shirt and into a clean one before tucking him back into bed. She paused at the door.

"You two need to learn how to be friends, not just brothers," she said.

They lay in their beds quietly after that, listening for whatever sounds were about to emerge from below. But Nick only heard the usual nighttime sounds: the hum of a house, the fade in and out of a passing car, his brother's breathing. Exhausted now, Nick was just about asleep when he heard a voice in his ear.

See what I mean, crybaby? Even Dad says you've got a little prick. Mom probably thinks so, too.

Nick smiled into his cup of coffee. Mike never passed up an opportunity. No wonder he did so well in sales.

He handed Marcy a menu. "You said something about Dad."

"You sure you wouldn't rather talk about Peggy Gallagher?" It was Marcy's peace offering and Nick was inclined to accept, but before he could respond, Marcy dropped the menu to the table and held up both hands. "Okay, okay, don't get your boxers in a bollix. I'll get straight to the point. I'm pretty sure Dad's dying."

The waitress appeared to ask if they were ready to order. Marcy signaled for Nick to order while she scanned the menu. After he ordered a BLT, Marcy snapped the menu shut and said she'd have the same and a cup of coffee. Black.

"What's he got?" Nick asked when the waitress left.

Marcy stared at him, wide-eyed. "That's it? *What's he got?*"

Nick looked away. "I know how that sounds, but we both know it's bound to happen sooner or later, right?" He waited a moment for his embarrassment to pass. "What makes you *think* he's dying?" he asked.

"He's being nice."

Nick leaned back against the vinyl padding of the booth. "Ah. The dreaded Nice diagnosis. How long's he got, Doc?"

Marcy closed her eyes. She shook her head and shoulders as if loosening up for a jog. She mumbled something under her breath, chantlike. Nick guessed this to be some sort of affirming statement. Was Marcy in therapy?

"Let's start over," she said.

And she did, telling Nick about the call from her father and the condition of his house. She spoke fast and in detail, hardly pausing for air or Nick's reaction. It reminded him of when they were younger and she used to come into his room—Mike was always out on a date by this time—to complain over the latest outrage committed by their father or to cry about how much she missed their mother.

Then, as now, he knew he should have tried to comfort her, but he couldn't get past the feeling that she needed to buck up, that she wasn't the only one fighting these fights. And so he'd sit on his bed, back against the headboard, and look away or down when she started to cry—even the night she came to him in near hysterics, complaining that one of her sleepover friends had called home to have her parents pick her up because the old man had come into the family room to tell Marcy something but fell to the floor, dead drunk. "Flat on his face," Marcy wailed. "He scared the shit out of her."

Nick had laughed. He hadn't known how else to react. Marcy's friend had nothing to fear, but even now there was something hilarious about the scene as Nick saw it: his father walking in, maybe swaying a little bit, about to say something, and then . . . *thunk!* What could anybody do except laugh?

"Are you hearing what I'm saying?" she asked now.

"Of course," Nick said. "What's your suggestion?"

"Goddammit, Nick, I knew you weren't listening. I just told you. Sunrise. It's an assisted-living facility. One of the girls in the office has her mother there and her mother loves it."

"Have you talked to Dad about this?"

"Not yet."

He chuckled. "Good luck with that one."

Marcy looked out the window. "Well, see, that's part of why I wanted to talk with you. I figured that if it was more than just me talking to him about it, he'll listen." She paused, and when Nick didn't say anything, added, "Especially since he's trying to get the three of us together anyway."

"The three of whom?"

"*Whom? Whom* do you think? Us. You. Me. Mike. So we might as well use his plan as an excuse to talk to him about ours."

"I'm confused," Nick said. "Who wants to see us?"

"Who have we been talking about, Nick?" Marcy now assumed a second-grade teacher voice he hadn't heard before but suspected his niece often did. His heart went out to her. "Your father? Remember him? He wants a get-together. That's another reason I think he's dying."

"He told you he wants to get together with the three of us?"

"You think I'm making this up? Of course he told me. Told Mike, too."

"He called Mike?"

Marcy waved her hand dismissively. "Don't get in a sibling rivalry snit, Nicky. He called Mike by accident, I think."

Nick fiddled with a sugar packet. Marcy wasn't telling the whole story. He felt it in his bones. "Let me make sure I've got this straight," he said. "Dad wants us to get together for some reason—maybe to recover all those happy memories he lost to Jack Daniels—and you want to take the opportunity to talk him into moving into a nursing home."

"It's an assisted-living facility and it's two separate issues, dickwad."

Definitely hiding something. Nick thought about something Marcy had told him a few minutes earlier, something about her spending a lot of time lately—sometimes with April—getting the old place "in shape."

"And what do you suggest we do about the house?" he asked.

Marcy's face reddened. "What do you mean?" she asked.

Bingo.

"Well . . . you've obviously thought all this through. Any thoughts on who might list the house, once Dad moves out?"

"You think that's what this is about?"

Nick shrugged.

Marcy stood. "I'll tell the old man you're too busy to see him," she said. "Call him if you change your mind."

Not wanting to watch her go, Nick turned his attention to the whirlpool he'd made in his coffee with his spoon. For a long while after Marilyn died, he believed she was somehow looking down on him, somehow transmitting encouragement and advice and helping him avoid doing things that would make her cringe. But what he'd just done convinced him, finally, that she wasn't hanging around in some other life-form or energy force. She was gone. She would always be gone. He was here alone, mucking things up all by himself.

He opened the portfolio he had brought with him. Inside was Bobby Gallagher's college essay. The prose was better than expected.

"I'll pay for those, but I've changed my mind," Nick told the waitress when she brought the two sandwiches. "Just more coffee, please."

CHAPTER NINE

The white panels of the emergency room ceiling reminded April of the Beatles song her father loved. She couldn't remember the name—something about a hole in the roof or filling holes in Albert Falls—but she could remember that he practically worshipped John Lennon. Heather's theory was that people put Lennon on a pedestal because he got shot, but Heather didn't know squat about music and, besides, that sounded like something Heather's parents might have said, not Heather. Still, in a way, it was cool that he got shot before he got a chance to sell out.

At one time April had started a list called TAD—Things About Dad—naming everything she could remember about her father. Singing Beatles songs was at the top, and second was the way he'd suddenly grab her and throw her up over his head before April realized what was happening. She'd be in the air, trying to catch her breath, and in the next moment she'd see her father's face suddenly in focus, his smile, the tiny gap between his two front teeth, and the scratchy feel of his kiss on her cheek. But the third entry stopped her short. She didn't want to include it, although skipping it would somehow make the entire list less credible, less real. And because it was a topic she didn't want to think about, much less write about, she abandoned TAD altogether.

The argument had started out to be what she thought would be an ordinary fight between her parents, but it grew so loud, and with so much crashing and stomping and crying, that April had hid in her room and tried to work up the courage to dial 911. By the time things quieted and she came out, it was too late. Her father had left without even saying good-bye. He called her a few days later and promised he'd be back someday. But even at eight, she knew the word, coming from him, meant never. And now, a few days past her fifteenth birthday—which he had yet to acknowledge—she also knew there was a reason someday was never, and that—any minute now—this reason would come bursting into the room, hair on fire with worry and hands on the side of her head and mouth wide, a big O, like that awesome painting of the weird guy on a bridge, screaming and asking questions and maybe crying about her baby, her baby.

As if this whole situation weren't embarrassing enough.

Three stitches above her right eyebrow, which actually looked pretty cool. She couldn't wait to show her friends. They'd gasp. She'd shrug it off. Keith Spinelli would be concerned. He'd want to comfort her in some way. She'd let him.

She wondered if there'd be a scar. She hoped so. She didn't want anything big and disgusting, just a small, white line, raised a little bit. Forehead Braille. Irresistible. An interviewer would ask her how she'd gotten it. She'd explain. People all over the country—the world—would then cut themselves just so, to look more like her. She'd then have to hold a press conference to tell kids not to do it. But they'd do it anyway.

She needed a story her mom would buy. *Yeah, I'm such a spaz. It was so cold that I wanted to get into the house fast and I walked right into that stupid storm door at the same time Grandpa was opening it.* She was sure her mom would go along with the scenario, just as she had when April told her that the "Life Lessons from a Mentor" essay was now her assigned final project for English. This proved to be the perfect cover for the driving lessons her grandfather was more than willing to keep secret. Like most people, her grandfather seemed a little afraid of her mother—which was weird, since he was her father and all. But April noticed that whenever her mom dropped her off or picked her up from her visits, he'd ask in almost a little-boy voice if she'd called Nick or Mike yet. To which she would let loose with one of her hanging-on-the-cross sighs and say she'd left messages and how many times did she have to tell him? And Grandpa, who'd recently been given billing as the first and only listing on Signs Of Intelligent Life, would jeopardize his standing on said list by nodding meekly.

God only knew what the woman would do to him now. But her grandfather had insisted on coming here. She'd tried to tell him no, that it would ruin everything. He told her not to worry about her mother, that her mother would be grateful that they were being extra careful, making sure everything was okay.

She wondered how a father could know so little about his daughter.

"You decent in there, kid?"

"Come on in, Grandpa."

Her grandfather pushed aside the curtain and glanced around as if he had expected to see someone else. He was still wearing his heavy plaid jacket—April called it his lumberjack special—and his hundred-year-old rubber galoshes, complete with the metal snaps down the front. "How do you feel?"

"Same as the last fifty times you asked. Fine. Can we get out of here?"

He nodded. "Doc should be by soon," he said. "He wants you to sit for a few minutes. Let me see those stitches."

April told him she didn't want to take the bandage off. There wasn't a chair in the tiny cubicle, so she scooched over on the bed and invited him to sit next to her. When he did, she could tell he'd been smoking his pipe. The smell, combined with the feel of his weight next to her, was both comforting and confusing. She suddenly wanted to cry. How lame would that be? A few stitches and she turns into a baby. Still, inside she was trying to will her grandfather into holding her tight so she could bury her face in his smelly plaid shirt.

"How bad's the car?" she managed.

The question seemed to take him by surprise. He had been staring straight ahead, the way he sometimes did while she was driving. *Earth to Grandpa,* April would call out. But she didn't trust her voice to do so now.

"A little banged up on the passenger side," he finally said. "The headlight works but probably needs to be replaced. All in all, not too bad."

The funny feeling had moved up to April's throat, threatening to explode. "I am so sorry."

"That car's had a pretty . . . what do you call it? . . . *charmed* life." Her grandfather patted her hand. He continued. "It's what—twenty-something years old? Never been in an accident. Somehow, that's just not right. You can't reasonably expect to live that long and not get dinged a few times. Sooner or later, there's got to be some sort of payback. It's like what Clare—your grandmother—used to tell me, that sooner or later—"

He stopped abruptly and stared at the floor. April wasn't sure what to do. This was one of those awkward moments that she found both baffling and annoying. Was her grandfather just putting a happy face on the fact that he was truly and mightily pissed off? Did he want her to apologize again? She wanted to. But he suddenly seemed on edge and she wasn't sure what effect her words would have. Maybe he'd tell her sorry wasn't good enough. Maybe he'd tell her he understood. Worst of all, maybe he'd tell her that the driving lessons weren't such a good idea, after all.

"Anyway," he said suddenly, "lots of people have trouble remembering which way to turn in a skid. Although most people don't normally assume the gas pedal is the answer."

He winked.

April wanted to laugh. She tried to laugh. In fact, she thought she was laughing. But she was crying and she put her head in her hands and leaned forward and sobbed and waited for her grandfather to wrap his arms around her, but he just seemed to sit there, which made her cry harder, but then, finally, she felt his hands on her shoulder and she was being pulled forward and someone was murmuring in her ear and she felt and then smelled the breath, but it wasn't smoky or tobacco-y but more garlicky . . .

Her mother.

It took a while for April to stop crying but probably less time than it would have taken if it had been her grandfather holding her and stroking her hair. When she stopped and looked up, she saw that her mother was squatting in front of her, giving her one of those meaningful I'm-looking-you-straight-in-the-eyes-to-show-I-care looks that she probably read about in *Parents* magazine.

"So. Tell me what happened."

"April's been working hard on this school assignment of hers," her grandfather answered. "So I thought she deserved some hot chocolate. The kind you used to—"

"I'm asking my daughter," her mother said, not taking her eyes off April's. Must have been a technique covered in the article—maybe a sidebar tip: Do Not Break Eye Contact When Interrogating Your Delinquent Teenager.

"You asked what happened," her grandfather continued. "That's what happened. We were headed to Friendly's when we hit a little ice. Knocked some poor guy's mailbox over. Accident. That's all."

Still staring at April but in a low voice that April knew was actually the first rumblings of an impending volcanic eruption, her mother said, "That's all?"

April felt her grandfather shift his weight.

"Yeah. We were going to Friendly's to get a hot chocolate like I said, and we got in an accident. That's all. No biggie, as you kids used to say."

Now her mother finally broke eye contact and stood, directing her death stare at her grandfather. April saw that her grandfather was smiling, but she knew—and it felt like a secret—that it was a phony smile. But his smile wilted as her mother stepped closer.

"Easy for you to say, old man, when it's someone else, not you, who needed stitches to close a huge gash just inches from her eye. No *biggie* for you!"

"Mom! Chill!"

"Don't tell me to chill. Do you have any idea how terrifying it was to get that phone call to come to the hospital? I'm in the middle of a meeting and I get this call and I have to rush to the hospital not knowing anything. Not knowing if you were alive or—"

"Uh, Mom? Since I'm the one who called you, I'm not sure you had to wonder if—"

"Don't smart-mouth me, young lady. You know what I mean."

April shook her head and looked away. She wanted to sleep.

Her mother turned her attention back to her grandfather.

"Let's cut to the chase, old man. Were you drinking?"

April watched her grandfather smile sadly. He looked down and didn't answer. If it hadn't been for his white stubble and the gross gray hair in his ear, he would have looked like a little boy—a little boy who needed to be rescued.

"Mom, Grandpa's the one who insisted we come here. I wanted to go home."

"Well, bully for him," Marcy said. "For the first time ever, he demonstrates more sense than a fifteen-year-old. Stop the presses."

The sudden silence that followed her mother's remark reminded April that they were in the emergency room of a hospital. She supposed that their argument was helping the other patients take their minds off their pain, if only for a few minutes.

"Which Friendly's?" her mother asked, locked in on her grandfather.

"You know which one," he replied. "The one on Forest."

"Oh! The one on Forest."

"Right. The one we used to go to. On Forest."

"The one on Forest that closed five years ago? That one on Forest?"

April tried not to look over as her grandfather reached down to fiddle with one of the snaps on his boots. "Really? Didn't know that. Guess we would have found out when we got there."

Her mother snorted so loudly April thought she might honk out half her nose. "You are so full of it," she said.

"Leave him alone, Mom."

"I will! And so will you! You're not to get in a car with him again."

"Jesus, Mom."

"I'm not going to tell you again. Don't 'Jesus' me." Marcy turned to her father. "Okay, Billy Boy, here it is. You can't take care of your house, you can't remember that Friendly's, a few blocks from your house, closed years ago, and April tells me you sometimes forget her name. It's time to stop driving."

April felt the flush again—not at her mother's assholeness, but at her own betrayal of her grandfather by mentioning the memory lapses. To April's immense relief, her grandfather, head still bowed, tilted his head toward April just enough to make eye contact. He looked like a playground coconspirator. He winked.

Her mother's cell phone rang. She glanced at the display.

"Mortgage broker. I've got to take this."

"Uh, mom?"

April pointed to a sign on the wall: ABSOLUTELY NO CELL PHONES.

"Stay here," Marcy said.

As if I have a choice, April thought.

She and her grandfather sat quietly for a few moments. A heavily accented voice on the PA called for a Dr. Woodson.

"Thanks for lying for me," April said.

"Who lied? I told your mom we got in an accident. Truth."

"The hot chocolate . . . Friendly's . . ."

"That's true, too. I just didn't tell you I was going to treat you. A surprise. You like surprises, don't you?"

"But Mom thinks you were driving. And now she thinks you're too old to drive. And she thinks this is all your fault."

Bill reached over and patted April's hand. His hand felt thin and papery.

"Two things. First, your mom is right. It *is* my fault. Second, you can't control what people think—no matter what you say or even do. Sometimes it's not worth the effort." He winked again. "Life lesson number whatever."

There was a sudden swish of the curtain opening and closing, and a white coat appeared before them, worn by a short, rotund man with a few wisps of hair and a nose exploding with red veins.

"I'm Dr. Brennan," he said, and extended his hand to April's grandfather. "And you are . . . ?"

"Yes, I still am. Plan to be for a while."

The doctor frowned. "Your relationship to the young lady here?"

"Grandfather. Plan to be that for a while, too." He gave April a playful jab in the side with his elbow. Definitely coconspirators.

"And her mother or father is . . . ?"

"Her mother is outside on her cell phone. She'll be back in a second. Never mind about her father. Out of the picture."

April's grandfather smiled at the doctor as if he'd just remarked on what a beautiful day it was. The doctor seemed confused.

"I see," he said. "Well, I have to get to a consultation, so if Mom has any questions, she can call me." He turned to April. "In the meantime, young lady, you should take it easy for the rest of the day. Tylenol for the pain, if you need it. Any questions?"

"Nope," her grandfather answered.

The doctor glanced at him, then back at April. "I was asking the young lady," he said.

"No," April said. "No questions."

"See?" her grandfather said. "She's tough. Like her granddad."

The doctor didn't seem to be listening. He jotted something on the chart. He then clicked his pen and put it in the front pocket of his white coat. He looked at April seriously, and she had a feeling he was about to do her the immense favor of dispensing some wise and kindly doctorly advice.

"You should see the people who come in here who don't wear a seat belt," he intoned. "They often don't walk out. Judging from that cut and the bump on your head from the steering wheel, it's a good thing you were wearing one." He turned to leave, which was fine with April. The guy gave her the creeps. But just then the curtain opened. April didn't even look up. She could *feel* who it was.

"And you are?" the doctor asked.

"Marcy Shea. Her mother. Can I have a word with you, Doctor?"

She didn't give him much of a choice, April saw, as her mother grabbed the doctor by the elbow and led him out into the hall. April looked up at her grandfather. He winked at her.

"Don't worry, kid. We'll get through this."

Before April could respond, her mother was in front of them, staring hard at April.

"So. You were driving."

"Look, Marcy."

"Shut up old, old man," her mother said. "I'm speaking to my daughter. I already know—oh, god, do I know—that you're a liar. I need to find out if my daughter is."

Was this it? April wondered. Was this the moment she had been planning for, the moment she had been writing about in her journal, in her songs? The moment, finally, to use the word that she knew would hurt her mom most. *Failure* as a mother. *Failure* as a wife. *Failure* in careers. In her daydreams of the event, she delivered the verdicts calmly, her mother cowering, cowering, until she begged for forgiveness. They would be in a restaurant, and she pictured herself standing up suddenly, towering over her mother, and finally walking away to leave her mother staring at the half-eaten Chilean sea bass or whatever.

Later, when April thought back to this moment in the hospital, she wondered if her grandfather, her coconspirator, had somehow sensed what April was planning and had decided, as April had a few minutes earlier decided for him, that she needed to be rescued. Because it was he who spoke up at this point, not April. He looked calm, but sad.

"Your daughter is not a liar, Marcy," he said. "She's a good kid. You've done a great job."

Her mother's reaction was exactly what April had been hoping for in her fantasies: surprise, shock, and—best of all—silence.

And then, without a look back—no nod, no conspiratorial wink, no nothing—her grandfather walked down the hall. April and her mother watched him go. He looked tall to April. Tall and strong, even in that ridiculous jacket and those embarrassing galoshes and even if he took small steps and had to pause at the end of the hall, right beneath the exit sign, to figure out which way to go.

CHAPTER TEN

Marcy winced when Hank smacked his lips after a sip of merlot and leaned forward, nearly upsetting his water glass.

"It's time," he said, looking serious. "It won't be easy. But you've got to do it."

She was reminded of the old joke that the best way to tell if a lawyer is lying is to see if his mouth is moving. Substitute "male" for "lawyer" and you've got a pretty good rule of thumb.

She didn't want to think that way about Hank. After all, Hank had done nothing but help her get acclimated to the office, offer tips on showing houses, and warn her about some of the more obscure legalese and shady tactics she'd run up against during closings. He'd asked her to dinner several times and was in every way a gentleman, focusing all his attention on her: how she liked her job, what she liked to do when she wasn't working, even what she preferred to talk about when she was with a "nosy old sales hound like Hank Johnson."

Hank Johnson made her laugh. Given the crap she was going through with April—the moods, the long silences, the threats to someday ignore her the way she, Marcy, was ignoring the old man—Marcy appreciated anyone who could make her smile. And he listened, too. He didn't pretend to listen as a prelude to boasting about the glory days as a high school football star or some such puerile bull. He asked questions about what she had just said. He actually knew how to *converse.*

Still, Hank Johnson was a male. And most males, particularly the one she had been married to for nearly ten years, eventually and inevitably revealed their small personality quirks, like lying, avoiding responsibility, and trying to stick their dicks into . . . well, anything. She couldn't let go of what that woman had said about Hankering Hank.

"Did I say something wrong?" he asked now, jolting back as if he suddenly realized he was getting too close to the shock line of an invisible fence. "I should mind my own business. Forget what I said."

"No, no," Marcy said. She refolded her napkin for about the fourth time. "It's just that I don't think we're going to get much for it. The way he's let the place go, the value must have dropped by at least 50 percent. My brothers and I are going to have to . . ."

Hank was shaking his head like a bobble doll.

"What?"

Hank held up both hands just above the table. "I wasn't talking about the house," he said. "I'm just saying you need to go see him. I know it won't be easy, with what happened with April and all. But from what you've told me, he's trying to reach out. Making a mess of it, but trying. . . ."

Marcy was caught between smiling and crying. He knew so much more about her than she did about him. But then, he asked a hell of a lot more questions of her than she did of him. And he was right about her father.

The son of a bitch.

And so early the next afternoon she found herself on the familiar street, driving slowly and trying to observe everything she saw from the fresh new perspective she was determined to take during her overdue, unannounced visit. There were still traces of dirty snow on the side of the road, but people were out and about, taking advantage of the thaw. She passed a father and son digging a hole next to a damaged mailbox, their dedication to home improvement a sharp contrast to what she encountered a few minutes later as she approached the front walk of her father's house, where signs of early spring life—to say nothing of spring cleaning—were nowhere to be seen. She saw through the picture window that he was watching television. He didn't notice her even when she threw her hands up in the air to regain her balance on the wet leaves, extra slick from months under snow.

"Never did rake the goddamn yard, did you?" she called out in a mock-angry voice when she walked in the house.

The only reply came from the television. Her father was asleep in front of it, pipe in his lap. It looked—and now she noticed the smell—like he'd been smoking it recently.

She went to touch his shoulder when someone on the television said, "What have you got to say for yourself, Bill?"

It was a Jerry Springer–type show. Marcy had no idea who the host was. She wondered if her father did. She wondered if he actually watched this crap every day. The Bill in this case was a pale, skinny, twenty-something skinheaded neo-Nazi. Facing him in a chair opposite was a young black woman, a young nebbish-looking man, and a priest.

"Bill?" the Jerry-host asked.

What have you got to say for yourself, Bill? Marcy imagined herself sitting on the stage, flanked by Nick and Mike. Jerry would look into the camera and say, "Now let's hear Dad's side of the story." The old man would walk onstage to a chorus of boos. The camera would zoom in on a few beefy security guys snapping to attention, ready if the crowd rushed forward. Her father would take his seat, the camera capturing every twitch while the studio audience catcalled.

And now, Bill, the Jerry-host would say, preacher now, stern or-chestrator of this Come to Jesus moment, *You've heard what the children, your children, have said. You've heard in their voices the pain in their hearts, a pain that hasn't diminished even after all these years. Now it's your turn. I'm going to ask you a simple question. You owe your children a simple, straightforward answer. This is your opportunity, once and for all, to clear things up, your chance to tell your side of the story. And the question, Bill, is simply, finally, this: Why, Bill?*

Go ahead, Bill.

We're waiting, Billy Boy.

How do you respond, old man?

"What in holy hell?" Her father suddenly stood, brushing away ashes from his trousers.

"Christ almighty, what are you doing, sneaking up on me like that?"

"Sorry," Marcy said. "You were asleep. I was about to—"

"What's wrong?" he asked. "Is Marcy okay?"

Marcy couldn't help feeling touched by his concern and therefore put aside the twinge of worry she felt at the misnomer. "She's fine, as you can see. Do you mean April?"

"You know who I mean."

"I'll let you know if I ever have a civil conversation with her." Marcy took off her jacket and threw it on the newspapers that covered the couch. "Since when did you become a Jerry Springer fan? Or whoever?"

"Ah, turn that off, will you?"

"I see that you've kept up with your cleaning," Marcy said, fishing through the clutter for the remote. She swept her arm around her to extend her judgment beyond the piles of newspapers to the discarded tobacco pouches and the dirty glasses, cups, and mugs. But the old man merely sat back in his chair and gazed indifferently at the mess around him.

"Shall I make coffee? Or has the health department cordoned off the kitchen?"

"Have you decided to forgive me about April?"

"No."

"Well, that answers that, I guess. So to what do I owe the pleasure?"

Marcy pushed aside her coat and an armful of newspapers to make room on the couch. She rubbed her hands together, not quite sure why her pulse was racing, why she was finding it so difficult to begin.

"Spill it," her father said, smiling.

"Huh?"

"You've never had trouble speaking your mind before," he said.

True enough. But this was different.

"Have you tried Mike and Nick again like I asked you to?"

The "like I asked you to" was enough. She almost thanked him for it.

"Two things," she said. "First, if you want to get together with me and Nick and Mike, you're going to have to call them yourself. I already tried Nick, like I told you months ago. At least three times I've told you this."

"I know that. I thought you were going to ask him again."

"I did. He wants to know why you want a family reunion. I don't know why, so I can't tell him. Only you know why."

Bill nodded. Marcy wasn't sure how to interpret it. Was he being condescending or coy?

"So you want to tell me why?" she asked, almost surprised she wasn't yelling. Yet.

"What's the second thing?"

"It's time to think about moving out of this dump."

Her father's eyes flickered, as if he finally recognized the tactic she had always taken with him: talk about something else, something completely unrelated to the request she was about to make, and then suddenly let it fly, as if simply underscoring the need to correct a glaring and prolonged injustice. *It's time to let me sleep over at . . . It's time to let me start dating . . . It's time to extend my curfew . . .*

She imagined the technique was cute when she was a little girl. Less cute when she was a teenager. Maybe not at all cute now.

"That how you sell houses?" he asked. "Time to sell this dump? This *dump,* by the way, used to be your home."

"Ah. So you remember what I do for a living."

Her father looked startled, as if he had been caught in a lie—or, at the very least, was trying to figure out the connection between what he'd said about selling houses and his daughter's vocation. He looked like he was trying to figure something out. Almost as if he'd said the thing about selling houses without realizing what he was saying.

"Of course I remember," he said, putting his pipe in the ashtray with a *ping.* "Getting tired of you asking me that."

"It was a statement, not a question," Marcy said. Why was it that every time she came into this house she immediately turned twelve again?

"I'm talking about respect," her father said, his eyes boring into her. "I built this house, you know—"

"Boy, oh boy, do I," Marcy said, feeling herself losing her grip. " 'I'm your father! Respect me!' " she mimicked. "Well, you know something, Billy Boy, being able to produce kids doesn't automatically earn you—"

"That's not what I'm talking about. I'm talking about this house! I built this home for your mother, and even though I couldn't know it back then, I built it for you kids. I don't remember it being such a hellhole. I don't recall a time you didn't have this roof over your head. The heat never got cut off. There was always food in the fridge. Your mother loved this house. Show it some fucking respect!"

Marcy sat up straight. Her father had always been strictly a hell-

and-damn kind of cusser. She didn't recall him ever dropping the f-bomb. And she couldn't recall ever seeing him look *hurt.*

"I'm sorry," she said. "Truly."

When she looked up, she saw that her father was watching her carefully.

"Now," he said, his eyes narrow, as if trying to decide if she was putting him on. "What about that granddaughter of mine?"

She held his eyes for only a moment before looking away.

CHAPTER ELEVEN

Nick sat at the Gallaghers' country-style kitchen table and marveled at how so many fathers managed to raise sons without strangling them.

Across from him, arms folded against his chest, hands clenched into fists beneath his biceps, lips set to sneer, sat Bobby Gallagher. Next to a plate with a half-eaten pizza slice was a marked-up copy of the latest version of his college application essay. He'd barely glanced at it.

"Your mother said tomorrow's the deadline, right?" Nick asked.

Bobby gave a half nod.

"Well, then. Are you interested in reviewing the suggestions?"

Bobby had never been what anyone would describe as polite in the three months since they'd met, but he'd never before been so openly hostile as his glare made him out to be now.

Maybe he was just angry that he couldn't procrastinate any longer. Maybe he was upset that Nick had the nerve to make even more suggestions after two previous drafts. Maybe Bobby thought—as Nick had to admit was often his own attitude when he submitted his articles to the magazine—that the essay was perfect as is and resented any feedback that questioned its brilliance.

Not that previous occasions had given Nick reason to expect any sign of gratitude. Whenever Peggy wasn't involved in some charitable event or dealing with a family issue and agreed to "get together"— a strange way to describe a date—Bobby preferred to ignore Nick rather than subject himself to his mother's orders while she "made some final adjustments" in getting ready for the night out. Without exception, those orders were to review progress on the essay with "Mr. Warrington," and almost without exception, Bobby had barely changed a word of it since the previous visit. But since it was obvious the two of them weren't going to discuss batting averages or the NFL draft, Nick usually just edited the thing while Bobby scowled.

Nick actually liked the piece more than Bobby seemed to. Instead of waxing grand on why he wanted to expand his horizons during his forthcoming university years, Bobby had written about a homeless woman he saw frequently on the streets of Woodlake. He described her vividly, if ungrammatically, along with his "feelings of uneasiness" at driving by her in an expensive automobile. And rather than rant against the injustices of today's society and how an education at the University of X would prepare him to someday address these important issues, which have always been of burning importance for him blah blah blah, Bobby took a different tack. He "confessed" that the old lady living in her cardboard box did *not* change his desire to earn money—lots of it. But what the old lady *did* do, he wrote, was make him realize that he was one of the lucky ones. And even if he worked for a huge company and made a lot of money and even if he in some direct or indirect way helped widen the gulf between the rich and poor in this country, he would always remember that, compared to that lady and thousands and thousands like her, he was lucky. And with luck came responsibility to not screw it up.

"Losers," Bobby wrote in his final sentence, "blow it."

While Nick appreciated the essay's youthful candor, he wasn't convinced that an admissions officer was going to chase after a candidate whose primary motivation was to avoid making a mistake. Recognizing the irony of his own eagerness not to "blow it" with Bobby, Nick had originally decided on a tops-of-the-trees revision strategy. He'd gently suggest rephrasing some of the sentences to put a more positive spin on the piece without sacrificing its voice or its vibrancy. He'd demonstrate the proper use of the semicolon, the correct placement of a comma or period when used with quotation marks, and the logical structure of a powerful, persuasive argument.

Bobby, of course, couldn't have cared less. He treated Nick with the disdain of a jock listening to the class nerd explain the dangers of dangling participles.

Even now, feeling the seventeen-year-old bore holes in his face with his glare, Nick chalked it up to the understandable suspicion that any teenager might have about a man dating his mother. He was pretty sure he wouldn't like it if his own widowed father started dating a woman tomorrow, and he hadn't so much as spoken to the man in a year. Of course, Bobby's dad wasn't dead, which probably made seeing his mother with another man all the more upsetting. He once asked Peggy if this might be the reason Bobby seemed at times—Nick chose his words carefully here—*offended* at something about him or perhaps at something he had said.

"I doubt his father has anything to do with this," she said, waving her hand in dismissal. "It's probably oedipal."

"Oedipal?"

"Yeah, you know—the guy who had sex with his mother."

"Yes, yes, I know what it means." But his unasked question was this: Did all mothers consider the possibility that their sons wanted to sleep with them, or did Peggy have some deeply subconscious and creepily incestuous but unrealized belief that all men found her attractive, even her son?

Whatever the reason for Bobby's insolence, Nick couldn't help growing increasingly irritated every time his attempts at small talk were met with a grunt, shrug, or eye roll.

But then, three nights ago, he received an e-mail from Peggy with her son's essay attached. *Finally got him 2 get off his a** and input your suggestions. Wld u mind taking one FINAL (promise) peek? Dedline in 3 days. Any suggestions will b appreciated!!! Me*

It was the promising "Me" that spurred Nick to open the document, print it, and get to work immediately. Bobby had indeed made a few changes, but missed quite a few others, which Nick reiterated in the margins and then wrote what he thought was a congratulatory note at the end, telling Bobby it was a fine essay and wishing him all the best with his application. But judging from the way Bobby was ignoring the paper now, it would be a while before he read that hopefully rapport-building message.

"Something wrong?" Nick asked, finally.

"Just wondering," Bobby said.

"Oh?"

"Yeah. I'm wondering," Bobby said, slowly, "what kind of loser agrees to correct some kid's spelling . . . just so he can have sex with that kid's mother."

Nick sat back. Clearly, it had been a long time since he'd been a teenager. But didn't a few generations have to pass before things came to this, when even the kids from "good" homes so easily and profanely expressed their disrespect and disdain?

He heard noises overhead. Peggy, getting ready for their night out. The sounds of her footsteps, of a door or a drawer opening and closing, somehow spoke to the accusation. Why else had he, Nick, called Peggy last night to say that he'd read the essay and caught a few typos and was ready to review it with Bobby—and, oh, by the way, did she like jazz? Nick blushed, which only stoked his anger. What did this kid, this spoiled near-illiterate, know about his intentions? While the idea of having sex crossed Nick's mind more and more frequently as he continued seeing Peggy, the act itself was far less alluring to him than being with Peggy. Releasing sexual tension, he'd shamefully rediscovered after Marilyn's death, wasn't all that difficult. What *was* difficult was being alone. The more he saw Peggy, the more he realized how much he missed just being with someone, spending time with a friend. Well, not just a friend: a woman. Just to feel, if only for a few hours, like part of a couple, to smell perfume, to marvel at smooth skin and delicate lines and softness.

"Look, Bobby," Nick said, quietly, looking directly into Bobby's sullen eyes. "I've been doing this as a favor to your mom. She apparently believes you're much smarter than this essay would lead someone else—such as a university or college admissions officer—to believe. If you don't want my help, fine. But if you intend to sit there with your hands in your armpits and insult me and, by inference, your mother, then screw you."

Bobby's eyes widened, but only for a moment.

"I'm not changing this into some phony, kiss-ass essay." He sounded to Nick just a little less sure of himself.

"Have I ever suggested that?" Nick asked. He pointed at the paper. "What you've got there is good. But it won't work with too many typos and too many disjointed thoughts. If you want me to help you fix those, fine. If not, that's fine, too. Enjoy minimum wage."

That finally elicited the reaction Nick had all but given up hoping for. Bobby actually laughed.

Nick moved to the chair next to Bobby's and began walking through the paragraphs. He explained how to correct a few run-on sentences that had been pointed out before, the proper use of "it's" instead of "its," and—here he started losing Bobby again—how to correct several confusing disagreements between pronouns and antecedents. He resisted, as he had during previous reviews, the frequent temptation to ask Bobby, "Didn't they teach you this stuff in grade school?" When they finished reviewing the paper, Bobby didn't

exactly rush off to revise his work and get it ready for submission
the next day, but he did grumble a "thanks" before calling out to his
mother that he was going out.

Now the kitchen was empty. Nick hoped Peggy would be ready
soon. They were running late as it was, and he'd paid a lot for the
tickets. He was especially eager to hear Sonny "Bones" Markham,
billed as a top up-and-coming jazz pianist. Marilyn had always loved
jazz; it was after a jazz concert, in fact, that she snuck Nick up into
her dorm room to spend the night with her. It was most excellent
foreplay, she had said of the jazz. From that point on, Nick got serious
about his collection.

"Nick?"

The voice startled him.

"Next to the fridge, on the wall. The intercom."

Nick chuckled as he found it. He wasn't sure he'd ever before
been in a house big enough to need an intercom. He pressed the talk
button. "Kitchen to Base. Do you read me? Over."

"Nick, I'm so sorry."

What was she was apologizing for? Her lack of appreciation for
his corny intercom talk? Her tardiness? He reflexively checked his
pocket for the tickets, and then pressed the talk button again. "Everything all right, Peg?"

"It's just that I can feel another of these damned migraines coming on."

Migraines had been among the worst aspects of Marilyn's ordeal.
She started getting them when she began chemotherapy. When one
set in, she needed to stop moving immediately. It freaked Nick out,
the way she'd lie there, so still, barely breathing on the bed, or on the
kitchen floor, or in the upstairs hallway, wherever she happened to be
when the attack began. He wanted to lift her up and cradle her head,
or just settle next to her and hold her hand, the way they often did at
night as they fell asleep. But Marilyn would plead with Nick to just

block out the light. All light. He would do his best, stepping around her as quietly possible. He always felt he was getting an unwelcome preview of what was ahead: Marilyn on her back, eyes closed; Nick looking down at her, helpless and hopeless. And then she would ask Nick to leave.

So much for seeing Bones Markham tonight.

He pressed the button. "How can I help?" he asked.

"It's not bad yet, but I know from experience that it's going to get worse." Her voice sounded staticky, but strong. "I'm so sorry, Nick, but I just don't think I can go out tonight."

"Don't worry about it. Just feel better. Marilyn used to get these and she—"

He let go of the button. When was he going to stop making this mistake? It was pitiful, really, this constant referencing.

He pressed the talk button. "Can I bring you a glass of water or something?"

"It's okay, Nick. Really. I've found that these things just take time. I'm glad you understand. And I'm sorry, but can you show yourself out?"

"Of course. Feel better. I'll call you."

He waited for her reply, but it didn't come. She must have collapsed back on her bed, awaiting the agony. He wondered if he should take a glass of water up to her, but decided against it. She needed complete quiet. He picked up his keys from the kitchen table and took Bobby's dish with the pizza scraps to the sink. Since he knew firsthand that the last thing Peggy would want to see if she came downstairs to get aspirin or something stronger was a pile of dirty dishes, he found a dish towel, threw it over his shoulder, and got to work.

It was nice, actually, standing at the kitchen sink, in front of a window that looked out onto a nicely maintained backyard. The hot water was calming, the task of drying somehow important, and the feeling of someone else in the house was incredibly comforting. He took his time.

Since jazz wasn't on the agenda, he needed a new plan for the evening. There was the article that Ginny had just assigned him, but why ruin the evening completely by even thinking about Ginny Eastland?

A perfectly nice young woman, Ginny. Early thirties. Good figure. Probably married to some yuppie broker or software genius, judging from the clothes she paraded about in, clothes that most people on the editorial end of publishing can't afford. It wasn't her fault that the industry was changing. She wasn't to blame for last month's reorganization. She might even be excused for the condescending way she'd described to him the "new direction" of the company by explaining her suggestion that Nick give the "telecommute thing" a try. The message was clear enough: telecommute or terminate. "We want fresh," she'd said. She also encouraged him to freelance on the side, which only a complete buffoon would confuse with anything other than an undisguised hint that the squeeze-out was on. But she kept sending him assignments, and he had to be grateful for that. Hadn't he?

Focus on the positive, he told himself as he dried his hands on the dish towel and draped it along the rim of the sink. He let himself out of the house, careful to close the door quietly. Even the slightest sounds were murder on migraines.

In his car, he turned on the Bones Markham CD he had planned to play for Peggy on their way to the concert. He was about to make a right turn at the stop sign at the end of her road when a car making a left went way out of its lane and nearly hit the front of Nick's car. Nick slammed on the horn. The other driver didn't even turn his head as he gave Nick the finger.

He was sure that his headlights had made it impossible for his own face to be seen, much less recognized. But Nick definitely saw and recognized the other driver.

A car that had pulled up behind his tooted gently.

"Fuck you!" Nick yelled. He had to wait for a line of cars coming from the left to pass before he could execute—to less friendly honking now—a U-turn back onto Peggy's road.

Can't be him, he said as he drove back toward the house. I'm being paranoid.

But there was a car in her driveway and a shaft of life emanating from the front door as he drove by. Careful to maintain a non-stalking speed, he saw Peggy, dressed in a sleek black cocktail dress, stepping aside to let Peter Jackson enter.

He used a driveway a few houses down from Peggy's to turn around. He made his way home slowly, focusing carefully on the posted speed limits. He maintained a safe distance from the car in front of him. He kept the radio off. He declined the option of turning right on red, with caution, unless there was a car behind him. Whenever he moved his foot from the gas pedal to the brake, or vice versa, the tickets in his pocket cut into his thigh.

He hesitated at the front door. Inside, the house was ready in the event that the outcome of the my-place-or-yours decision was his. Nick had spent most of the day scouring the downstairs bathroom and especially the master bath, paying particular attention to the toilets and the floor around them. He made sure the kitchen was spotless, the refrigerator free of old cheese or other malodorous items. A bottle of chardonnay sat expectantly on the bottom shelf of the refrigerator door. He had vacuumed the bedroom rug and dusted the dressers and bedside tables, apologizing to Marilyn as he put the pictures of the two of them inside drawers, out of sight. Now, as he let himself into the house, he felt the need to formulate another apology, as if she were sitting on the steps just inside the front door, waiting for his explanation.

When he and Marilyn had bought the house, he'd wired it so that the music he selected from his system in the den could be heard throughout. In this way, he and Marilyn were able to "christen" the house by making love in each room, accompanied by John Coltrane or Miles Davis. Nowadays, Nick always left the radio on whenever he left—not to fool a potential burglar, but because he hated the silence of returning to an empty house.

He craved that silence now. Slamming the door behind him, he went to the den and turned the music off. As he did so he saw, on one of the shelves, a picture of Marilyn. The picture had been taken at the Indiana Dunes on Lake Michigan. It had always been one of his favorites. She was sitting on the beach at sunset, hugging her knees, smiling at him like a promise.

He grabbed the picture, lifted it high over his head, and, after a half-second hesitation and with a downward swoop of his arm, threw the picture on the floor in front of him. It landed face up, the glass cracked but not shattered. A jagged line ran across Marilyn's knees; the sun behind her now the center of a glassy spider's web.

CHAPTER TWELVE

April improvised to her footsteps as she made her way home.

I'm finally out, finally free.
Summer's here. Just you and me.
We'll make the most of the time we've got.
I'm gonna love you, babe. Gonna love you a lot.

April frowned. Well, that sucked. But she'd just finished her last day of school and she'd have plenty of time to concentrate on her songs, her singing, and finding a band that wasn't too lame. She saw herself performing in one of those outdoor concerts by the lake. Keith Spinelli would hear this incredible music and wander over to see who it was and would be amazed to see her, April Shea, up there onstage, front and center. She might point to him, a special crumb, as she acknowledged the wild roar of the crowd.

She couldn't wait for the long days ahead. She and Heather would do some serious tanning—forget what her mother said about skin cancer. Why couldn't her mother, the only dark cloud on the summer horizon, be more like Heather's? Why couldn't she be more like anyone else's mother?

She considered the options that would keep her away from home as much as possible. She couldn't hang out with Heather all the time or her IQ would drop a few hundred points. Kelly Honaker lived nearby, but she was such a preppy, two-faced slut that April might catch an STD from just being with her. The inseparable Chandra Zahm and Allyson Cagley were nice, but they had been best friends since kindergarten and had their own strange language that kind of freaked April out. She concentrated on the rhythm of her footsteps to crowd out the thought that when it came down to it, she didn't really have a best friend besides Heather.

She stopped when she saw the car parked halfway up the driveway to her house. She didn't recognize it, not being a car nut like her grandfather, who liked to go on and on about his precious Impala. The thought of him brought a pang, since she hadn't been allowed to see him after the accident, but she forgot all about her grandfather when she got closer to the car and saw that it was a Mercedes. Who did her mother know that drove such an expensive car?

Of course! She ran toward the house. He'd made it big. And he came back, just as he said he would.

April slammed the door behind her.

"Dad?!"

She smelled the perfume her mother used to wear when she and her father would go out. As a kid, she always associated that scent with babysitters and desperate grabs at her departing parents, and over the years she'd occasionally slipped into her mother's room to open and breathe in the fragrance from the small square bottle— always three-quarters full—that rested on the top of the dresser.

But almost as soon as she smelled the perfume, she saw that the man sitting with his back toward her, facing her mother on the couch opposite, was not her father.

It was Hank Johnson.

Her mom seemed nervous. "Hi, Sweetie," she said, stepping forward and then back. "You remember Mr. Johnson."

April took it all in as she approached them: her mom's nicest dress, the string of pearls, and—now that she was close enough to smell it—Hank's pukey cologne.

"Hi, April," he said, standing. "Been a while, hasn't it."

April nodded slightly as she shook the hand he extended and got an unsolicited lesson in the basics of a hearty handshake: eye contact, ear-to-ear shit-eating grin, and a bone-crunching grip.

"Mr. Johnson and I have to meet with a potential buyer, and then we have a business dinner, April," her mother said. "I put your dinner in the fridge. All you have to do is pop it in the microwave and—"

"The Mercedes," April said. What she had wanted to say was, *You drive a Lexus. So the car outside isn't yours.*

"You like it?" Hank asked. "Drove it off the lot not more than an hour ago." He looked at his watch, and then at her mother. "We've got some time, Marcy. Why don't the three of us go for a ride?"

April looked at the strand of pearls again, then turned and walked toward the stairs.

"April?" her mother called out.

As she took each step, slowly and deliberately, April heard her mother mumble something to Hank Johnson. Hank Freakin' Johnson's reply was quite clear. "Not to worry," he said. "I was one myself."

She lay on her bed and waited. A moment later, the room filled with her mother's perfume. April closed her eyes. She heard the door being closed softly.

"I cannot believe what you just did," April heard. She hadn't opened her own eyes yet, but she could already feel the heat from her mother's. "Just where do you get off being so incredibly rude like that?"

"You cannot keep going out with that creep." April felt the words come down from the poster on the ceiling and through her mouth.

"Sit up and look at me. And keep your voice down. He'll hear you."

"I hope so."

"What is going on with you?"

April waited. She was determined to wait, to not say a word. Let her mother draw her own conclusions. Let her stand there forever if she wants. April would not speak. "Do you have to wear those pearls?" she asked.

"What about these pearls? What's wrong with them?"

"Nothing. I'm sure Dad would love to know you still wear them."

Now her mother paused for more than a moment.

"Let me explain something, young lady. First, your father didn't buy me these pearls. He preferred to spend his money on other things. Other people. These pearls were my mother's. Second, I am not *going out* with this man. We have a business dinner. I've told you: Hank— Mr. Johnson—is a very successful realtor. He's been in the business a long time. He's given me all sorts of advice. He's been a huge help to me. And this is how you act?"

April tried to keep her face blank. Indifferent. Repulsed.

"I'm trying to keep things together, April. This is the first job I've had where I don't have to bow and scrape or clean up after someone. I have to make this work. We've got expenses. You're going to college in a couple years and someone's going to have to pay for that."

"I'll ask Dad."

"Ha!"

"Why do you hate him so much?"

Her mother held her breath. Her features softened. "I don't hate him. Not anymore. But we'll talk about that later. In the meantime, as

I told you, I'm going to a meeting and then to a *business* dinner with Mr. Johnson. He's doing me a favor. Just remember, in case you're tempted not to like him, that in a way he's doing both of us a favor."

"And what favor are you doing him?" April asked.

She hadn't expected the slap, so it didn't hurt at first. But after she heard her mother walk back downstairs and talk with Mr. Johnson and the front door close and the house grow silent, her cheek started to burn.

She held back her tears. After a few minutes, she booted up her computer and opened her PITS list. At the top of the list, above her mother's name, she typed in her father's. She pressed hard on the keys: P-A-T-R-I-C-K S-H-E-A. She stared at her father's name. Then she selected it and deleted it. Then she did an undo. Then another cut. Another undo. A final delete. She closed her computer and lay back on her bed.

Her mother made everything suck so much.

She had to get away. As soon as freakin' possible.

Roxie's expression seemed to have changed. She was no longer into her music. She was looking directly at April. It was clear Roxie didn't like what she saw: a wimp who let her mother get away with slapping her for no good reason. A loser whose own mother would rather spend time with a *salesman,* for chrissake.

And who had Roxie been? Only someone—a woman—with the guts to take her life into her own hands, to pack her bags and head to North Beach in San Francisco and not let anything or anybody stand in her way.

April turned on her stomach. What could she do? She didn't have money to take a plane or bus or train to San Francisco. And it would be—the rest of June, July, August, and most of September—*four freakin' months* before she could even get a learning permit.

Fine, Roxie called down from the ceiling. *Enjoy your summer with Marcy and Hank.*

April slapped her hand against the bed next to her head. She'd rather be with anyone else, live anywhere else.

She sat up as if Roxie herself had reached down, grabbed April by the shirt, pulled her upright, and started singing at the top of her lungs:

What you thinkin' 'bout, Mr. Ear Hair
Sittin' all alone in your newspaper chair?

CHAPTER THIRTEEN

Mike Warrington watched his boss. Wayne tried to be subtle, but Mike had known him too long and too well not to see how his eyes surreptitiously followed the waitress after she delivered a Jack on the rocks to Mike and the check to Wayne. She couldn't have been more than a few years older than both their daughters.

"Time's have changed, old friend," Mike said.

"Who are you calling old?" Wayne asked, smiling. He took his wallet from his inside jacket pocket as he inspected the check.

"Wasn't all that long ago that you'd be testing lines. Like, 'How long have you worked here? Got a boyfriend? What time do you get off work?'"

Wayne offered up a rueful chuckle.

"Last time I tried one of those, I had hair."

Mike forced a small laugh. He recognized Wayne's line for what it was: an engineered, self-deprecating nugget intended to say to others, *You're talking with someone comfortable in his own skin, a man who doesn't feel the need to impress, a leader who understands the power of poking fun at himself.* It was quips like those—used frequently with customers, strategically with superiors, and occasionally with colleagues and subordinates—that helped Wayne get to where he was: senior vice president, sales, North America. Mike was one of ten of his direct reports and dozens of indirect reports. But it was not a line, Mike felt, that Wayne should have used with him. Mike heard it as, *I may think about that stuff, but I don't talk about it like a frat boy. I've grown up. You might want to give that a try.*

Mike had not wanted to get into sales. In fact, he had been determined to avoid any calling or occupation that smacked of following in the old man's footsteps. He had managed to get high numbers in the draft lottery and so didn't have to even consider joining the service. His father encouraged Mike to get into sales—*Sky's the limit when you're on commission*—and so he promptly took the first non-sales job he was offered, which was with a large regional bank. Soon afterward, however, eyes bleary from columns of numbers and head filled with incomprehensible jargon about equity and float and discrete compounding, he found himself thinking the military might have been a better choice. Then he began scouring the classifieds.

He and Wayne started as sales reps on the same day. For the first months—almost a year—they teamed up to make cold calls to small to midsize machine shops scattered throughout Ohio, Michigan, Indiana, and Illinois. Wayne had more than just hair back then. He had drive. He was the one who pushed them, at the end of the day, to call on one more metalworker. He was the one who shamed Mike—*Do you want the business or don't you?*—into entertaining boorish prospects each night at steak joints and pasta palaces. *Whatever it takes,* Wayne would say. A customer wanted to get hammered? Wayne would pick out the lounge, get stinking with him, and still be ready for an eight o'clock meeting the next morning. A customer liked strip clubs? Wayne made sure he had plenty of singles for G-strings. And on those rare occasions when they weren't entertaining customers, Wayne put his schmoozing skills to work, usually successfully, on receptionists, waitresses, store clerks—even, once, a tollbooth attendant.

As Wayne had just pointed out, it was all a very long time ago. Still, that year had been a valuable one for Mike. As Wayne moved up, he helped Mike move up. He always returned Mike's calls—at first, out of loyalty to that year in the trenches; later, Mike came to believe, mainly because Wayne knew how much dirt Mike had on him. Mike didn't mind the shift. In fact, he encouraged it. Through friendly reminders of past exploits, Mike made sure Wayne remembered there was always the possibility that Mike might someday—at a corporate affair, perhaps, or an event that included wives—mention (accidentally, of course) one of Wayne's early-career indiscretions.

And so Mike was curious to know what tone and approach Wayne would take when he finished totaling up the bill and signing the check and finally raised the subject that led to this increasingly rare get-together of old sales hounds. Wayne was taking a long time to add things up.

"Less hair, maybe," Mike said, trying to make his voice smile. He put his glass of whiskey to his lips. "But you still have all the other requisite equipment, don't you? We're not that old yet, are we?"

The waitress appeared. Wayne handed her the signed receipt and thanked her. This time when she moved away from the table, Wayne's eyes focused on Mike.

"We've heard from Stephanie Kraus," he said.

The whiskey burned in Mike's throat more sharply than usual. A typical Wayne move: get to the point when the other person least expects it—something he'd coached Mike on when Mike had started managing others. The first reaction, Wayne always said, tells you everything you need to know.

But Mike had been prepared. He swallowed smoothly and placed the glass down in front of him slowly. "Oh?"

"More accurately, our lawyers have heard from her lawyers."

Mike nodded. It was important to remain calm. Or, at least, appear calm. He hadn't expected that. He thought Stephanie might complain to Wayne, maybe even file a complaint with HR. He didn't think she'd go straight to lawyers. And after only a few days. Even so, Mike had all his bases covered. He'd kept her on for a few months after taking away the Transcon account. He had raised everyone's quota, not just hers. And he had stopped going to Cranston.

You don't really think you're going to get away with this, do you?

She could prove nothing.

Still, he wished he'd ordered a double.

"What's on their minds?" he asked. He liked the tone and evenness of his voice. Cool. Unconcerned. No big deal.

"About two million," Wayne said.

Mike snorted, perhaps a little too loudly. "That's ridiculous," he said. "She was deadweight, Wayne. Nice-looking deadweight, easy-on-the-eyes deadweight, deadweight with great tits, but still deadweight."

Wayne shook his head. "I know it's just you and me talking here. We go way back. I'm no prude, as you know. But you might not want to describe her that way if you have to give a deposition."

"Won't come to that," Mike said, feeling his way toward his stride, suddenly the legal savant. "She only had one account that was bringing in any sort of revenue. *One,* Wayne. And it wasn't even enough to keep a rep assigned to it. So I turned it over to telesales."

"Yes, I saw the numbers," Wayne said. "They didn't seem to me to be all that awful."

"They were less than everyone else's on the team. I have to be fair. As a manager."

"I understand," Wayne said. He always recited that little empathetic acknowledgment whenever he was about to disagree with someone. "It's just that it doesn't *look* fair. Especially when you get a cut of future telesales and she doesn't, since you took the account away from her. And now you've fired her."

Wayne was starting to irritate him, as Stephanie had, although she had been more direct. *Fair? Give me a fucking break. You're nothing but a parasite. You can't cut it in sales anymore, so you're making a living off the commissions others generate. How fair is that, asshole?*

After all and as always, Wayne had apparently gathered and mastered the pertinent facts and figures. Mike could see him ordering Judy, his assistant, to bring in the records. He had no doubt spent hours poring over them, looking at the situation from every conceivable angle. He wouldn't be caught short. Wayne should've been a goddamned lawyer himself.

"Wayne, you've always told me to run my territory the way I see fit. And remember your memo about head count? Every region had to cut back—even if it meant some of our high-potential people had to go. Stephanie was my most inexperienced rep. She had a lot of potential, but she wasn't pulling in the numbers the other guys were. I gave her every opportunity to make up for the loss of Transcon. I kept reminding her to fill the pipeline. I kept her on as long as I could. But I can't let her affect the overall performance of the team. I had no choice."

Blow me, she had said.

Mike saw the skepticism in Wayne's narrowed eyes. But, so far, nothing had been said that would incriminate either of them. The figures—when presented in a certain way—could be used to justify his actions. From a legal standpoint, anyway.

"That's it?" Wayne asked. "Everything I need to know?"

Good old Wayne. Just making sure his ass was adequately covered.

"What else would there be?" Mike asked. He couldn't help himself. Instead of just saying, *Yep, that's it, old buddy,* he had to push it. Move closer to the line.

"Just wanted to make sure," Wayne said. He put his wallet back in the pocket of his blue suit coat and stood. The meeting was apparently over.

"I can back you on workforce reduction. But if there are any other, ah, surprises . . ."

Mike nodded. "I understand," he said. "I hate surprises, too."

But as he drove home, Mike thought about that particular lie. He didn't hate *all* surprises. He liked, most especially, the ones that came with unbuttoning, unzipping, unclasping.

But could those really be considered surprises? He had long ago ceased being astonished when women consented, some almost eagerly, to be with him. So the seduction itself was not novel. Maybe it was the variety he enjoyed: the varying fullness of lips, the different shape and sway of breasts, the different reactions to his touch, the responses to that first moment—the grabbers, the guiders, the aggressive, the passive, the moaners, the laughers, the shouters, the shudderers, the sighers. That was it, he decided: He liked variety, not surprises. So his mood darkened considerably when he saw Stephanie Kraus's car parked on the street in front of his house.

He stopped halfway up the driveway to make sure it was her. After all, there were plenty of Volvos in the state of Illinois; hell, there were plenty on his own street. The summer sun was low in the sky now, casting shadows, and he couldn't tell if someone was sitting in the driver's seat. He pulled the car into the garage. He turned off the ignition and sat for a while, thinking what he might say to her. Nothing came to him. He'd just have to wing it. He got out of the car and walked outside, starting down the driveway at a steady, confident, no-nonsense pace. But the car was gone.

What was she up to? She had driven two and a half hours for . . .

what? Mike stared at the spot where the Volvo had been parked, as if it might suddenly reappear. And now the words came to him. *Can't take things so personally, Stef. Don't let your anger get the best of you. You can't prove anything. My word against yours. Nothing personal. We both had some fun while it lasted, didn't we? Why don't we leave it at that?*

Colleen's back was to him when he entered the house through the kitchen, lugging his overnight bag and briefcase. She was scrubbing a pot. He smelled . . . hamburger? Pizza?

She glanced over her shoulder when the door closed.

"Hi, hon," she called. She continued scrubbing.

So much for "hail the conquering hero," Mike thought. When he was little and his dad came home from work, his mother would stop whatever she was doing—cooking, washing dishes, whatever. She'd wipe her hands on her apron, walk over, put her arms around his neck, and wouldn't let go. No perfunctory kisses. Real kisses. Long kisses. No embarrassment when Mike and Nick came in to greet their dad. They'd see their mom, her slip showing a little as she reached up and held on. Their father would laugh and squirm and eventually their mom would go back to whatever she was doing, with a look on her face that Mike would remember years later and, only then, recognize as one of anticipation.

"How was your trip?" Colleen asked, turning back to the pot.

"Fine," Mike said. What to do: go over and kiss her neck, maybe reach around and give her a friendly little double squeeze, or unpack? "I stopped for a drink, a meeting with Wayne." Mike almost laughed: this time, the truth.

"How's he doing?" Colleen asked, still scrubbing.

"A little balder. A little fatter."

Colleen laughed. She turned off the water, grabbed a sponge, and kissed Mike on the cheek as she went to wipe down the table. "Not everyone can stay as buff as you, dear," she said.

Was she being suggestive . . . or mocking? Mike made an effort not to pinch his midsection.

"Where are the kids?" he asked.

"Upstairs. Homework. Whatever."

Whatever was Clare on the phone texting or talking with several friends. *Whatever* was Ty on his computer—maybe doing homework, probably surfing porn sites. This didn't alarm Mike. If the technology had been available to him when he was Ty's age, he would never have left his room. *Whatever* they were doing, gone were the days when they'd hide in the mudroom or the dining room or family room, waiting for him to come home and call out to them, yelling to Colleen to call the police, that someone had *absconded* with their children.

Absconded? Colleen would yell back, theatrically.

Absconded! Mike would reply.

He'd hear them giggling, waiting for the run-and-catch to begin.

Mike looked at Colleen as she sponged down the table. Since he'd walked in the door, he'd seen more of her backside than of her face.

"Guess I'll go unpack," he said.

"Oh, wait. I can't believe I forgot this. You'll never guess who called today."

Mike felt a jolt of adrenaline, but in the same moment reassured himself that if Stephanie had called, Colleen wouldn't have waited to confront him. She would have been sitting at the kitchen table when he'd walked in. Waiting.

"Who?" he asked.

"Your brother," she said.

This couldn't be good, either, but it would be a cakewalk compared to the first scenario. Mike assumed the call was related to the letter he'd gotten—and promptly thrown, unopened, into his briefcase. Maybe he should have read it. But it had been enough to see his father's handwriting to make him decide he'd deal with it—whatever *it* was that his father was writing about—later. Maybe he'd started sucking down Jack Daniels again.

"Mike? Are you listening to me?"

"Sorry. Just thinking about work." He put his overnight bag down. "So Nick called?"

"Yeah. It's been so long, I wasn't sure who it was at first. And it was kind of a strange call."

Strange call. What was strange was that Nick had called at all. He usually fobbed his messages off on Marcy. Like the one about Marilyn's death. Awful for Nick, sure. Nick was going through a tough time, obviously. But he couldn't call his own brother himself with the news? He had to go through Marcy? What had he ever done to Nick that was so awful? When things got tough, Nick always seemed to run to Marcy. And she always ran to Nick. What was *that* all about?

"Are you all right, Michael?"

"I'm fine. Why?"

"Don't you want to know why it was kind of a strange call?"

Mike laughed to hide the wave of annoyance rising up inside him. "Why was it kind of a strange call, Col?"

Colleen picked up the pad that she kept by the wall phone. "Well, he said everything was probably okay, but that you need to call him right away about this message your father left him."

She handed the note to Michael. *10-10. Gate 8. 2 p.m. June 17.*

Mike knew—immediately—exactly what it meant. But whatever was supposed to happen on June 17—tomorrow—was obviously going to have to happen without him. He should have read the letter from his father. He hoped it was still in his briefcase.

"Michael, what's this all about?"

He could truthfully have said he didn't know what this was all about, but he wasn't sure it would appease her this time around. Something in the way Colleen asked the question resurrected the niggling message from somewhere deep inside his consciousness that, after twenty-three years of marriage, she deserved to know more about his family than he was inclined to share. Mike had become so expert in cordoning off this topic that months could pass before he even entertained the notion that he was—as Colleen had long ago accused him—being selfish with this part of his life. She had learned to live with it. But now Nick, with a phone call, was threatening to fuck it all up.

The front doorbell rang, and Mike heard a thump above him.

"I'll get it," Clare screamed, followed immediately by the sound of her footsteps running down the hall and down the front steps.

Mike looked at Colleen. "New boyfriend?" he asked.

"Not that I know of."

"Maybe *I* should ring the doorbell when I come home," he said.

Colleen laughed.

"Mom?" Clare called from the front door. "Someone for you."

Colleen frowned. "No idea," she muttered. She wiped her hands on a dish towel and patted her hair into place. "So are you going to?"

"Going to what?"

"Do what we've been talking about. Call your brother!"

Colleen left the kitchen, passing Clare on her way out.

"Hi, Daddy. How was your trip?"

Mike hugged his daughter. "Fine," he said. But he wasn't thinking about his trip. He was thinking that he needed to find that note right now.

"Excuse me, honey," he said, letting her go. Released from her perfunctory hug, she was already out of the kitchen when he opened his briefcase and started riffling through his files.

He froze when he heard a familiar voice coming from the front hall. Not Colleen's, he told himself, as if undertaking a complex process of elimination. Not Clare's; she was probably already back upstairs and on the phone or online. Certainly not Ty's voice, which was getting deeper every day.

"What are you saying?" he heard Colleen ask.

There was now no mistaking the voice that answered. Deep. Husky. The voice, he once told her after they'd made love, that could launch a thousand erections.

CHAPTER FOURTEEN

Bill thought he'd gotten away with breaking wind, but a few moments after the silent event, April rolled her window down.

"Hot in here," she said.

Generous, Bill thought; more so than he would have been. And it *was* hot. But it was mid-June and this was the Midwest, after all. Without turning, he watched her adjust the earbuds of her gizmo. He patted his shirt pocket, then his pants pockets. Where'd that damn pipe go?

"How long are we going to sit here looking at this ugly thing?" April asked.

The ugly thing was Spartan Stadium. They had been sitting there—specifically, near Gate 5—for an hour.

"Not much longer," Bill said.

He wasn't sure yet how much of his plan, if any, he wanted to share with April. Fact was, he was making it up as he went along, ever since she'd shown up on his doorstep more than a week ago, yellow duffel bag in hand, asking if she could "crash" for a while. Bill had made her call her mother to let her know where she was and that she was safe. But when April handed him the phone, apparently at her mother's insistence, and he tried to reassure Marcy that everything would be okay and that everyone just needed a little time to cool off, Marcy had just two words for him before slamming the phone down: Keep her.

"You want to tell me what this is all about?" he'd asked April as he threw her a clean pillowcase. He'd put clean sheets on his bed and insisted on bunking out on the living room couch.

"No," April said, punching the pillow—pretty hard, Bill noticed—into the pillowcase. "Yeah. It's all about me getting as far away from that bitch as possible."

Bill stopped smoothing the top sheet and looked at her. "That's your mother and my daughter," he said. "Never call her that again."

He waited until April nodded.

"This your first stop? Seeing as how you want to get as far away as possible and all."

He'd been down this particular road before. Nick had once come into the kitchen one evening when he was half April's age, lugging a suitcase nearly bigger than he was, and announced that he was running away from home and nothing they could say would change his mind. He and Clare had exchanged glances. Clare was signaling that he should not laugh. "You all set with bus fare?" he'd asked Nick, who stared at both of them for a moment, then stomped back upstairs, the suitcase banging against each step as he did.

"You know what 'far away as possible' is for me, Grandpa?" April asked.

"Shoot."

"California."

"Makes sense," Bill said as he put the top cover back on the bed. "Can't get much farther without getting wet."

"I'm serious, Grandpa. This singer I know? With this band? Well, I don't actually know her—she got her start in San Francisco. There are lots of bands out there looking for singers and songwriters."

Bill nodded. He remembered Clare's admonition against laughing.

"Sounds like a plan," Bill said, not knowing what else to say that wouldn't sound like a smart remark.

"I wish it were," April said. "I got no money, no way to get there. I'm pretty much stuck with this pathetic existence in Loserville until I'm old enough to get a job, get a car, and get the hell—heck, sorry— out of here."

By morning, however, there was indeed a plan firmly in place, thanks to a lumpy couch and Bill's inability to shake from his mind the dual problems of an unhappy granddaughter and three children who couldn't seem to find a good reason to visit him.

Well before dawn, he'd gotten off the couch, found some paper, envelopes, and a pen, and written letters to his children. In the letters he assured them, especially Marcy, that April was safe. But—and he wrote the "but" in all capital letters—if they wanted to reunite mother and child, it was going to have to be a family effort. Sometime soon, he wrote, one of them would receive a clue about a location that he and April would soon be visiting. Chances were, he advised them, that the person who received the clue would not understand it; however, one of the others would. They'd actually have to TALK TO EACH OTHER to figure it out. And then all three of them would have to travel to the specified destination, where Bill would "deliver" April to them. But ONLY if all three were present. Mike. Nick. Marcy.

The arrangement he presented to April, however, was a bit different. He told her he'd get her to San Francisco—even resume teaching her how to drive along the way—if and only if she agreed to make some stops—at least three of them. She also had to promise that she wouldn't try to talk to her mother again until he gave the okay.

April agreed almost before he finished his first sentence.

To allow time for the letters to reach all three of his kids, he told April she needed to spend a few days brushing up on her driving skills—in parking lots, this time, so as not to risk being discovered or cause injury to any local mailboxes. But today, the seventeenth, they'd set out for Spartan Stadium.

Bill found his pipe, filled it, and lit up. He wondered how the conversation between Nick and Mike had gone. His first clue—*10-10. Gate 8. 2 p.m. June 17*—had been included on a small, blank postcard that he sent along with the letter to Nick. Seemed that those two had the most trouble talking to each other.

He could understand why they'd stopped talking to him, but he had never figured out what had driven a wedge between the three of them, or at least between Mike and the others. Didn't they realize how lucky they were? Bill thought of Jack, his only sibling, ten years older, who had been killed in the final days of the Second World War. Bill never got to know his older brother as an adult, the way his own kids could know each other now. For Bill, Jack was always—even now—the older, heroic brother. He was the reason Bill joined the marines, the reason he wanted at least two boys. When Clare wanted to try for a girl, Bill readily agreed but secretly hoped for a third son. If something should happen, god forbid, to one of the boys, the remaining two would still have a brother.

Hearing a scratching sound, he looked over to see April hunched over a small notebook of some sort, scribbling away furiously.

"What are you writing there?" he asked.

She didn't hear him. She still had those damned earbuds in. It seemed as though they'd been in her ears since they'd left Woodlake and arrived in East Lansing.

10-10. Gate 8. 2 p.m. June 17.

It was a beautiful clue, he thought. But he also knew it was perhaps the riskiest one, since the only person who'd be able to figure out the clue was the one least likely to care. Still, may as well take the bull by the horns.

Bill kept his attention on Gate 8. He had parked at Gate 5 so that he could drive away if just one or two of them showed up. If they wanted April back, they had to play by the rules. There were plenty of cars parked near the gate—probably summer session commuters—but there wasn't anybody out walking about, looking around the way people do when they're meeting someone. He opened his window all the way now. There wasn't much of a breeze.

The small, tinny sounds suddenly grew louder as April removed the earbuds. "I know I promised I wouldn't ask too many questions," she said. "But why are we spending so much time in Lansing or East Lansing or whatever this city is? And why are we staring at that?" She pointed at the stadium.

"*That* is where the greatest game in the history of college football took place," Bill answered. "November 19, 1966."

April turned to look at him. "Football is stupid," she said.

Bill laughed. "Exactly what I would tell Manny, just to get his goat."

"Manny?"

Bill hesitated. What could he tell a fifteen-year-old about a war buddy? How would she be able to understand, sitting in a hot car on a warm summer day, the winter of '52? A hole somewhere near the 38th parallel. Dig or die: That was the rule. He and Manny dug. They dug with a crappy little shovel and, at times, frozen hands with broken and bloodied nails. And there they'd sit, wrapping and rewrapping horse blankets around themselves. Between mortar rounds, when all they could do was tighten their sphincters and hope that a shell wouldn't land in their laps, they talked. *Swapping lies,* as they liked to call it. Manny talked about growing up poor in East Lansing. About how he worked hard to get through high school and then through Michigan State. How proud he was to enlist after graduation. How stupid he realized he'd been.

Mostly, though, Manny talked football. The Spartans, specifically. How when—*if*—he ever made it back home, he'd get season tickets and watch the Spartans kick ass all season long. Especially Notre Dame's ass.

When Bill found out that Manny hated Notre Dame, he became an immediate Fighting Irish fan. A subway alum. He told Manny that if he, Bill Warrington, ever had a son, that son would someday be a Domer. Getting his goat was the best way to keep Manny from saying things like *if* we ever get out of this goddamn foxhole.

Manny did get out of the foxhole, but he never made it back to East Lansing. As he shook Bill's hand the day he shipped out, he told Bill that he was going to live in California. Or Arizona. Anywhere snow wasn't.

They'd kept in touch for a while. Manny settled in Los Angeles and became a cop. They exchanged letters, replaced later by Christmas cards, later nothing. Until one day Bill received in the mail two tickets to the Michigan State–Notre Dame game—the game all the newspapers were touting as the Game of the Century.

The tickets were sent by Manny's widow. *Used his old service revolver*, she wrote. *Couldn't leave Korea.*

"A buddy of mine from the war," Bill said to April now. "He gave me tickets to the game. Notre Dame was ranked number one, Michigan number two. They were both killing their opponents all season. The national championship was on the line."

April nodded, but Bill could tell she wasn't really paying attention.

"Your uncle Mike and I went."

April turned. "Uncle Mike? Was he even born then?"

Bill laughed. "He was ten or eleven at the time. And he was a diehard Notre Dame fan."

It was true. Bill didn't know how it happened. Mike didn't get it from him. The only time Bill ever even mentioned Notre Dame was when he talked about the war and Manny, and he never talked about the war. But somehow, Mike had fallen in love with the Fighting Irish. He even had a poster on his bedroom wall of Ara Parseghian, his image superimposed against pictures of the Golden Dome and Notre Dame Stadium.

Bill remembered how Mike thought his father was teasing him when he told him he had tickets to the game. Then, when he realized it was true, he hugged his father. Every night before he went to bed, Mike told Bill how many more days there were until November 19.

And then, suddenly for Bill but not for Mike, it was November 19 and they were in the stands with seventy-six thousand other people, screaming and cheering and laughing.

Bill spent more time watching Mike than he did the action on the field. Mike grimaced when Regis Cavender scored for MSU. He groaned out loud when Bubba Smith knocked Terry Hanratty out of the game. Bill thought Mike might start crying when All-American Nick Eddy left with a shoulder injury.

But then, early in the fourth quarter, Mike was jumping up and down and hugging his father when the Irish kicker tied the game at 10 with a field goal. And he actually grabbed his father's hand when, with a minute and ten seconds left in the game, the Irish had possession of the ball on their own 30-yard line.

"Here we go, Dad," Mike called up to him. Bill had never seen his son so happy. "Here come the Irish!"

But the Irish stayed where they were. Parseghian decided to run out the clock.

On the way home, Mike kept asking Bill how he could do that. "How could he settle for a tie, Dad? Why didn't he go for it?"

Bill explained, as Parseghian himself later did, that a tie would still keep Notre Dame in the running for a national championship. That he couldn't risk a turnover. That he had to do what was best for the team.

"But he should have still gone for it, right, Dad? *You* would have gone for it, right?"

Bill couldn't answer. The words rang loud in his ears. *You would have gone for it.* All he could do at that moment was reach over and pat his son's knee.

The following week, the Fighting Irish stomped on USC, 51–0. But Mike didn't watch the game. Nor did he comment when the Irish were, after all, named national champions. Parseghian's strategy had worked. But a few weeks later, Bill noticed that the poster of Parseghian was no longer on Mike's bedroom wall.

"Never settle," Bill said to the smoke that rose up before him. "Never."

April had put her earbuds back in and was writing away in her composition book. A diary? Bill wondered. Was she writing about football? Old stories? Pipe smoke and farts?

Why hadn't he kept a diary, a journal? How many adventures and people had he forgotten over the years? A journal could bring them all back. The stories he'd be able to tell! In the end, he figured, that's all you had.

They sat for another half hour. He looked one more time at Gate 8 before starting the car.

He and April were quiet as he drove to the hotel Bill had picked for their first night on the road.

CHAPTER FIFTEEN

April didn't mind waiting for her grandfather. Any amount of time behind the wheel was cool with her, even at rundown gas stations in the middle of nowhere. At the moment, nowhere was on some back road in Illinois, a few hours west of Chicago.

She made a vow to return someday to Chicago. They had only driven through it, but her grandfather had insisted she at least see it since they were so close. April was glad they did. She couldn't decide what to look at: the long expanse of beach and blue waters of Lake Michigan to her right, or the forest of skyscrapers to her left. It dawned on her that she'd never seen real skyscrapers, at least not like this, all lined up against the ocean-lake, as if to say, "This isn't just land, baby. This is *Chicago.*"

"This is so cool," she'd said to him, but her grandfather, who had taken over the driving in Indiana, hadn't responded. April saw that he was hunched over the steering wheel, gripping it as if he might otherwise be pulled up through the roof and tossed onto the congested highway. She'd never seen him so tense. Usually, he seemed more relaxed in the car than out of it, smoothly executing the hand-over-hand turn, demonstrating the proper way to check the rearview and side mirrors, checking the blind spot without moving into the next lane prematurely. But as she turned to try to find the Sears Tower, he seemed to be looking only at the car directly in front of them. April doubted he had even noticed he was driving practically on top of one of the Great Freakin' Lakes. When she asked him if he was okay, he nearly bit her head off, telling her to zip it so he could concentrate on keeping them from getting killed.

They survived, although judging from her grandfather's swearing, just barely. He drove another couple hours before turning into this gas station, telling her he needed to take a leak and for her to "take over." So she'd gotten in the driver's seat while he hit the bathroom.

April decided that she'd definitely need a signature look before they got to California. Riding around in a Chevy Impala wasn't a great start, but whatever. She gripped the top of the steering wheel with her right hand and rested her left arm on the window so that her elbow stuck out. *Too butch.* She tried the ten-and-two grip. *Too old lady.* She tried the hand at the top again, but this time with her left elbow inside, resting on the leather enclosure for the door handle. She gripped the wheel with the top of her fingers, and extended her thumb along the inside part for easier steering. *Bingo.* People would see that she was driving, but the driving was secondary to whatever thoughts—lyrics—she had on her mind. That was the difference between the elbow in and elbow out. Elbow in: thoughtful, skilled, important. Elbow out: pretentious, amateurish, lame.

She belched. She and her grandfather were eating at too many greasy fast-food joints. Her mother would have a cow if she knew all the crap they were taking in: burgers, French fries, home fries, Pepsi with scrambled eggs. Wasn't her fault, though; Grandpa chose all the restaurants. And he was a million years old, so this stuff couldn't be all that bad for you. She felt a slight twinge in her stomach. She belched again—a nice, loud boomer—and felt better.

She looked into the rearview mirror to get another look at her sunglasses. She couldn't decide if they said "driver" or "dweeb." She had picked them up a few weeks earlier, bored to death while Heather shopped for shoes. April couldn't understand her friend's obsession with shoes. Boys never looked at a girl's shoes. Not that April made fashion decisions based on what boys wanted. If she did that, she'd end up looking like Kelly Honaker. That slut.

Something caught her eye. She looked away from the mirror and saw that the man behind the cash register was staring at her. She squinted to see if he was really looking at her. Maybe he was just reading something, the book or magazine—porn, probably—at an angle that made it seem like he was looking at her.

No. He was staring at her. Definitely. And he didn't turn away when he could obviously see that she had caught him staring.

Or had he? Maybe he couldn't tell because of her sunglasses.

April caught her breath. He was definitely staring at her. She started to look away but then decided that wouldn't be right. *She* wasn't the one staring. *She* wasn't the perv. And she wasn't some *kid*. She was on her own. Pretty much. She was *driving* across the whole goddamned country. No skinny, probably toothless gas station attendant was going to stare her down.

Just as she set her jaw in anticipation of a stare-down battle, she won. She saw the attendant pick up the phone and turn away from her. She laughed quietly. He was faking it, she was sure. The phone probably hadn't even rung. He had sensed something about her, something *strong*, and backed off.

Her victory was short-lived. The man hung up the phone and resumed his creepy staring.

Where was her grandfather? Normally, she didn't mind that he took his time in public bathrooms. Better to take care of all possible business there than in their motel bathroom. But he'd been in there longer than usual and the freak was still staring. It looked like he was smiling: a gross, up-skirt kind of grin. April wished Keith Spinelli was with her. All she'd have to do was casually mention that the gas station guy was staring at her, and he'd go in and kick the crap of out him.

Actually, no: Keith was too nice a guy. Too mature. He'd tell her to ignore him. She tried to take the imagined advice, but the perv's eyes were starting to freak her out.

Where the hell was her grandfather? She thought for a split second that he wasn't in the bathroom, after all. That this was some sort of setup. Her mother liked to say that he always had something up his sleeve, a hidden agenda. Was he setting her up in some way? Was her mother about to appear from around the corner of the gas station?

"Ridiculous," April said out loud. She decided he was just having the kind of trouble described in disgusting detail on those TV commercials for stuff to help old men piss better.

She considered moving the car. Her heart was beating faster now. Her hands were sweaty. What if they slipped on the steering wheel as she started to move the car and she drove into one of the gas pumps? Explosion. Yellow and red and orange shooting toward the sky.

I should write that down, April thought. *Sweaty hands, balls of fire.* As soon as the perv stops staring.

Her grandfather finally appeared from around the corner of the gas station. He was squinting even though he was in the shade, looking as if he were trying to locate the car. Strange. But, as she was learning, old people did a lot of strange things. She took a breath. Her hands were steadier now. She was about to turn the key and drive over to him when he walked to the car.

"Took you long enough," she said, annoyed but hugely relieved. She glanced over to see if the perv was still staring. Her grandfather was sweating profusely.

"Grandpa, what's wrong?"

"Little warm," he said, out of breath.

"It's not *that* hot," she said, not wanting to argue but needing to talk. "Especially for June. It's usually way hotter."

"Well, it is for me," her grandfather said, sharply.

Maybe it was another old-person thing, April thought, although she had always assumed that old people preferred the heat. Otherwise, why did they all haul ass down to Florida?

"Whatever," she said. She turned the key in the ignition. The car, thank god, started.

"Do me a favor, willya, Clare?" Bill said. He reached into his pocket, pulled out a bill, and handed it to her. "Get me some water. Poland Spring or whatever they got."

"It's April," she said, correcting him for about the hundredth time. She wasn't really angry about his mixing up her name with her grandmother's or maybe her first cousin's. She just wanted to get the hell away from that gas station. "What happened to 'good old tap water'?" she asked. When they had first started out, her grandfather made fun of her frequent requests to buy bottled water, saying that he'd been drinking good old tap water all his life and it hadn't hurt him—or his wallet. "Why didn't you have some good old tap water when you were in the john?"

"Came out rusty," he answered, still huffing a bit. "I'm a little thirsty, is all. Get one for yourself, too."

From the way he seemed to be having trouble catching his breath, April saw that her grandfather was more than a little thirsty. Not a good sign. They hadn't been on the road that long, and already her worst fear was coming true: The old man would have a stroke or die or something and the ambulance and the cops would come and ask all sorts of questions and find out about her and suddenly she'd be back home, getting nagged to death when her mother wasn't laughing hysterically at one of Hank Johnson's embarrassingly corny jokes. Hank and his jokes were making a slow but steady climb up her TITS list.

"Before I pass out?" her grandfather said.

April switched off the ignition.

The air inside was cool but clammy. A radio was blaring a ball game.

"Hi there," the attendant said.

April decided she needed to pay close attention in case she would later have to describe the scene to the cops. He was old—probably in his thirties. Skinny, black hair. No glasses. She would check for eye color when she paid for the waters.

She grabbed two bottles from the cooler. Heart pounding, she tried to appear nonchalant as she put them on the counter. The attendant didn't move. He didn't even look up from the newspaper spread out before him. This gave April the opportunity to take in more details. She forgot to check his eyes, as she was distracted by the tattoo on the right side of his neck of a heavily fanged dragon whose tail disappeared beneath his dirty blue work shirt. *No name patch, officer.*

He turned the page with a snap and looked up suddenly, acting all surprised. "Oh, I'm sorry. You're still here?"

April wasn't sure if she should smile or what.

"Um, yeah," she said. A nervous little laugh forced its way out of her.

"See, I'm surprised because when I said hi to you a few seconds ago, you didn't say anything. I assumed you left."

April felt her face start to burn. "Oh," she said. "Hi."

"There! That wasn't so hard, now, was it?"

No missing teeth that April could see. Actually, a nice-looking man, she had to admit, if you were into tats. His smile seemed warm, genuine. She pushed the bottles toward him.

"Anything else I can do for you?" he asked. He sat with his arms crossed. He didn't move in his chair. He was, suddenly, no longer smiling. He was staring.

The skin on the back of April's neck prickled. "That's it," she said. She tried to sound cool, in control. She slid the bill that her grandfather had given her onto the counter.

The attendant glanced down at it, barely moving his head. Maybe, April thought hopefully, he's a paraplegic.

"Can't change that," he said.

April saw now that it was a hundred-dollar bill. *Shit.* She'd have to go back out to the car, ask her grandfather for something smaller, and then come back in and deal with this creep again. But then she knew, somehow—*beyond all shadow of a doubt,* as her mother liked to say—that there was plenty of money in the register.

"Sorry," April said. "That's all we've got." She emphasized the "we."

The attendant snorted. "You and Gramps, eh?"

He stood and took a step to his right so that he was standing in front of her, the counter and the waters and the hundred-dollar bill between them.

"Well, I'm sorry that's all you got. But I still can't change it." He looked at the bill. "We don't usually get people in here flashing a lot of money around." He leaned forward. "*Unfriendly* people."

"I'm not flashing anything around." Something about what she'd just said didn't sound quite right to her.

The attendant smirked.

That did it for April. There had to be another gas station or 7-Eleven down the road, even though this one was the first one they had come across for miles. Her grandfather would just have to wait. It was his own freakin' fault. He'd wanted to take the back roads, for some reason. Stare out the window at passing trees. She was sorry he was thirsty, but there was no way she wanted to spend another second sharing space with this weirdo.

"I just wanted to buy some water. But . . . whatever."

She reached for the bill. As she touched it, the attendant slammed his hand on half of it. The tips of his fingers touched hers. April pulled back.

"Maybe we can work something out," he said.

The coolness on the back of April's neck zoomed down her back.

"I mean, we have several options here," he said. "I could pretend that I thought you handed me a ten-dollar bill. Didn't see that third zero. You'd get water, and a few bucks' change to boot. I mean, if your grandpa got this kind of money, he probably wouldn't even miss it."

"Can I please just have my money back?" April said, her voice small.

"Of course you can." But the attendant didn't move his hand. "Nobody here saying you can't. Still a free country. But then you wouldn't have your water, and you ain't gonna find another station or store or nothing on this road for miles and miles."

She knew that he was telling her something, with that "miles and miles." She just couldn't process it at the moment.

"In fact, you're the first ones to stop by since about six o'clock," he said. "Sometimes I go through the whole shift and nobody comes in here."

"That's okay," she said. What was okay? "I guess we'll just have to go without." Another of her mother's sayings: *go without.*

"Well, now, hold on," the attendant said. "Like I said, we got options."

He leaned back to look out the window at their car. April did the same. Her grandfather was sitting with his head against the window, the way he did when he dozed off while she was driving. The attendant smiled again. He leaned closer. April smelled tobacco. Her stomach felt funny again.

"You do something for me," he said, slowly, his eyes wandering, "and I'll let you have those waters for free."

Leave, April heard in her head. *Turn around and get out.* But she couldn't. Even as she knew she should, she couldn't. She would never again make fun of a horror movie where the victim stood immobile while the knife or hatchet or whatever was about to kill came closer and closer.

The attendant smiled again. "What do you say?"

Things were starting to spin. The attendant, his left hand still on the bill, moved his right hand to beneath the counter. April heard a zipping sound.

"Check it out," he said. "You want your water, don't you?"

When she and Heather were both about nine years old, Heather found a stash of porn in her older brother's closet. Among the lurid magazines was a videotape. She showed it to April one afternoon after school. April still remembered the title: *Back Door Booty*. And she remembered getting sick to her stomach when the camera zoomed in on the eponymous action.

"What's the matter with you?" the attendant asked, his face red. "Look!"

April lurched forward, grabbing onto the counter. It was a vomit projectile of *Exorcist* proportions. The attendant yelped and jumped back. He looked down at the dark, wet Rorschach-type pattern that had suddenly soiled his shirt. But what April saw—as the attendant jumped about, looking for something to wipe himself with—was a fantastically ugly thing, a swollen veiny worm made uglier still by splotches of sickly brown and green.

The dragon on his neck strained to get at her. The attendant opened his mouth to yell again but another spasm seized April and she let loose with the second liquid missile. It wasn't as powerful a stream as the first, but, because he was standing away from the counter, it hit him lower, a direct hit. He jumped back farther and hit his back against the rear counter where he kept coffee and cigarettes. April saw the coffeepot jiggle and splash. He screamed in pain.

"Get outta here!" he screamed. He hadn't been able to stuff himself back inside his pants, and April was surprised at how suddenly vulnerable he was, how powerless he looked. She knew without actually forming the thought that he couldn't come after her, couldn't make a call, couldn't do *anything* until he took care of his goddamned penis. *"Get the fuck out!"*

April wiped her mouth with the back of her hand. She saw that she had leaned far enough forward to avoid soiling her clothes. She also saw that the hundred-dollar bill had largely escaped, but the two water bottles had taken a severe hit. She grabbed the bill.

The attendant was still hopping about, screaming, trying to zip up.

April shoved the bill in her pocket and started toward the door. Before she reached it, though, she stopped, turned, walked to the cooler, and took two clean bottles of water. Then she walked out.

It took all her willpower not to run. It seemed important not to do so, although April wouldn't have been able to say why.

"Nice and easy," she said softly, using the words her grandfather used when first teaching her to drive. "Smooth and steady."

Her grandfather was apparently asleep, his head against the passenger-side window, mouth forming a small O. April wondered how he had slept through all that, as if what had happened a few moments ago had raised a ruckus that could be heard for miles.

"Grandpa," she called. He didn't respond. She called his name again, but he didn't move. She tried to see the rise and fall of his chest, to make sure he was breathing, but her own breathing was so heavy that she didn't trust her initial impression that he was completely still. Dead still.

Her hands were shaking, but she managed to get the key in the ignition. Swallowing the bile that rose up in her, she forced herself to think only of the immediate task at hand. *Foot on brake. Turn the ignition. Shift into drive. Ease up on the brake—nice and easy.*

Check mirrors. Check 'em again. Press down on the gas pedal, smooth and steady.

She turned left—hoping that she was now driving in the same direction she and her grandfather had been traveling before they stopped. It had to be. She remembered turning left into the gas station. So she should turn left to get back on the road in the same direction.

"Grandpa, is this right?" she asked. "Am I going in the right direction?"

Her grandfather didn't move.

Keeping her eye on the road, she reached over and, hesitating at first, fearful of what her action might confirm, poked her grandfather.

"Is this the right way?" she asked again. Again, no response.

She gripped the steering wheel tighter and forced herself to take a few deep breaths. She tried to deny what she knew to be true: God or someone somewhere hated her and everything was crashing down around her. Her grandfather was dead—dead!—and she had not a clue about what to do. She was in the boonies filled with pervs. Her dreams of singing, of San Francisco, of escape from Woodlake, Ohio . . . all gone. And what had she been thinking, anyway?

She tried to focus on staying to the right of the white lines, tried to empty her mind. They—she!—had a full tank of gas; she was bound to end up somewhere before the tank ran dry. But then what?

Maybe she should count, out loud, the divider lines in the middle of the road, the way she did as a little girl at the start of a road trip with her parents. She knew it drove her parents, especially her father, crazy. Out of the corner of her eye she could see, as she counted, the turn of their heads toward each other, the palms-down motion that her mother made to signal her father to keep calm. But at about number 50, he'd ask that April not count so loud; it was hard for him and her mother to talk—as if they ever did. At around 150, he'd "suggest" that she count to herself. But April would protest that she couldn't keep track that way. Her father grunted and let her continue for a while, but she never made it past 223 before he ordered her to sit back in the seat and be quiet, and let others enjoy the ride, too.

Now April couldn't count at all. The numbers got jumbled. She bit her lip to stop the tears. She told herself to be strong. Can't pull over and cry like a little girl. She wasn't in the back of her parents' car anymore. She needed to take care of things herself, *handle* things. She tried to form a plan. But what could she do? She didn't know where they were, where a hospital was, *nothing*. She sure as hell couldn't turn around and go back to the gas station for help.

The thought of that gas station almost knocked her off the road.

And then, suddenly, her grandfather sat up. He looked ahead, as if trying to spot a landmark, then turned to April.

"Did you see that? Did you see him hit that ball?" he asked. He was smiling, his eyes wide with wonder. "Maybe he's not a fruit, after all." He sat back and stared ahead, his eyes fixed on something far away. "Wasn't that great, Clare?"

A few minutes later, April heard him breathing deeply and knew that he had fallen back asleep. Or had never awakened. She kept her eyes on the road, which seemed to stretch out before her forever.

Sweaty hands, balls of fire.

Balls on fire.

April started laughing so hard she thought she might have to pull off to the side. That sobered her up. She had no intention of stopping until the tank was dry.

CHAPTER SIXTEEN

Marcy found herself in April's room. She'd been wandering through the house again and ended up here, as she often did when her mind would not slow and her eyes burned and her legs screamed out for movement. She'd been home alone plenty of times when April was at school or sleeping over at a friend's, but the house had never seemed as empty as it did now.

She stood at the foot of the unmade bed. The first thing she would tell her daughter when they returned home would be, "Now, go up and make your bed." April would see the light. She would see that her mother wasn't one of these soccer moms who caved in to their children, who cried at the first tough situation. She would see that right was right.

The closet door was open, where April's clothes hung haphazardly on hangers or were piled in wobbly stacks on the shelves or lay in multicolored puddles on the floor. Her desk, though, was highly organized: pens in their holders, notebooks stacked neatly in the corner, photographs—April and her at the beach, toddler April and Patrick in front of their home, a dozen or so pictures of April and her friends, cheek to cheek—were taped collage-style on the wall behind the black computer monitor. Her keyboard and mouse sat on the desk surface, waiting. Those were the only things Marcy had touched in April's room for years, other than the clothes she rearranged when she brought in new ones. Things would be different now if she hadn't touched those things. But she'd had to do it, she told herself whenever the question popped into her head, which was often. No use thinking about it.

But she did anyway.

She'd had the right to do what she did. She was the mother.

Marcy started out of the room. Maybe she should clean it up a bit, a sort of welcome-home gift for when April came back.

No. That would be rewarding bad behavior.

What she really should do, she thought, was trash the place. Strip the bed, upend the mattress, throw the computer monitor through the window, and rip down all the posters.

Those posters. Those goddamned posters.

She looked above to the one she hated most: the skinny pervert holding the guitar between his legs, the skanky singer with her hand on the neck of the guitar as if she were holding his dick. Why on earth had she allowed it to stay up there, where April could stare at it while lying in bed, all the time in the world to be brainwashed into how much fun these people were having, how rich they were, how popular and how okay drugs and promiscuous sex were. April had of course challenged her, asking how she, Marcy, knew that they were into drugs and sex, insisting that for all she really knew, Don't Care was a Christian band.

All the more reason to believe they're into drugs and orgies, Marcy had responded. Ever heard of Jimmy Swaggart, Jimmy Baker, all those other . . . Jimmies?

But that wasn't the argument that had led to all this. The argument that started all this began, as the huge ones always do, unexpectedly. It was the day after The Slap, as Marcy had come to think

of the first and only time she had ever struck her child. April was in
the family room watching TV while Marcy was putting some clean
clothes in her closet. On the way out of the bedroom, she noticed that
April had left her computer on, with her e-mail program open.

Marcy didn't hesitate, and a few minutes later yelled down for
April to come up immediately. When April arrived, Marcy pointed
at the computer and told her that she had opened the "Sent" folder
and read several of the messages. And she wanted to talk about the
one she had sent to a boy named Keith Spinelli, the one that sounded
a little too forward, a little too available, a little too goddamned
slutty.

Marcy's shoulders slumped now as she stood in front of the computer. She recalled how April's eyes went wide, her face red. She
seemed unable to breathe for a moment.

*How could you? It's not enough you slap me around—you have to
pry into my personal stuff, invade my privacy?*

April had chosen the very words that would trigger an avalanche
of guilt and doubt. She had only slapped April once.

I'm the mother. I have the right. I don't have to apologize.

Marcy had turned and walked out of the bedroom. April put
her whole body into slamming the door, achieving the ear-splitting
thwack that echoed in Marcy's head even now. A moment later, she
heard the *click* of the lock. She felt this, too, like a gob of spit in
her eye.

The thing to do, she figured, talking herself down, was walk
away. The thing to do would be to wait, to give April time to work
out for herself the realization that, when it came to the happiness and
well-being of her daughter, Marcy would do anything.

Proud of her response, certain that she was reacting with more in-
sight, more maturity, more plain old common sense than most mothers would in similar circumstances, she went downstairs, yanked

out the vacuum cleaner, and started in on the family room carpet that she had vacuumed the day before. As she pushed the machine around, every now and then she thought she heard a noise, and she'd switch off the vacuum and turn, expecting to see April—red-eyed, sniffly, apologetic. But no, the sound must have been something in the vacuum cleaner, something she hadn't noticed before. Maybe it was dying—another thing she'd have to take care of. When she'd vacuumed the carpet twice, she sorted the laundry. An outside observer would have guessed, given her pace and industriousness, that she was the hired help, eager to finish for the day. Marcy had wondered, as she created piles of T-shirts, underwear, and dark socks, if April would ever truly appreciate the incredibly mundane ways that her mother demonstrated unconditional love. She wasn't like the other mothers. She didn't belong to a country club—didn't want to, even if she could afford it—and sit around gossiping and drinking instead of paying attention to—*taking care of*, for chrissake—her family. Instead of lounging about, she worked. She always looked for ways to bring in more money for her and April, better ways to earn a living, to create a life. What was she guilty of? Being a good example? Marcy slammed the lid of the washer down and started a load of whites.

Marcy asked herself if she had appreciated all the things her own mother had done for her? Had she even considered the question before? As the washing machine groaned and swished, it occurred to Marcy that her mother's death had wiped out almost all the memories of her mother doing motherly things. She'd forgotten about the mother before the visits to the hospital, before the long naps during the day, before the hospital bed and the other equipment moved in. And what did she remember from the mother before? Only one recollection cooperated. Her mother had come into their TV room. She'd sat on the couch and bent over to tie Marcy's shoes while Marcy rattled on and on about a television show. Marcy looked down at the top of her mother's head and then leaned back a little so she could see her mother's face, and she noticed it was splotchy, her eyes red.

"Are you crying, Mommy?" she asked.

Her mother finished tying Marcy's shoes.

"Go out and play, honey," she said. "Stay in the yard."

That was it. That was the most vivid interaction Marcy could remember before her mother fell sick. Maybe her mother, wherever she was now, in whatever realm, had something to do with this inability to conjure up other memories. Maybe her mother was telling her still to stay in the yard.

She had planned on veal cutlets, which happened to be April's favorite. But after this, maybe she should just heat up some frozen lasagna. No, she'd gone out of her way to stop for fresh veal. She breaded the cutlets, threw them onto the frying pan, and started making a salad. How many mothers even bothered with a goddamned salad?

The scent of veal usually brought April into the kitchen to ask when dinner would be ready, but Marcy wasn't terribly surprised when it didn't happen this time. So should she go call up to April, tell her to wash up for dinner, as if nothing had happened? Hell, no. The ball was in April's court. She knew the food was there. If she wanted to eat, she needed to come downstairs.

Marcy set the table for two. She let the veal fry a little longer than she normally did, waiting for April. Finally, she took one of the cutlets for herself, put the other on a plate, and put it in the oven to keep it warm. She put some dressing on her salad and ate that first. The kitchen was quiet. No noise from upstairs filtered down. Finally, Marcy ate the veal, cleaned the kitchen. When she was done with the dishes, she was so angry that she took the cutlet out of the oven and threw it in the trash.

After she finished with the dishes, she turned on the network news and sat in front of the television April always complained was too small. Midway through, not having seen or heard anything, Marcy turned it off. She threw another load in the washer and folded the clothes she'd left in the dryer the previous evening. She then went into the den to sort through the bills, then decided she'd pay them another time and went back into the kitchen. She sat at the table and snapped through a magazine. At around ten, she decided to go up. She stood outside April's door, listening. Then she knocked.

"April, I'm going to bed." She didn't add the usual "I love you." Nothing.

"April?"

Another minute. Marcy knocked.

"At least say something, let me know you're okay."

Now she pounded on the door.

A moment later, she heard April call out, "What?" Marcy realized that April was probably lying on her bed, ears plugged with her iPod, staring at the ceiling and the poster.

"I'm going to bed. Good night."

Marcy read in bed for a while, waiting for April to come in to apologize. After an hour, she turned out the light.

She was on phone duty the next morning at the realty office. She didn't see April before she left for work. When she got home at about noon, she saw the note on the kitchen table.

I'm not the slut, it read.

Marcy knew—even before she ran upstairs clutching the note, calling her name—that April was gone. She hadn't taken much. The piles of clothes on the shelves and on the floors were pretty much the same. The yellow duffel bag was gone from beneath the bed.

By the time April called from the old man's house, Marcy had reread her daughter's note so many times that she'd already run the gauntlet, several times, from indignation to guilt to disgust at April's cruelty.

She and Hank had been so careful—too careful, Hank some-

times said. Before the day of The Slap, they were never even in Marcy's house together unless April was there—and there before Hank
walked in. Instead, they did it at Hank's condo, during the day, after
a joint call. Or they'd do it at night, but early, so that Marcy would
be there when April got home after visiting a friend. They'd even,
with much laughing and embarrassing grunts and groans as they
struggled to position themselves accordingly, tried to do it in Hank's
car on a deserted stretch of road near the Woodlake Reservoir. They
did it, yes, but given all the prerequisites Marcy'd insisted on, they
didn't do it all that often.

So where did April get off making such horrible, nasty insinu-
ations? What right did she have to pass judgment? Even if she and
Hank had been less discreet—hell, even if they had been doing it on
the couch in front of the picture window with the lights on—what
right did this teenage kid have to call her mother a slut?

"Put your grandfather on," she'd said when April finally called
that evening to tell her where she was. It was the smugness in his
voice, the incredible nerve of *him* telling *her* that everyone just needed
to cool down, that sent her over the edge. After everything she'd had
to put up with from him and from her daughter, how dare they mock
her now. "Keep her," she'd said, and with that she'd hung up.

Marcy was certain that April would soon get so grossed out by
her grandfather's living conditions that she'd crawl home, promise to do anything, even clean the toilets from now on, if only her
mother would forgive her and let her back in. Let them play their
little game.

But the ridiculous letter that had arrived two days later had sent
her running to Nick, who said that, yes, he'd gotten the same letter,
except there was an additional message about some gate somewhere,
the number 10, and the date June 17. Nick said he'd already left a
message with Mike's wife, and they'd just have to wait until their

older brother got around to returning the call. "At least we know she's safe, Marcy."

"We do?" Marcy had said, voice rising. "Are you sure about that? Would *you* be so goddamned eager to wait for the next note if it was your daughter? And why the *fuck* did you call Mike instead of me? This is *my* goddamned daughter!"

Nick kept assuring her that everything was going to be all right, not to worry. But someone had to take the brunt of all this. Marcy felt she would break in two if she had to bear this entirely by herself— including the guilt she felt in any role she'd had in the old man's decision to play this idiotic game.

Now, sitting on April's unmade bed, staring up at the hideous poster on the ceiling, she pulled out her phone and called the only person she knew would be most likely to help lighten her load.

"This wouldn't have happened if you'd listened to me," Marcy said when Nick answered.

The pause. "Pardon me?"

"I told you we had to do something about him. I told you the old man was losing it, remember? But you didn't want to do anything, remember?"

"Are you, in some way, blaming this on me, Marcy?"

Yes, she thought. I am blaming it on you. And I am blaming it on Mike. And the old man. And goddamned Patrick Shea.

"Marcy?"

She hung up on him.

But Nick, being Nick, called her back. He had news, he said. Mike had, in fact, heard from their father about their first chance to get April back. He said he had no idea what their father meant by his clue. But—surprise, surprise—he wanted to help.

"Mike's on board, Marcy," Nick said, and Marcy started crying.

Still keeping the phone to her ear, she slipped her shoes off and stood on the bed now. She reached up for the poster with her free hand and felt along the edges for some give, a spot where she could rip the goddamned thing down, burn it. She found it. She tugged but let go and smoothed the edge, and sat down on the bed. The sheets were warm from the sun streaming in the window, and it almost felt like they were warm from April's body. She lifted the pillow to her face and smelled it, deeply.

"We'll find her, Marcy," Nick said. "We'll find them both."

CHAPTER SEVENTEEN

Every now and then Bill's head bumped up against the window as the tires hit a seam in the road, but for the most part the ride was smooth. The steady drone of the engine might have put him to sleep had he not been so terrified.

He knew that for some reason his granddaughter was nervous, too. She kept calling over to him to ask if they were going in the right direction. He'd nod, unable to find the energy to respond verbally. At one point he didn't answer fast enough, apparently, for she poked him—to make sure, he supposed, that he was still breathing. Gradually, he felt himself become a little less agitated, and his panic slowly morphed to something more akin to curiosity. He wanted some time—and some peace and quiet, thank you—to work out everything that had just happened.

"I thought you were thirsty."

Like a kid who'd finally realized the futility of arguing with his mother against eating his vegetables, Bill opened one of the bottles and took a sip.

"And here's a news flash, Grandpa. Not everybody has change for a hundred."

Bill wiped his lips with the back of his hand. "I gave you a hundred?"

"Yes, you gave me a hundred! And let me tell you—that . . . jerk . . . was not pleased."

Okay, Bill thought, so maybe she got a little grief for not having something smaller. Was that what she was all worked up about?

"It was not a pretty scene," she said.

Bill took another sip. Did she want to compare pretty scenes? How about one with an old man in a gas station bathroom who, feeling pretty good about things for no particular reason—euphoric, actually—looks into the mirror, starts sweating profusely, and feels his legs giving way as he realizes that he suddenly has no idea where he is or what he's doing.

"Strange," he said.

"What's strange?"

Bill was surprised that he'd said that out loud. "Oh, nothing really," he said. Maybe talking about it would make it less strange and more logical. But Bill never did like talking about things unless he was pretty sure he knew where the conversation was headed—or, at least, where he wanted it to go. And there was simply no way to predict how his granddaughter would react if he told her that in those first few minutes after looking in the mirror, he felt the panic as if it were a living being hovering over his head, about to consume him. He'd taken a quick inventory to fight off the panic—something he'd learned to do but didn't know where or when. He was Bill Warrington. He was in a dirty restroom somewhere. He was sweating. What else? Nothing joined together for him.

"You don't want to talk, fine. I can live with that."

Bill looked over. She talked just like Marcy. But, especially in profile, she looked like Clare. The thing he found most curious of all at this point—downright baffling, actually—was that he couldn't remember her name.

He knew she was his granddaughter. He knew they were going somewhere together. But the name was playing games with him, staying just beyond his reach, teasing him.

That's what was happening. He wasn't losing his memory; he was letting his memories have full rein, and, as a result, they simply took over sometimes. Like at home, when he'd make up his mind to fix a squeaky door or clear off the kitchen table but something would remind him of one of the kids, and, next thing he knew, hours would have passed and he'd find himself sitting in front of the TV, staring at a show or at nothing at all. Or like a little while ago in the gas station bathroom, when he'd been leaning up against the door trying remember what was outside it, and he suddenly thought of Clare. The thought became a presence—so clear and so vivid that he was certain she was at that very moment waiting for him just outside. And everything seemed to return, even though it hadn't. He was Bill Warrington. Clare Warrington was his wife. And Clare Warrington was standing just beyond that door and she would smile when she saw him and hold out her hand and he'd take it and slide his fingers between hers the way they always did it, the way they had done hundreds of times.

"No, *thousands* of times."

Bill saw his granddaughter look over. He closed his eyes.

Memories could also turn on you, he thought, just as they had when he'd reached for that doorknob—he would have used a paper towel, but of course the bathroom didn't have any—and he knew in that instant that Clare would not be outside, she would not be there for him, that she was gone and somehow, in some way, he was responsible.

He leaned his head against the window.

And there she was again, leaning against their new Oldsmobile Vista Cruiser. The kids loved that car. They sat transfixed, staring through the skylight over the second-row seat. They were about to go somewhere special, because Clare was wearing her flowered dress, the one that accented her slim waist. Bill loved being seen with the woman in the flowered dress. But, no, she wasn't wearing the flowered dress. She was wearing tight black pants and no socks and a pair of sneakers and she was telling Nick to hurry up or they would miss warm-ups. And then Nick was in the backseat, wearing his baseball cap and his Woodlake Drugs T-shirt and reading a Hardy Boys mystery. *We're on our way to a baseball game,* Bill called back to him. *Think about the game.* But Nick continued reading. Seemed it was all he did. Or write little stories that he liked to read to the family at dinner. He wasn't like the other boys, or even his older brother. One day when Nick was younger, Bill had found him in their room, sitting at Clare's vanity table, sitting next to his mom, putting on lipstick as his mother did. Clare had told him to relax after Nick ran out the door, crying as he always did. *You're going to turn him into a queer, doing stuff like that,* he said, but Clare said Nick was just curious, a sensitive child, and Bill was going to make him neurotic. And now Bill was talking to a doctor and the doctor was saying nothing was wrong and Bill yelled that something was definitely wrong and Clare was in a hospital bed, her lips bright red, as if she had just applied lipstick, her face a jaundiced yellow. The doctor poked him in the arm and asked him if he was all right. But now Bill and Clare were running. They were running away from the hospital and Bill had brought the flowered dress and Clare was in it now, asking him if this was the right way, and her skin was yellow, her lips terribly chapped, and she sat in the stands at the baseball game alone, looking small. But then Bill was next to her and he was yelling at Nick, out there in left field, to stop daydreaming and pay attention to the batter. And Clare grabbed his hand and intertwined her fingers and told him to stop it, you're going to embarrass him. Bill looked over and Clare smiled and her lips were still red but her skin was perfect now and he heard the crack of a bat and Nick had hit the ball over the head of the pitcher and it dribbled over second base and the short stop and second baseman were confused about who should field it but it was a clean hit, a base hit, no question about it, and after a moment's hesitation, as if surprised he had actually hit the ball, the coach yelling at him to run, Nick scampered down to first base.

"Did you see that? Did you see him hit that ball?" Bill yelled. But now they were back in the car. He didn't recognize the road. "Maybe he's not a fruit, after all." He sat back and stared ahead. He was afraid to look to his left. He was afraid he wouldn't see anything familiar, anything at all. "Wasn't that great, Clare?" he asked, but he knew it was not Clare sitting next to him.

He closed his eyes again. It was April. April! How could he have forgotten a screwy name like that? And with what felt like a breeze across the top of his head, everything came back to him: their trip to East Lansing; his children's no-show; the doctor.

He heard April turn on the radio and then turn down the volume. A good kid. Considerate, the way her mother used to be. Still was, most times. April hummed along with the song. After a while, she started singing softly.

"Louder," he said, opening his eyes.

April glanced over. "Did I wake you? Sorry."

"Sing louder, April," he said.

April shook her head. She pushed some of her hair behind her ear. Bill saw from her profile that she was smiling.

"Why not?"

"Feels weird, singing to just one person."

"You want to be a whatchamacallit and you're shy?"

"Singer-songwriter."

"Huh?"

"I want to be a singer-songwriter."

"Well, I know you write," Bill said, nearly ecstatic over remembering how she loved to doodle in that little notepad she kept in her pocket. "So sing."

April exhaled noisily, as if she'd been asked to weed the garden. She turned up the volume. "It has to be loud," she explained.

Suddenly, a sound so loud and so ghoulish filled the car that he wondered if they'd crashed into the back of a semi and he was already dead and on his way to hell, the voices below reaching up for him.

"Meet the new boss," April yelled, shaking her head violently as she drove. The scream, Bill realized, had been his granddaughter's. *"Same as the old boss."* A few noisy codas later, the song ended. April turned the volume down.

"Well?"

Bill worried about his eardrums. "I like Sinatra, Bennett, Peggy Lee . . . those guys," he said. "What do I know?"

"C'mon, Grandpa. Tell me the truth. Remember our deal."

Bill nodded. Yes, he remembered the deal. And he was very grateful that he remembered the deal. Things weren't nearly as bad as they'd seemed just a few minutes earlier. In fact, the more he talked with April, the more he seemed to remember.

"Grandpa? You're not falling asleep are you?"

"Are you kidding? After what I just heard, I may not be able to sleep for a week!"

April glanced over at him. Bill got ready to apologize.

"Now I know what my mom means when she says that you're about as subtle as a kick in the crotch," April said. "I sounded that bad?"

"Like a tomcat with his testicles caught in a fence."

"Grandpa! Gross."

"A grizzly in heat."

"All right," April said. She was laughing now.

"A dachshund in a foot of snow."

April looked over at him.

"A *male* dachshund," Bill said. "Think about it."

"I get it," April said. "My singing sucks."

"I didn't say that," Bill replied. "I just told you how it sounded to me. And isn't that how it's supposed to sound to someone my age? Wouldn't you be more worried if I actually liked it?"

April didn't say anything for a half mile or so. "I guess you're right."

"I know I'm right. Listen—your mother came home one day. She was about your age, maybe a couple of years younger. She ran upstairs and started playing this record full blast. She showed me the album cover and asked me, just like you did, how it sounded. I said they needed a haircut and they'd never convince a producer to make another of those records. Guess who."

"The Beatles."

"How'd you know? Aren't they before your time?"

"My dad. Whenever one of their songs came on the radio, he'd get all serious and tell me the Beatles changed the world."

"He blamed them, eh? Well, you get my point. Doesn't matter what I think. You get up on that stage, sing your heart out, or your head off, or whatever."

April drove a few more miles before saying, "I'm starting to think that all this is, you know, a mistake?" She waved her arm in front of her to include him, the car, the road.

He waited a while before he answered.

"Well, I guess this is where I tell you that chasing a dream is never a mistake, right?" he said. "That everything's going to be all right. That you've got what it takes to be a huge—"

"Singer—"

"—*Songwriter*, but what do I know? All I can say is, we'll see. And we won't be able to see if you don't give it a try, right?"

"Right."

It was getting darker now. Bill suggested that maybe April would want to turn on the headlights. She did. A few minutes later, she asked, "Where are we going, Grandpa?"

Bill didn't even need to think about the answer, for which he was grateful.

"You'll see when we get there. You're going to love it."

"And then west?" April asked. "To San Francisco?"

"You bet, April. Definitely. Golden Gate, cable car to the stars, the whole bit."

They drove on. It was almost completely dark now, and Bill could see that April was getting a little nervous about the headlights coming at them. He suggested they start looking for vacancy signs.

"Grandpa?"

"Yeah?"

"Thanks."

"For what?"

"For remembering my name."

Bill didn't know how to respond. He stared into the darkness.

"Grandpa?"

"Yeah?"

"Can you tell me a story about my mother?"

"What kind of story?"

April shrugged. "I don't know. Maybe a story about when was she about my age." She paused. "Maybe a time when she got in trouble."

Bill laughed. "We could drive to California and back and I'd still be talking," he said. "Your mother was a first-class pain in the ass."

CHAPTER EIGHTEEN

April tried, surreptitiously, to crack open the driver's-side window. Her grandfather hated having any of them down while they were driving. He claimed the racket hurt his ears. She didn't want him to be uncomfortable, but the air conditioner wasn't working, despite his insistence otherwise, and his stale pipe tobacco smell, his old-person smell—he hadn't taken a shower in two days—and his more than occasional farts were nearly suffocating her. Fortunately, he had lapsed into another of his storytelling jags and didn't seem to notice the sudden sharp and steady low whistle of air.

"We were driving along I-80 in the middle of Iowa, just as we are now," he was saying, squinting into the sun as they headed west. "Your mother sees this sign for Arnolds Park on Lake Oko-something-or-other. An amusement park. Well, that was it. She wanted to go to Arnolds Park. She made it her mission, no matter what we had planned.

"I told her to forget it, that it was miles out of the way. But those damned signs kept showing up along the road, and the begging and the pleading would start all over. 'Look at the roller coaster! A Ferris wheel! Bumper cars! Please, daddy, please!'"

Her grandfather chuckled, and then grew quiet. April wondered if he'd pick the story up again, start another one, fall asleep, or announce that he needed to take a leak, in which case she would have to pull onto the side of the road and let him out so he could take care of business then and there.

"Right now," he'd said when she'd first suggested they wait for a rest area, "unless you want me to piss my pants." She was pretty sure it was illegal to urinate right there on the side of the road, so she nervously checked the rearview mirror for cops whenever her grandfather had to "answer the call," as he put it. She guessed that they'd both be in a lot of trouble, she for driving without a license; he for indecent exposure or something.

It appeared that this was either a pause or a prelude to sleep, for he wasn't fidgeting the way he normally did when he needed to relieve himself. She hoped it was just a pause. She enjoyed the stories he told of her uncles, Mike and Nick, but she didn't know them well enough to imagine them as little boys or as anything but older men. She sometimes daydreamed while her grandfather talked of them, but when the story featured her mother, she had no trouble paying attention, no trouble picturing her as a little girl.

"Then she started in on her brothers," her grandfather said after a mile or so of silence. " 'Wouldn't you rather be on a roller coaster than looking at some dumb lake full of salt?' she asked them. 'If you had your choice, would you rather sit by a stinky lake or smash cars into each other?' " He laughed. "She was unrelenting. Here she was, the youngest of the three of them, pretty much telling them what to think. She never did take a backseat to anyone."

"That's for sure," April said. "She's always gotta be in the driver's seat. Drives me crazy."

"Watch how you talk about your mother," he said.

She didn't understand. Was this how adults made conversation? It was okay for them to trash someone, but don't *you* dare try. She wanted to say she was just agreeing with him. But he didn't give her the chance.

"She doesn't let up," her grandfather said, as if that awkward little exchange had never happened. "She kept working on her brothers. 'Who cares about some stupid natural wonder? Mountains are boring. What about roller coasters and go-karts? What about fun? That's what vacations are supposed to be about.'

"I told Clare to get her to shut up, but Clare didn't have any more luck than I did. Besides, she was on to me. She knew, without my telling her, what my plans were. She was like that. We were like that. Didn't need to talk our feelings to death. So finally I pulled off to the side of the road. I turned around and told her that if she said another word, we'd turn the car around and head back to Ohio and she wouldn't see anything. I told the boys the same thing went for them, even though they hadn't said anything. I looked each of them in the eye and asked them if they understood. They all nodded."

Her grandfather snorted at the empty road ahead.

"Here's the thing: April knew she had won. And so she kept her mouth shut. If she suspected that she had lost, if she thought that I wouldn't make the turnoff and take us to Arnolds Park, she would have kept whining and complaining. I'm not saying I would have turned around and headed back to Ohio. But if she had kept complaining, I would have stayed straight on I-80 to Salt Lake City."

"You mean Marcy."

"Huh?"

"You said April had won. You meant Marcy."

Her grandfather looked over at her. "I'm talking about your mother. Not you."

"I know that, Grandpa. I was just saying what you said."

"You don't need to tell me what I said. I know what I said."

He occasionally yelled at her like that. But then he seemed to forget it after a while, so April just chalked this up to his general crankiness.

"Anyway, I drive hundreds of miles out of our way so that April can see this damned park. And when the kids figured out—signs would tell us we're headed in the right direction for Arnolds Park, just sixty miles ahead, then forty-five miles, ten miles—well, they couldn't sit still. They were jumping all around the backseat. We didn't put people in jail back then for not wearing a seat belt. April leaned over and hugged me from behind and nearly made me drive into the other lane in front of an oncoming semi."

April didn't bother correcting her grandfather.

"We get there and of course the kids go bonkers. They want to ride every ride. But the ride they want to ride most is the roller coaster. What the hell was the name? Legend! That's it. The Legend. That's the first thing they want to do. Ride the Legend. And the boys challenged Clare, thinking that she'd be too scared to go on it. That's probably when the boys realized that their mother wasn't scared of anything. She wasn't scared of standing up to her father when her father told her she could marry better than a Warrington. She wasn't scared when she lost most of her blood delivering Mike. She wasn't even scared of the crap that killed her."

A short pause. April scrambled to think of something consoling to say that wouldn't push the old guy further down the black hole he'd just brought them to. But then he resumed, his voice lower, a little softer. "It's been so long, I sometimes forget some of the things she did," he said.

"Like what?" April asked.

"Anyway," he went on, as if he hadn't heard—or decided to ignore—her question, "we all went over to the roller coaster. But at the entrance to the line, there was one of those signs that says you must be this tall to ride this ride. And your mother wasn't tall enough. Not nearly. She raised holy hell, and I tried to talk the attendant to let her through. I didn't get anywhere until my pal Abe Lincoln somehow found his way out of my wallet. Before you knew it we were being strapped down into one of the cars."

He paused. "Actually, we weren't being strapped down. It was one of those bars that they lower to your lap. It was good and tight across my lap, but there was lots of space between the bar and your mother's lap. The attendant saw this, and I thought he was going to tell us to get off. I put my arm around your mother to show him that everything was going to be fine, that she was all nice and secure. What did he think? I was going to put my daughter in danger? I winked at him, and he kind of nodded and shook his head at the same time and moved on to check the other cars."

Her grandfather turned his head to look out the passenger-side window. For the next few minutes there was just the sound of the tires on the road, the wind whistling through the small crack in her window, and her grandfather's loud breathing. She was afraid he might have fallen asleep.

"What happened?" April asked.

"Huh?"

"On the roller coaster, remember? The story you're telling?"

"Of course I remember," her grandfather said. "What do you think, my brain is Swiss cheese? Let me get a breath every now and then, will you? You're just like your mother: in a hurry to be in a hurry. What's the rush? We've got a thousand miles or so to go."

He fell silent again. April figured he was going to punish her by keeping quiet. This game was starting to get on her nerves. Okay, he was an old man. Fine. He was having a little trouble with his memory. Actually, more trouble than maybe anyone realized. But there were times when he was so sharp, so funny, that she was convinced there was no way he was losing it. So when he got quiet in the middle of the story or seemed to lose his train of thought, April could never be sure if he was pulling some sort of stunt on her or if he was just being ornery. That was the word her mother used most when she described him: *ornery.* The word fit. April could see that now. He was being ornery. She didn't like it. After all, she was doing all the work lately: all the driving, all the explaining or apologizing to front-desk clerks and waiters and waitresses when her grandfather got cranky or forgetful. But a lot of the time he was completely cool—*charming,* an older person might say. It was like traveling with a freakin' bipolar.

"Come on, Grandpa. What happened?"

She waited for the angry outburst, but it didn't come.

"I kind of hate to even think about it, even now," he said. "But I guess you're going to hound me to death, aren't you?"

"Hey, you're the one who started telling the story in the first place. Don't start something unless you intend to finish it."

It was a line directly from her mother's mouth, and April thought that that might be the reason her grandfather looked over at her, eyebrows raised, the hint of a smile on his face.

"So you're the one giving life lessons now?" he said.

Like that, April thought to herself. How can he be losing it but remember stuff like her English essay, the imaginary essay that, in a lot of ways, started the two of them on this road together? It just didn't make sense. Her grandfather had to be playing games with her.

"Like most roller coasters," her grandfather said, "this one started off with a big hill. You know, to build up the tension, the excitement. And there were signs along the way as the cars were slowly pulled up the hill: 'No turning back now.' 'Hold on to your hats.' That sort of nonsense. I read the first one out loud to your mother. But when I looked down I saw that she was scared. I held her a little tighter and told her that this was going to be fun. A blast. But then I looked up and I could see that the hill was pretty steep. The sign at the top was 'The Point of No Return.' Suddenly, your mother felt tiny sitting next to me. I held her tighter, tried to reassure her that everything was going to be fine. I tried to make a joke.

"But then she looked up at me and said—and I'll never forget this, we were about halfway up the hill at this point—she said, 'I don't think this is such a good idea, Dad.' And of course she was right—it wasn't. And I felt stupid for what I'd done—even as I tried to convince her, and myself, that everything was going to be all right. When she said that, she sounded like a grown-up. The grown-up I should have been.

"I tried to reassure her, and I held her even tighter. But as we continued up that hill, she kept sliding down, slinking down, lower in the seat. So I tried to pull her up. But we were on such a sharp angle it was difficult for me to move.

"And then we reached the top. Of course, we weren't there but for a second, maybe less. But from there, near the top and at the top, you could see everything: the other rides, the picnic area, the parking lot, and the surrounding farms. And the lake. And a town not too far off in the distance. A few buildings.

"It was quiet for a second. And I heard it again: 'Dad, I don't think this is such a good idea.' I don't think your mother actually said it again. I just heard it in my head. Or maybe I'm just thinking that's what happened. It's been a few years.

"And then your mother slipped off the seat entirely, beneath the bar, and into the area for your feet, between the seat and the front of the car."

He took out his handkerchief and mopped his brow.

"Underneath the safety bar?" April asked.

"She was such a skinny thing," her grandfather said. "And I couldn't reach her."

He paused again. April had to restrain herself from asking what happened.

"Oh my god, the scream that came out of her as we went down that first hill. I was thrown back in my seat, but even after that there was no way I could reach her. The safety bar was locked, and the curves threw me back or to the side. I couldn't reach over the bar. She was sliding back and forth at my feet, banging into the side of the cart. She was screaming and crying and I was yelling for the operator to stop, but of course my screams were drowned out by the others. There was no way the kid could see us, anyway. Oh, sweet Jesus. Those jerks and curves were knocking her around like a Ping-Pong ball. I tried to use my legs to push her against one side, but the ride was just too jerky. I couldn't keep still. I tried to put them over her so she wouldn't fly out of the goddamned car, but there was never enough time before the next curve or dip. Oh my god, the way your mother screamed. And then she stopped screaming."

How was it that her mother had never told this story? April tried to think of the few times they had gone to amusement parks, Cedar Point or Six Flags. Her mother had always been a bit overprotective and kept telling her to be careful, but she didn't make a bigger deal out of it than any of the other million things she nagged April about.

"Was she knocked out?" April asked.

"As soon as the safety bar was released, I picked her up and started running," her grandfather said. April knew he hadn't heard the question. "She was out cold, and bleeding from a cut on her forehead. She was a real gusher. Blood everywhere. All over her, all over my shirt and pants. People screamed when they saw us.

"Clare and the boys were there, right where they were supposed to meet us. They were laughing, probably about how much they had enjoyed the coaster. But then they saw us. Clare . . . the look on her face . . . I think that if she'd had a gun on her, she would have shot me. No question. No explanation. I had hurt her little girl. That was the one thing about her that scared me: the way her feelings could suddenly turn, go cold. You became insignificant, a little speck of nothing. In this case, I was worse than that. I was evil.

"You know how people sometimes ask that stupid damned question about what you'd do differently if you could do it all over again? Some people say they wouldn't change a thing, which is baloney. You go through life and you don't wish you could change anything? You haven't been living. For me, it was the moment I slipped the kid a fiver. Because from the look on Clare's face, I knew she was capable of hating me. Or maybe I knew I was capable of making her hate me. In either case, I thought I'd lost them both. So that's the thing I'd change. Even more than what happened much later, when I actually *was* losing Clare."

April was afraid he was diverging again. But she dared not speak up or ask a question. He was getting off track. And what was he talking about wanting to change much later, with Clare?

"I was screaming at people, asking where first aid was. But I guess they were so shocked at the sight: a man with a little girl in his arms, blood everywhere, a woman and two young boys chasing after him. No one could give me an answer. So I decided to just run to the car. We'd get in the car and drive to a hospital. I'd seen the town from the top of the roller coaster hill. There had to be a hospital in there somewhere. Clare was yelling at me to stop, but I kept running. We got to the car and the boys jumped in the back. I got in the passenger side, still holding Marcy, and told Clare to drive. Clare started arguing with me. She wanted to see Marcy. She started shouting, asking what had happened. The boys in the back were crying now. One of them asked if she was dead."

He shook his head and leaned back. He grew very quiet. A few minutes later, April heard the deep, rhythmic breathing. There was no reason to wake him to finish the story. The end of the story was that her mother had been fine. The end of the story was that her mother kept on being a little girl for a while, then went to high school and met her father and eventually—too soon, she'd heard her mother say more than once—she'd had her. And now this trip. This trip was pretty much the end of the story.

CHAPTER NINETEEN

Mike Warrington could not get used to the disinfectant. He had stayed in plenty of hotels over the years; he knew the smell, had always been able to ignore it before, but not here.

Maybe his sensitivity to it was heightened by the thought that he might be in this cramped, two-room unit for more than the night or two he had promised Clare and Ty he'd be gone. Why, after all, *had* he selected a hotel that billed itself as the "extended-stay luxury option" if he didn't think that things would not be getting back to normal soon? The olfactory evidence of the much-touted daily maid service seemed to trap him, the unpleasant, almost smoky scent not only giving lie to the hotel's "home on the road" marketing slogan, but also mocking him.

The smell was strongest in the bedroom, perhaps because of the adjoining bathroom. He was having enough trouble sleeping without having to deal with *that*. After the first night, he had called down to the front desk to request a different suite. The monotone at the other end of the line informed Mike that the only available units were the "Executive Studio Suites," which meant that the bed was in the same room as the couch, vinyl easy chair, television, "work-ready" desk, microwave oven, minibar, and clothes bureau. Too cramped for Mike's tastes. Besides, what if he brought someone back to the room—that young headhunter he had met a few days earlier, for instance? He knew this was a ridiculous thought, given his current situation. But why not? You never knew what might happen. And if something like that did happen, could anyone blame him? What could Colleen say, after all? She was the reason he was in this dump.

The front-desk clerk, in a surprising burst of above-and-beyond service, told Mike that a two-room suite would be available in ten days or so. Mike thanked him, asked him to tell the maids not to use so much Clorox, and hung up. Damned if he'd be here in a week. In a week he'd be back home, comfortably inside the 3,800-square-foot house whose mortgage payments had nearly killed him when he bought the place twenty years ago, mainly to please Colleen. She'd wanted a big house, and he'd busted his butt to give it to her. Well, all right, she wanted a big family more than a big house, but you couldn't stuff a big family into a shack, right? And, yes, she had expressed some concern about being able to afford the monthly payments and by "big family" she had meant more than one—three or four, tops— since she had been an only child, but Mike knew she loved that house and he loved it and he was young and ambitious and all you had to do to motivate Mike Warrington was to tell him he couldn't do something or might not be able to handle it. And so he traveled all week, from before dawn on Monday through late Friday night. He started beating his quotas, his commissions started increasing, and soon meeting the monthly mortgage nut got easier. As he developed his customer base, the bigger sales started coming in, huge orders from customers who admired his work ethic and who knew he'd always push their orders through at the plant. He and Colleen put an addition on the house. They found themselves paying luxury taxes on their cars. And a few years ago, after receiving the largest bonus he'd ever gotten or, as it turned out, would ever get, he paid the remaining mortgage off in one fell swoop. His accountant had advised him not to, with his locked-in interest rate so low. Mike knew the accountant was right, but screw it, he wanted to pay it all off anyway.

Mike loosened his tie, removed the fifth of Jack Daniels from the brown paper bag, and poured a couple fingers—then a little more—into one of the little plastic cups provided by the hotel. He sat in the faux easy chair, knowing what Colleen would have thought at the sight of the dark brown fabric: God knows what germs are harbored in *there*. He channel surfed and considered all the people he wanted to tell off. He wanted to do it to their faces, just for the sweet pleasure of saying it out loud. He'd start with the headhunter. Good smile, firm handshake, nice rack, wrong attitude.

Another older one, he knew she was thinking as she showed how she could shake hands with the best of 'em. *No way anyone's gonna hire this fifty-whatever.*

"Have you considered the possibility of the service sector?"

Have you considered the possibility of blowing me?

Wayne would be next. *Can't help you out, buddy,* he'd said, moments before he became Mike's new ex-boss. *She's really pushing this lawsuit.* Wayne had delivered this news on the telephone while Mike was having a drink at a crowded bar at O'Hare. He said Transcon couldn't afford to take a hit like that, then apologized for delivering this kind of decision over the phone, and then asked if Mike had anything to prove she was lying, because, well, that was his only shot, given their zero-tolerance policy about this sort of thing.

Yeah, I got something for you, Wayne, you backstabbing mother-fucker. Bend over.

And Stephanie. Oh, Stephanie! How Mike wished she were in front of him at that very moment. What he'd say! What he'd do!

What, exactly, would he do? Stand up? Hit her? Or would he do something on par with what he had done when Colleen had confronted him—teary but calm, invoking the sake of the children—after Stephanie's visit.

He'd listened. He'd nodded. He was gone within the hour.

He decided to leave his bag packed, keeping it on the aluminum luggage rack next to the dresser unit. He'd picked clothes out of the suitcase both mornings, closing it afterward as if he were going to check out that day. He smiled, thinking of how he would return home, call Ty into the bedroom to watch him unpack.

Didn't I tell you I'd be back, he'd say to his son. *Didn't I tell you there was no need to look so sad, so disappointed?*

Mike refilled his plastic cup. Jack Daniels.

"Why Jack Daniels?" he said out loud. His voice bounced off the wall and back at him, slurred from the impact. Jameson from now on. Or Jim Beam—drink American, at least.

Mike sat back in the chair, sipped at his drink, and stared at the television.

His father had started with Jack Daniels after a few months of drinking six-packs each night. Somewhere along the line, the beer wasn't doing it for the old man. It took a while for Mike to notice the transition, because after his mother died and his father started drinking, Mike had perfected ways to stay out of the house and away from the stony silence that seemed to have descended along with the lid of his mother's coffin. It was his senior year in high school. After football or basketball practice he would grab something to eat with a buddy, and then head over to Angela Monroe's house to "study."

Study sessions. The Monroes had a partially finished basement, perfect for Mike and Angela's course of study. Mrs. Monroe would leave the basement door open as she went about her business. Mike could tell that she didn't like him. But how do you forbid your daughter to see a classmate whose mother had died? And how do you, as a seventeen-year-old, refuse to hang out with a girl who came to your mother's wake and told you—even though you hardly knew her, hardly even noticed her since she never went to any of the games or dances—that she'd always be there for you.

He learned later that her mother and father had divorced. Rumor was that the father had pretty much walked out. Something about a secretary. Finances were tight, so Angela worked after school. He discovered this one night after practice when he stopped at a drugstore and there she was, behind the counter. He thanked her for coming to his mother's wake. She said she understood what it was like to lose a parent.

Mike nodded, but he thought to himself that she had no idea what it was like to lose a parent. Sure, her father had walked out on them. But he was alive. His mother was dead. Big difference. He was about to point this out to her when she said that if he ever wanted to, you know, talk about it, she'd be willing to listen.

He got hard, then and there. He imagined a sympathetic session. He'd pour out his heart. She'd nod sympathetically. She'd hold his hand between hers, empathizing. He'd drop his head; she'd offer her shoulder. Mike would say he wanted to hold her, just hold her, but it was uncomfortable to do so sitting down. They'd move to the couch.

The study session would begin.

Just mentioning something about his mother's death alone was enough to get them making out the first couple of nights. Then one night he said, enigmatically, that his family was "screwed up," which proved good enough for an under-the-shirt feel. For weeks, it didn't get much further than that. But then one night he discovered the formula that would serve him so well throughout his college years and beyond.

"I've been a complete asshole," he said to Angela one night, removing his hand from her warmth as if he were suddenly ashamed.

"What do you mean?" she asked.

"Here you've been so good to me, listening to me moan and groan.

And I haven't listened to you. Things haven't exactly been easy for you, have they? Tell me. I want to know."

Angela didn't say much. But what she did do, after a long kiss, was stand and walk to the bottom of the stairs. After making sure her mother wasn't nearby, she returned to Mike. She stood above him. She put her finger to her mouth to signal that they needed to be quiet.

It was fast. It was furtive. Afterward, she cried.

Mike, sitting in the hotel, laughed out loud. He supposed he should thank his mother for dying and his father for drinking: These little developments had helped him get laid. The dying-and-drinking story served him well throughout college, but not once he'd gradu-ated and gone out into the real-world bars and bedrooms of Chicago to start his life. By then he'd polished other tactics, and the women had their own needs and agendas. Mike had come to accept that most women wanted it just as bad as he did. And so his approach—straightforward but nonthreatening, expeditious but not rushed—worked more times than not.

Another surprise—usually not unpleasant—was that the women seemed as willing to move on as he was. One of them—Shelly? Sherry?—seemed so nonchalant about "breaking up" that he'd had to ask why.

"You're like Oakland," she said.

"What does that mean?" he asked, thinking of the Oakland Raid-ers or the Oakland A's. Which sports hero had he reminded her of?

"Gertrude Stein," she said. He stared at her blankly. "Look it up," she said.

He didn't bother. But some years later, on an airplane, he came across a profile of Oakland in the in-flight magazine. The lead for the article was the Stein quote: "The trouble with Oakland is that when you get there, there isn't any there there."

But during those first few years in Chicago, long before he ran across the quote, Mike had plenty of reasons to think that whatever women wanted there, or anywhere, he had it.

Until he met Colleen.

He first saw her at a trade show of Chicago-area businesses. She was one of several people staffing the advertising agency booth next to his company's. During move-in and set up, he watched as she made sure the signs were in the right place, that the brochures were displayed properly, that the company's logo and tagline would be the first thing people would see when they turned down that aisle. She was obviously in charge, bustling about with authority. But judging from the way the others—a couple of guys and another woman—reacted to her requests, she wasn't bossy. The men obeyed immediately, meekly. Mike knew that they hoped she'd notice them, praise them, and eventually reward them in the way that all men want to be rewarded by a long-legged beauty like Colleen. He saw them watching her when she wasn't looking: bending over to pick up a box, talking with the other woman, unconsciously reaching inside the top of her blouse to adjust a strap.

Later, years later, after they had been dating for a while and throughout their marriage, Colleen insisted that he had approached her. But Mike always said that it was she who had made the first move. Her male colleagues were at lunch or on a break. Mike was setting up a display of drill bits when he heard someone behind him. He turned to see Colleen. She smiled shyly and pushed a loose strand of hair behind her ear. He hoped it would fall loose again.

"Can you tell me where the men's room is?"

Mike raised his eyebrows and smiled.

"I just need to know if people ask," she said, reddening. Mike thanked God for thinking of the blush response.

Colleen's recollection was that Mike had offered, several times, to buy her a cup of coffee—even after she informed him that she was not a coffee drinker. That he then tried to get her to join him for lunch or for a drink after dinner.

"It was so obvious," Colleen would say. "The girl with me said you were like a puppy dog, furiously wagging your, uh, *tail* for attention."

However it happened, Mike and Colleen had their first date at a convention center snack bar. He asked her to a Bulls game, which she accepted, and then he'd had to tap every contact he knew—not all that many at the time—to get tickets. How could you not fall in love with someone who loved sports and who seemed to attract the attention of everyone—male and female—in the arena?

Mike stopped seeing other women. For perhaps the first time, he wanted to be with a woman for reasons other than simply getting her into bed. He loved the way Colleen smiled when he picked her up for a date, her quiet laughter, her perfume. He loved being seen with her. Of course he tried, repeatedly, to sleep with her. But when she let him get only so far and no farther, he didn't even think of moving on to someone else, someone less challenging. He would be patient. His patience, he was sure, would pay off. One night he'd find the right words, the right touch, the right moment.

The moment came a month or so into their relationship. At that particular moment, sex was the last thing on his mind.

They were in Colleen's apartment. Mike was on the couch, watching the news on TV while Colleen got ready for their date. One of the reporters was doing a review of *Reversal of Fortune,* the story of Claus von Bülow and his alleged attempt to murder his wife. In the movie clip they showed, the camera closed in on Jeremy Irons's face as he measured out the insulin. Suddenly, Mike was back in Woodlake, passing by his parents' bedroom when, through the partially closed door, he saw his father at his mother's dresser, counting out the pills he was about to give her. He watched as his father stared at the pills, as if he weren't sure about something. And then he saw his father shake out a few more pills into a separate pile. He pushed those into the original pile, and stared at them. Mike must have made a move, or perhaps even gasped, because suddenly his father looked up and saw Mike looking in.

It wasn't his memory of his father's resemblance to the actor's expression that set Mike off. Because the door was nearly closed, all he could see of his mother was the pyramid her feet formed over the covers. She was obviously on her back, waiting for her husband, trusting her husband, to give her the pain pills. But even that wasn't what caused Mike to break down on Colleen's couch. It was his memory of quickly moving on past the bedroom and on to whatever insignificant thing he was doing, without a word to either his father or mother.

Colleen, hair brush in hand, came out of the bedroom to see what was wrong. Mike told her everything.

Colleen comforted him.

The next morning, Mike left her apartment before she woke up. He couldn't bear the thought of seeing her after he'd made such a fool of himself, breaking down like that. He didn't call her that day. Or the next. But on the third day, he needed to see her, be in her presence. When he reached her on the phone, she hung up on him.

It took several days of trying, but she finally agreed to meet him for lunch. He apologized. He tried to explain that what he'd shared with her was something he'd barely acknowledged to himself. And he was ashamed of how he reacted.

"Spare me the macho crap," Colleen said.

Mike was astounded at her coldness. Was this the same woman who had cried with him, who had undressed him slowly, tenderly, kissing him as she unbuttoned, unzipped, whispering that everything was going to be all right?

Mike remembered several endless days after that. He sent flowers. He left long, apologetic messages on her answering machine. He begged for another chance. Somewhere along the line, she agreed to start seeing him again. But the sex had been a mistake, she told him. Not again . . . until they got married.

It was so old-fashioned, so incredibly out-of-date, so uptight that Mike decided that this was definitely the woman for him.

And now, he'd once again experienced her ability to suddenly shut him off—even after all these years. Mike sipped his whiskey and the image of her face—her expression as she turned after closing the door when Stephanie left—replaced whatever was playing on the television.

So many close calls over the years! Who was the first? Of course he remembered. You don't forget the first time you cheat on your wife. It was Ty's kindergarten teacher. The name escapes. Then there was Barb Thomas, one of Colleen's friends on the Welcome Wagon committee. After her, one of the front-desk clerks at the Indianapolis Marriott, where he used to stay when he handled the GM account. At the same time, usually the same road trip, there was Rita, the glass-ceiling-shattering purchasing manager at American Aeronautics in Louisville. Mike thought for sure that she would call Colleen once he'd decided it was time to move on; no man got the best of *her*. A transfer to the West Coast saved him.

The closest call had been Cary Walcott, the adult supervisor of the youth group at the First United Church of Christ. Whenever Mike attended church, which was not all that often, he noticed that Cary was involved in some aspect of the service—leading the hymns, reading from the Bible, making announcements at the end of the service. She had a nice figure and a demure demeanor, but Mike always suspected that beneath the churchy exterior was a delightfully inventive sinner. So when Cary contacted him to take out an ad in the church bulletin, he volunteered to deliver the check to her personally. She came to believe that their adulterous tryst, because it had taken place in the office in the basement, the *church* basement, was blessed by God. She talked a lot about God. How God disapproved—and yet how God *must* approve, since He'd made her fall in love with Mike. How God wanted them to end the deceit. How God wanted them to get married. But then God sent a lump to Cary's right breast. Mike stopped hearing from her when her husband started taking her to Minneapolis for treatment.

Works in strange ways, Mike thought, pouring some more Jack into his plastic cup.

There were others. He used to keep track. Then he stopped keeping track. When he started with Stephanie, he didn't pretend that she would be the last. He didn't plan on anyone being the last. He guessed he'd just keep going until he got caught—or didn't.

And now it had happened. He thought of a picture he'd seen in the newspaper of the funeral of that French president or prime minister or whatever. His mistress and illegitimate child were right there at the casket, weeping, identified, plain as day. The French got a few things right.

Mike closed his eyes. He thought he should put the cup down on the floor next to the chair. He didn't want to spill the stuff in his lap as he had done the night before, jerking awake to a cold, wet crotch. He focused on the warmth of the whiskey, the buzz. And then he felt an actual buzzing: his cell phone, which he'd put on vibrate so it wouldn't ring during his interview with the nitwitted, nice-titted "search specialist." He sat up quickly, spilling the drink on his lap, after all. It was only after he stood up, looking for a place to put the cup, that he realized he'd had too much. By the time he pulled the phone from his pants pocket, the caller had hung up. He checked the missed-calls feature and saw that it had been Colleen. Damn! She was calling to beg him to come home. He started to dial her number—their number—but then stopped. Maybe he should call back later, let her sweat it out. He went to the bathroom, used one of the hand towels to soak up some of the whiskey from his pants. When he finished that, he felt another buzz—the voice mail signal. He smiled to and congratulated himself for not getting in touch with her first. He was tempted to start packing, go home, surprise them all.

But first, he decided to call voice mail. He wanted to hear the remorse; better yet, the begging.

It's me. I got a call from April, Marcy's daughter. She sounded strange. She wouldn't tell me what was wrong. You need to call her on her cell phone. Call her right away. Here's her number . . .

That was it. No *Come home, the kids miss you,* I *miss you.* Nothing.

Mike refilled his plastic cup. As he replayed the message—several times—so he could jot down the number, he analyzed Colleen's tone, searching for hidden messages, signals. Nothing.

Cold bitch when she wanted to be.

Through the whiskey haze, the name April jarred him. For the past week, he'd chosen to forget all the nonsense developing back in Woodlake, but with the missing person herself dialing in, he didn't see how he had a choice in the matter. He needed to make the call, which, given the number of times it took for him to dial the right numbers on the keypad, was looking more dubious by the minute.

"Hello?" The voice sounded older than he'd expected. Mature, but uncertain. No, that was how all teenagers talked these days, he reminded himself, ending all their sentences with question marks.

"April?"

"Yeah?"

"This is Mike. Your . . . uncle. Uncle Mike."

"Oh. Hi." She didn't sound upset. She almost sounded surprised to hear from him. What was going on?

"April, where are you?"

There was a long pause.

"April?"

"I can't tell you. It doesn't matter."

"Your mother is worried sick." Mike hadn't talked to Marcy, but he guessed this was a safe assumption. "I don't know what your grandfather is trying to—"

"He wanted me to give you a message."

"What?"

"He said he was supposed to mail it to you. But he forgot. He gets kind of mixed up." Now Mike heard in her voice the "strangeness" that Colleen had referred to.

"April, tell me where you are."

"I can't. But Grandpa wanted me to tell you this."

"Tell me what?"

"I don't think this is such a good idea."

"Of course this is a good idea. You have to tell me."

"That's the message."

"What's the message?"

"I don't think this is such a good idea."

"That's the message. You mean, from my father?"

"Yeah."

"Put him on, please, honey." He tried very hard to enunciate very clearly.

"He's sleeping."

"Wake him up."

"You want me to wake him up?"

"Yes. Will do you that, please?"

"Hold on." There was muffling, some voices. "Uncle Mike . . . Grandpa . . . Wants to talk to you."

"Who is this?" The voice was scratchy. Mike remembered it well from his childhood, his father waking up after he'd fallen asleep in front of the television.

"Dad? What in the hell are you doing? Do you have any idea—?"

"Who is this?" his father asked again.

"Mike. It's Mike."

There was silence. Mike decided to fill it.

"I don't know what you think you're trying to do, but all it's doing is worrying Marcy. What is it with these messages, Dad? What are you trying to prove? Is there any reason we shouldn't just call the cops? You're kidnapping your own granddaughter, for chrissake."

There was another silence.

"Dad?"

"Who is this?"

Mike shook his head to ward off the chill he felt creeping up his spine. "It's Mike. Let me talk to April."

"Did you get my message? I told Clare to give you the message. I should have mailed it."

Clare? "Dad, I don't understand. Something about a bad idea . . . ?"

"Get a pencil, dipshit. Write it down exactly."

Dipshit?

"The message is: I don't think this is such a good idea, Dad."

" 'I don't think this is such a good idea, Dad'?" Mike repeated.

"That's it. Wait. That's not all. Tomorrow. Noon."

"What are you doing? Please put April back on."

"She's in the bathroom."

"Look, Dad. I don't understand what's going on here. I don't understand your message."

"Then call someone else," his father said. "She might know."

"Tell me where you are."

There was a series of tones. Then he heard his father say, his voice far away, "How the hell do you shut this damned thing off?" and then the line went dead.

CHAPTER TWENTY

Marcy Warrington laughed when she nearly sideswiped an Escalade. She laughed when the guy in the Escalade nearly lost control of his tank as he leaned over to give her the finger. She laughed because she was going to be late for her flight and if she missed it she was screwed because there weren't any more flights out that night and if she didn't laugh she might scream and drive the Camry that April loved to hate right up the back of the Suburban that had stopped short at a light.

"Doesn't anyone drive a normal goddamned car anymore?" she screamed, gripping the steering wheel so tight her wrists hurt. She was having trouble sitting still. "Move it, douche bag!" she yelled when the light turned red. Marcy jumped into the right lane as soon as there was an opening and floored it. She checked her rearview mirror. The guy driving was on a cell phone, shaking his head in disgust—obviously at her. Marcy flipped him off and stepped on the gas.

This was all Hank's fault, Marcy thought, fuming as she tried to pass a garbage truck straddling both lanes. Hank had wanted to come. Couldn't understand why she didn't want him to. Nothing against him, she'd explained. It was between her and April, something she had to take care of herself.

"But you're not doing it yourself," he had said as she finished packing, his hurt-little-boy look really starting to irritate her.

"For chrissake, Hank, Nick is my brother!"

Hank looked away, his bon voyage visit apparently falling short of expectations. Marcy had no doubt that he had packed and stashed a valise in the trunk of his car, ready to go should Marcy give the word. "So where was he when you needed to talk so much about April?"

Marcy slammed her suitcase shut. "What are you saying, Hank? That because you sat with me, listened to me, consoled me—things a boyfriend, a lover, should do, by the way—that you have a right to something that's frankly none of your goddamned business?"

Hank stared at her. "So that's how it is, after all this?"

Marcy looked back at him. And then the answer hit her: Hank was looking for an excuse. If he'd had a suitcase in the trunk of his car, it was for a weekend jaunt with some other woman he'd set his sights on. *Hankering Hank.*

"That's how it is," Marcy said. "We can talk about this when I get back." She picked up her suitcase. "Or not."

"Why don't you at least let me drive you to the airport? You're upset."

Vintage Hank, Marcy thought. *I'll protect you. You can't do anything without me. Don't even try.* How did this happen? When had he first started acting this way?

"I'm upset because I'm going to be late because you're acting like a love-lost teenager who can't handle the idea that his girlfriend has a brain and can actually survive without him!"

That caught his attention. His cheeks darkened, his eyes narrowed. He seemed to be weighing his words very carefully. "So go survive," he said.

Nick was waiting for her at the airport—on time, of course.

"You'd show up early for your own hanging," Marcy said as she hugged him.

"All set?" he asked. Marcy nodded into his chest. She was through with words. She was afraid she might start crying.

Nick picked up her suitcase, and his. He nodded toward the terminal. "What do you say we go get April?" he asked.

Marcy smiled—until she saw the line at the check-in counter.

"Holy shit!"

Nick laughed and told her to follow him. Marcy did so, passing dozens of other passengers as they made their way through the adjacent elite flier line.

"Guess you've been flying a lot," Marcy said.

"Writing travel articles," Nick said, "has its perks."

The agent smiled and asked Nick for his ID and what his final destination was. "Des Moines," he answered. "We're running a little late. Anything you can do to help would really be appreciated."

The agent frowned when Nick said Des Moines. She clicked away on her keyboard for a few more moments. "Did anyone call you, Mr. Warrington?"

"Call me? No. Why?"

"I'm afraid that flight's been canceled. Someone should have called you. I'm checking now to see if any other flights . . ."

Her words were drowned out by her furious typing and the blood that had rushed to Marcy's ears. "Canceled?" she said, knowing she was loud but unable to do anything about it.

Nick turned to her and held up his hand to calm her . . . or stop her.

"What's the problem?" Nick asked the agent. "Can't be weather. It's beautiful outside."

"Not in Chicago," she said.

"But we're not going to Chicago," Marcy said. "We're flying to Des Moines."

"Your aircraft is coming from Chicago, ma'am," the agent said. "I can put you on the first flight out tomorrow morning."

"We have to get there tonight!" Nick glanced at her. A warning. "What about a later flight?" he asked the agent. "Could just be a storm moving through Chicago and—"

"Yes, I'm checking that now," the agent answered. "There is only one other flight to Des Moines tonight, and it appears to be full. Overbooked, in fact. Would you like me to confirm those seats on the flight tomorrow morning?"

"I know you're in a tough spot," Nick said. "But, see, we need to get to Des Moines because my mother's dying. I'd hate to bump anyone off that flight, but I hope you understand the situation."

Marcy wanted to smile but was afraid it would tip the agent off. Who would have thunk Nick had it in him? It was the first lie she believed she'd ever heard from him.

The agent didn't look up. She kept typing and frowning at the computer screen. Marcy wanted to reach across the counter, rip the agent's little airplane lapel pin off her blouse, and jab it in her eye.

"I'm so sorry, Mr. Warrington. I wish I could help, but the first available flight is tomorrow at six thirty a.m. Would you like me to confirm those seats for you?"

"This is unacceptable," Marcy said, trying her best to remain professionally calm. *Assertively calm*, they had called it in a negotiation program she'd recently attended with Hank. But whenever she thought of the cancellation, she thought of April. "You have to put us on that plane."

"I'm sorry, ma'am. But I've checked everything, including flights through connecting cities. Everything is booked solid. When O'Hare shuts down—"

"That's not good enough," Marcy said.

Nick turned and glared at Marcy. "Let me handle this, okay?"

"Oh, great. Another man telling me he can handle it." She looked at the agent. "Come on, sweetie. I know you can do this. Get me on a goddamned plane. Tonight."

The agent stopped typing. Nick led Marcy a few feet away from the counter and grabbed her firmly by the shoulders. "I know you're upset, but—"

"You bet I'm upset. This is your fault. Couldn't get out until the last flight. Now look what the fuck has—"

"We're going to get there, Marcy," Nick said. "But you're about one curse word away from having security called over. Then we'll never get out of here."

He waited until Marcy broke eye contact, then walked back to ticketing. He spent a long time there, hunched over the counter. Every now and then he said something and the agent smiled. After an eternity, he turned, picked up the suitcases, and walked over to Marcy. Marcy felt a tear run down her cheek. "I guess since those suitcases aren't on that conveyor belt . . ." She couldn't continue.

Nick put the luggage down and smiled. "Oh, ye of little faith," he said.

"What? You got us on another flight? Another airline or something?"

Nick shook his head and pulled out his wallet. He removed a card and held it up to her.

"Hertz Club Gold," he said. "Another perk."

Marcy groaned. This was his solution? She wanted to sit on the floor, right there in the middle of the airport, and wail. "We'll never get there in time."

"We will if we drive straight through," Nick said. "We'll take turns driving."

"It's so far," Marcy said.

"Six hours to Chicago, another five or so from there to Des Moines. We can do it. Hell, Dad did it, by himself, when we were kids. And I don't fart nearly as often as he does."

They were just west of Toledo when Marcy finally got through to Mike. He had just cleared security and was walking to the gate for the flight to Des Moines, where the three of them were supposed to meet. Marcy heard the announcements of boarding and departure delays as Mike listened. She pictured him in a crowded terminal hall, people swirling about him like leaves as he stood with his cell phone to his ear. She imagined his brow was furrowed as he listened, in that serious way he looked whenever he talked on the phone.

"So what do you want me to do?" he asked.

Marcy was taken aback by the question. Until he asked it, she hadn't realized she'd expected Mike to tell *her* what to do. She'd always surrendered something—again, unconsciously—when she knew she'd be talking to her oldest brother. How old did you have to be before that reflex slackened? "I don't know," she said. "I'm worried we might not get there in time. Maybe we should just try to meet at the park?"

Now that she was aware of the dynamic at play, she was uncomfortable either way: accepting ideas from Mike, or suggesting them to him. Mike had never invited suggestions; he scoffed at them. He never waited for feedback on his ideas; he went ahead and implemented them. *Better to ask forgiveness than seek permission,* Marcy remembered him saying when she asked him—how long ago had it been?—if she should "forget" to ask her father if she could go to a party that she knew would be unsupervised.

"You don't mind, do you, Mike? I mean, normally I'd just tell you to forget it and go home, but the old man said all three of us had to be there, right?"

"Right," Mike said. "I'll be there."

"You're sure? I mean, can you take time off from work like this?"

"No problem there."

What was with these questions? Hadn't they already been answered when Mike agreed to travel with them to Des Moines after they'd figured out what her father's message was all about? He'd bought his ticket. He was standing at the gate.

"Great," she said. "See you tomorrow, then. Noon, right?"

Did Mike actually laugh? Or was it a passerby?

"High noon at the Legend," he said. "He's got a knack for the dramatic, eh?"

Marcy waited for more, but either Mike had hung up or the signal had been lost. She put her cell phone in her pocketbook.

"Something's wrong with Mike," she said. "He sounds different."

Nick made a sound; Marcy couldn't interpret it. Lately, whenever Mike's name came up, Nick grew quiet. She knew it was because Nick had somewhere along the line decided that their oldest brother was no longer worth the emotional investment he had been making: birthday cards never reciprocated, telephone calls not returned, Christmas cards with preprinted warmest holiday wishes from the Warringtons: Mike, Colleen, Clare, and Tyler.

"Different as in friendly?" Nick asked, after all.

"Exactly!" Marcy said. But then she realized that Nick was being ironic. She felt foolish.

Indiana welcomed them, according to a sign they now passed.

"Remember how the old man used to sing 'Gary, Indiana,' from *The Music Man*?" Marcy asked. "God, he loved that musical."

"Of course he did," Nick said. "Harold Hill, traveling salesman. Gotta know the territory. Dad loved Harold Hill because 'Seventy-six Trombones' is a far happier version of Willy Loman's shoeshine and a smile. But it still all boils down to the same thing: a con job."

Marcy tried to make out Nick's features in the dark. "Aren't we in a mood," she said. Then, after a while: "He put food on the table."

Now Nick made a sound Marcy could recognize.

"What are you snorting at?" she asked.

"I guess I just don't understand why you always defend him."

"I don't always defend him," Marcy said.

"Yes, you do. You can't blame him for *this,* at least?"

"This? What, this? I hate to say it, I really do, but April instigated this. You don't know what's been going on at home with her. The old man is in on it, that's true. But he's losing it. He's not entirely to blame. Can't you see that?"

"Here's what I see: I see a woman so confused that she feels compelled, for some reason, to defend the man she can't even bring herself to call Dad. Your anger repression is unhealthy, Marcy. And it's really starting to annoy me."

Normally, after a comment like that, Marcy would relieve the sudden surge in blood pressure by unleashing a string of invectives that a drill sergeant would envy. But Hank had taught her that when customers, for example, get upset and sometimes even verbally abusive, they're angry at the situation, not at you. The best course of action is to let the customers vent, acknowledge their frustration, not take it personally, and then calmly remind them of the benefits of working together. It worked. She knew it worked; she'd seen Hank do it . . . with her.

"Nick, I can tell you're frustrated. Maybe we should both take a breather for a few minutes. Then we can discuss this calmly. I'm sure we'll both benefit from a calmer approach."

Nick turned to look at her. Marcy saw, in the phosphorous green reflection from the dashboard lights, that her brother was incredulous. Still, she waited. And then, at the same time, they both burst into laughter. Nick nearly lost control of the car.

They didn't talk much for a long time. But every now and then, they'd start laughing. Nick started calling out the exits, and they'd break up at the mention of Indiana: Elkhart, *Indiana;* La Porte, *Indiana;* Valparaiso, *Indiana.*

When Nick called out Gary, *Indiana,* Marcy laughed so hard she thought she might start choking.

CHAPTER TWENTY-ONE

As the red and blue lights bounced off the mirrors and windows, Bill Warrington wondered how he might calm his granddaughter. She was gripping the wheel tightly, as if she were still driving.

"What's he doing?" she asked. "Why is he sitting there?"

"He's just running the plates," Bill said. "Making sure we're not car thieves, desperados on the run. Bonnie and—"

"This is bad," April said.

Something stopped him from reaching over and holding her hand—even though he knew that it was exactly what he should do. He remembered when dads starting hugging their sons instead of shaking hands. It began with those sissy, soul-brother handshakes. Strictly for draft dodgers and fags. "Shake hands like a man," he had said to Nick when he saw Nick greet a school buddy that way.

"Grandpa, you're not going to call him that, are you?" April asked.

"Call who what?"

"The policeman. A fag. You're mumbling something about fags."

Bill forced a laugh. Had he been mumbling?

A blue shirt and black tie appeared at April's window. An index knuckle rapped on the window.

"You have to roll the window down, honey."

April started pushing the handle the wrong way. "Why can't you have a car with normal windows?" she asked, her voice a millimeter from a cry. She reversed direction, shaking visibly.

The trooper stepped back so he could lean over to look in. Hard to tell these days, but Bill guessed him to be in his late thirties, early forties. Close-cropped hair. Smelled of aftershave. Couldn't tell the color of his eyes because of the hotshot sunglasses. Bill knew the type: hell-bent on protecting America from litterbugs.

"Everything okay, young lady?" the trooper asked.

"My granddaughter's a little nervous," Bill said.

"Oh? And why is that?" The trooper slowly looked away from April and over at Bill.

Bill smiled at his own reflection in the trooper's glasses. "Remember the first time *you* got pulled over by a cop?"

The trooper paused. "Hasn't happened yet," he said. "License and registration, please, miss." He stood and moved closer to the car as a semi roared by.

"What's the problem, officer?" Bill asked, calling out. "I didn't think we were speeding."

The trooper looked at April. "License and registration."

April turned to Bill.

"Well, see, officer, she doesn't have her license yet. I'm teaching her."

The trooper removed his sunglasses and narrowed his eyes at Bill as he continued to address April. "Then let me see your learner's permit, young lady."

"She doesn't have that, either," Bill said. "See, I guess I'm old-school. My old man taught me how to drive. Kind of a tradition in our family. Know what I mean? These fancy new driver courses aren't all they're fired up to be."

The trooper tipped his sunglasses to look over at Bill.

"Sir, if your granddaughter was in one of those courses, she'd know that driving thirty-five miles an hour on a highway is just as dangerous as going eighty. Do *you* have your license with you, sir?"

Bill struggled to get his wallet out of his back pocket. He finally found it behind some scraps of paper—receipts from gas stations that he'd been collecting for no good reason he could think of.

"Excuse me, miss," the trooper said as he reached across her to get Bill's license. Bill noticed the small tattoo on the trooper's wrist. "How old are you?" he asked as he examined Bill's license.

"Well, as you can see on the license, I'm—".

"I'm speaking to the young lady, sir."

The trooper looked up from the license at April, who squeaked out a "Fifteen."

"Fifteen, *sir*," Bill said. He winked at the trooper. "Just trying to teach her some respect. Kind of like they taught you in South Carolina."

"Pardon?"

"Saw your tat. Parris Island, am I right?" Bill asked, smiling.

The trooper shook his head. "San Diego."

Bill nodded. "Ah. No wonder."

"Sir?"

"Oh, nothing, really. It's just that a marine from Paradise wouldn't hassle a girl over going too slow. You sure you're a marine, boy? Not just another pussy recruit from Califagya?"

"Grandpa!" April yelled. "I'm sorry, officer," she said quickly, stuttering furiously. "He doesn't mean that. Sometimes—I mean, like, not like all the time or anything like that—he doesn't—"

"I know exactly what I'm saying," Bill said. He looked at the trooper and smiled again. "Just two leathernecks, swappin' lies, right? They teach you boys anything about the action in Korea? The Punchbowl? You want to talk cold? So cold you were afraid to take a piss, afraid the piss would freeze right inside your pecker. Vietnam, the Gulf . . . country clubs in comparison, am I right?"

The trooper tapped Bill's license against his knuckle. "Remain in your vehicle," he said, and walked off.

"Why did you say that?" April asked, still shaking. "Why can't you just be a normal old person?"

"Don't worry so much. He's okay. A little too spit-and-polish, but once a marine, right? He's just checking to make sure I'm not a mass murderer or something. So don't worry, I haven't killed anyone since . . ."

The words got caught in his throat. He had a sudden vision of Mike screaming at him. He had to feign a coughing fit. Goddamn these sudden flashes. Memories popped in front of him without warning, fresh, happening for the first time. And it wasn't just the memory: All the feelings he had felt at the time—the anger, shame, or exhilaration—compressed themselves into a small, clenched fist and popped him good. And they were becoming more frequent. Bill patted his pockets and found his pipe, only to remember that he'd wanted his handkerchief. He was sweating, after all. He didn't want April to see that. He fiddled with his pipe, put it back in his pocket, and wiped the sweat from his upper lip with his hand, pretending to yawn.

"This is bad," April muttered. "We're going to jail, I just know it."

Another knuckle tap. The trooper was back sooner than Bill had expected. April rolled the window down—successfully this time.

"Young lady, it's too dangerous to make the switch here, so I want you to drive to the next exit, pull into the first parking lot you see, and let your grandfather take over. I was watching you, and you were doing fine, just going too slow. But you're too young to have even a learner's permit. I can't have you driving on our roads."

"Yes," April replied. "Sir."

The trooper smiled and nodded. Then he looked at Bill. His smile disappeared. He reached across and handed Bill his license. "I don't suppose you know that your license expired two years ago?"

Bill smiled. "No idea," he said.

"Take care of it when you get back to Ohio," the trooper said.

"I will," Bill said. "So where'd you see action? Nam? Nah, you're too young. The Gulf?"

The trooper stood. "The minute you get back to Ohio, hear?"

A few moments later, Bill heard April exhale and the trooper's door slam.

"Semper fi," Bill muttered. "You and your faggot sunglasses."

"What should I do?" April asked.

Bill guided her back onto the highway.

"He's following us," she said, watching the rearview mirror more than the road in front of her.

"Just drive normally. Stay at fifty-five." He lowered himself in his seat so he could watch the trooper from the passenger-side mirror.

"How long do you think he'll follow us?" April asked.

Bill didn't answer. He was pretty sure the trooper was looking into the same mirror he was. No dummy, that trooper. Served his country. Probably even re-upped. Now he was just doing his job. A good man.

He looked back into the mirror and saw that the trooper had his left turn signal on. The patrol car eased into the left lane and then into a grassy strip between eastbound and westbound, just before a bridge.

"Perfect," Bill said. "He's setting up a speed trap."

April flicked on the turn signal.

"What are you doing?"

"Getting off at the exit, like he told me."

"Don't bother," Bill said. "I told you—he's gone. Just keep driving."

But April didn't. She did as the trooper told her. When they were in the parking lot of the Dunkin' Donuts next to the exit, she turned off the car and handed the keys to Bill. Something in the way the car suddenly went quiet, perhaps the tinkle of the keys, reminded him of a little ritual he and Clare shared in the early years. Whenever they returned from driving somewhere, he'd park the car, turn off the ignition, jingle the keys, and say, "Home, Clare. Safe and sound." These were often the only words spoken during long stretches of their trip. Another man's wife might fuss about the silence, about the lack of conversation. Clare never badgered him to "open up" with her, to "share." They never fought over silence. They never felt the need to examine each slight, each potentially inconsiderate implication. He sometimes thought that the most contented moments of his marriage were surrounded by those silences.

Home, Clare. Safe and sound.

Clare would reply, "My hero." She'd lean over and kiss him.

This continued for years, even as the kids in the back got older and would moan *Ewww!* or *Gross!* at the horrific semi-public display of affection. After a while, Bill couldn't pinpoint when, the kiss on the lips became a peck on the cheek. And after the diagnosis, he didn't feel quite right saying, "Safe and sound."

"And safe and sound is how I want to stay, Grandpa," April said, putting the keys in his hand before he even realized he was holding it open.

"I thought you wanted to learn how to drive."

"I do. I just don't want to get thrown in jail."

"No one's going to throw us in jail. Just keep driving the way you're driving, right on the speed limit, maybe a little over so they don't think you're running drugs, and we'll be fine."

He held out the keys. April crossed her arms and stared at him. Bill saw Marcy. But then he saw Clare. That look: fed up, expectant, patient, condescending, loving, hopeful.

"Goddammit," he said, flinging the keys into April's lap. "If you want to go to Seattle, then you're going to have to—"

"San Francisco."

"Whatever. If you want to get there, drive. You want to follow this big dream you're always moaning about? Then drive. You don't want to drive, you want to let some frustrated Rambo scare you, take away your dream—you want me to drive? Then we head back to Woodlake. You decide."

April's face fell. "Grandpa, why are you being so mean?"

Bill felt the sensation that he had come to dread coming over him. He braced himself for the little surges in his head, the tiny bright red and green lights that flashed in front of him, as when you press your fingers against your closed eyes.

Keeping his eyes locked on April helped. The shapes didn't appear. The pulsing sensation in his head ebbed. April looked as though she might start crying.

"You may have noticed that sometimes my mind wanders," he said, his voice soft, calm, defeated. "Sometimes I suddenly wonder what I'm doing. Wondering how long I've been doing it, how I got there. Even where I am. Or I can't do anything but close my mind and try to sleep. No matter what, I don't realize sometimes what I'm doing. Or I suddenly find myself asleep." He paused, caught his breath. "I don't think we want any of that when I'm driving, do we?"

It took a long time for April to respond.

"Grandpa, are you all right?" she asked.

"I'm fine, and don't start getting all concerned about me," Bill answered, feeling much better. "This stuff happens. No big deal. Now let's get back on the road. Unless you want a doughnut? Would you like one? I could go for one. I could definitely go for one."

April kept staring at her grandfather. Then she picked up the keys, inserted the correct one in the ignition, and started the car.

"No offense, Grandpa," she said, "but this definitely sucks."

As she pulled out of the parking lot, her cell phone rang.

CHAPTER TWENTY-TWO

Marcy had promised to stay awake and keep Nick company while he drove, but she had finally given in to her exhaustion and was breathing deeply, evenly. Every now and then she'd let out a small sound, a high-pitched *yip* of some sort. Was she dreaming about April? Was it the sound of relief? Or rejection? He wasn't a betting man, but at this hour—with the I-80 traffic backed up and creeping alongside the endless miles of predawn construction—Nick supposed he'd put his money on the latter. He'd never thought of himself as a pessimist, but Marcy's understandable inability to keep her promise had left him alone to deal—unsuccessfully thus far—with the self-lacerating thoughts that assailed him with each beam of light from the traffic zipping past in the opposite direction. For a while it seemed that each flash illuminated Peggy and her migraine in a sleek black dress.

Was something similar in store for Marcy, for all of them? The thought of yet another defeat—this one at the hands of his own father—was so unsettling that he now seriously entertained the idea of chartering a plane in Chicago to ensure they'd make it to Arnolds

Park in time, before the old bastard had a chance to make a fool of Marcy the way Peggy Gallagher had of him.

He'd thought being a gentleman was what women wanted. *No pressure. A nice guy.* Fool. How painful would it be if he were to drive into the nearest bridge abutment?

Maybe Mike had made the right decision to make himself as scarce as possible. Everyone has to find their own way of dealing, of coping. But in avoiding his father so completely, Mike seemed to have decided for whatever reason that it was necessary to cut himself off from the rest of his family, too. It was an arrangement Nick could never quite understand—and the reason now that he was skeptical of his brother's assurances that he would be at the park to meet them, the old man included.

And if the old man pulled another bait and switch on them, Nick vowed, he'd call the cops right there.

There wasn't much to remember about Arnolds Park itself from the family vacation all those years ago, so little time did they spend at the place. There was a lake nearby and a dock with the water that had once lapped his own puke up against the wood. The deadly combination of cotton candy and the Rotor had sent him out to the dock to hurl a second time—the first being, to his dismay, on the ride itself. Nick remembered specifically looking at the floor dropping beneath him, the yellow line that a few moments earlier had been touching his toes. He'd started feeling light-headed and was wishing the spinning would end when a collective groan arose. Thanks to the circular motion of the ride, Nick's vomit splatter covered a generous area. The attendant gave him a dirty look when the rotating stopped, and one of the riders, about Nick's age, gave him a push as they made their way down the exit ramp. Mike sucker punched the kid and grabbed Nick, and the two of them ran into the crowd toward the lake. It was right after this that something happened to Marcy on the roller coaster and they all rushed to the hospital for what turned out to be a butterfly bandage and an ice pack, but the whys and wherefores of that escaped him. That their father was summoning his daughter to the site of what was most likely one of her most traumatic memories struck him as both characteristic and appalling.

Why not have them gather at a place where he'd actually gotten it right? Such as the summer that just he and Mike and their father went on a camping trip to Presque Isle in Pennsylvania. Marcy was too young to go, and their mother didn't like camping, so it was just "us guys," as their dad said when he announced the trip. They had never been camping before, and Nick didn't know what to expect. He was amazed at the speed and ease with which his father erected a four-man tent, complete with bunk bed–style cots. There were other surprises. His father started a fire—a big one—without paper or lighter fluid. He handled fishing rods and bait as if he went fishing every weekend. He even showed them how to gut the fish they caught, filet them, and fry them over the fire. At night he let them catch lightning bugs while he had a beer and stared into the fire and got the tent ready for the night. In their sleeping bags, they'd beg him for a story. His father wasn't a storyteller, but it didn't matter much. They were so exhausted from swimming and fishing and playing in the woods that they fell asleep almost immediately. On the ride home, Nick asked his father where he'd learned all that outdoors stuff. His father grunted and told him that he'd learned it the hard way, the right way: in the marines.

The marines. The word had fascinated Nick. He'd associated it with his favorite color from his box of crayons: aquamarine. He imagined his father in a light blue uniform, standing in the snow. As he grew older, he started reading about the marines. His admiration for his father grew. The descriptions of boot camp were incredible, and they frightened him. He tried to imagine himself standing at attention with a drill sergeant screaming in his face; crawling under barbed wire; running an obstacle course; climbing walls and hauling himself up ropes. He knew he'd never make it. And somehow he knew, although he tried to dismiss it, that his father didn't think he would have been able to make it, either.

He'd make it in other ways, then. He forced himself to play sports and tried to convince himself that he enjoyed it. But he hated the cutthroat competition among both the kids and the parents, the pranks in the locker room, the ridiculousness of jockstraps and the humiliation of having your mother launder them. He was a fixture on the bench. He'd stand by the coach, hoping the coach would put him in, hoping that he wouldn't. He usually got game time only when his team was too far ahead to lose. One time, the coach actually pushed him aside, saying, "Come on, Warrington. You're in my way. Sit down, willya?"

There was one glorious moment, and it had happened way back in Little League. One day, he wasn't sure why, the coach put him in at center field. He spent the half-inning punching his mitt and praying that the batter wouldn't hit a high pop to him. In the bottom of the inning he came up to bat. With two called strikes, the catcher was hollering, "He's a looker, he's a looker, he's not gonna swing. Easy out, easy out." On the next pitch, Nick closed his eyes and swung. He felt something hit his bat; at first, he thought he'd hit the catcher's head. He opened his eyes and there was activity out beyond second base. The second baseman was running, the center fielder moving to his right, and all of a sudden people were screaming at him to run. He ran to first base, his legs moving furiously, as if in a dream. But unlike a dream, he was actually moving. The first base coach, one of his teammates, was windmilling his arm, the signal to go for second. When Nick neared second he heard people screaming at him to *hold up, hold up* and he stopped. He made sure his foot was on the bag and the relay came in and the second baseman tagged him even though he was safe by a mile and the ump yelled, "Safe!" and there was another crescendo of cheering. Nick looked over to the dugout and saw that everyone was standing and cheering, including the coach. And then Nick looked over at the bleachers and he saw his father standing and clapping and whistling. He saw his mother looking up at his father, and then out at him, smiling. She understood him. Thinking about it now, Nick had the strange sensation that even back then, as his mother smiled out at her son standing on second base, she knew that someday he'd be driving along, thinking about nothing and everything, and this moment would be relived.

Nick's eyes welled. They usually did when he thought about his mother—even more, perhaps, than they did when he thought of Marilyn. They all had idealized the woman, and though he was aware of the rose-tinted perspective brought about by her dying young—faults and idiosyncrasies forgotten in favor of more saintly reminiscences—Nick was hard-pressed to recall any flaws or even weaknesses. The only one he could think of—and it would be grossly unfair to call it a weakness—was her uncharacteristic complaining during her final days. But what could she do? Bone cancer, he'd read, was an extremely painful type of cancer. If she didn't have the right to complain, who did?

One night he was in his room, recording songs from the radio with a tape recorder he'd gotten as a Christmas present. He would spend hours taping the songs and keeping meticulous notes of the titles and artists. He used the machine's numerical counter to locate whatever he wanted to hear, but on this night, while recording "Stairway to Heaven," he heard his mother cry out. His bedroom was across the hall from his parents' bedroom. His parents were having an argument of some sort. Nick was furious with his father for arguing. Now, armed with something to document this transgression, he might have proof of his father's cruelty. He turned the radio down and let the recorder run until he heard the door to his parents' bedroom open and close and his father's footsteps recede as he walked down the stairs.

Nick punched rewind, then stop, and, putting in an earbud, listened to his parents' distant, muffled voices. His mother was sobbing
as he'd never heard before. *It's too much, Bill. The kids will only remember this. I never ask you for anything. But I'm asking you to do this.*
He also heard more crying. But it wasn't his mother. He ejected the
tape and put it in the top drawer of his desk. He sat for a long time,
trying to figure out what they had been arguing about.

After the funeral, he took the tape down to his father's work-
bench in the basement. He grabbed a hammer and, before he could
change his mind, smashed the cassette. He grabbed some grass
hand-clippers and cut the tape into tiny pieces, then put the whole
mess into the garbage. He never mentioned the recording—or its
contents—to Mike or Marcy.

"We're not going to be there in time, are we?" Marcy asked. The
sun was rising and they were still in Illinois.

"How long have you been awake?" Nick asked, caught off guard,
as if his sister had been listening in on his thoughts.

"Don't dodge the question," Marcy said. "We're not going to make
it in time, are we, Nick?"

"Sure we will," Nick said, not at all sure.

An hour later, they stopped for a bathroom-and-coffee break.
While he was waiting for Marcy, his cell phone rang. It was Mike.

"Not sure where you two are, but you may as well turn around,"
his brother said.

Nick almost laughed. Mike wasn't one for small talk. Since they'd
talked just yesterday and exchanged cell phone numbers, Mike probably figured they were up to speed—or at least as up to speed as Mike
wanted to be.

"We missed them?" Nick asked. "I thought he said noon."

"He did," Mike said. "My flight last night got canceled. I was
rebooked on the first one out this morning. I decided to call April to

make sure they would be there. She didn't have any idea what I was talking about."

"What do you mean?"

"Just what I said. I think the old man is keeping her in the dark."

Nick tried to digest all this while thinking about how he would break it to Marcy. "I don't get it. Where the heck are they?"

"I'm not exactly sure," Mike said. "But it sounds like they're almost through Nebraska."

CHAPTER TWENTY-THREE

April studied the road map while her grandfather was in the restroom. They had started early and already driven five hours. Her grandfather had slept most of the time. But at exactly noon, he'd opened his eyes and announced, "I need to piss and eat."

She was tired, but pinpointing their location on the map revived her. They were just about at the Wyoming border, finally free of Nebraska, just two states away from California. She couldn't believe how much time it was taking. During her long hours behind the wheel, April considered creating another list: STS—States That Suck. The people were friendly, though. The waitresses didn't seem as hurried or as angry and frumpy as they were back home. She wondered if people got friendlier the farther west you went. That would make San Francisco the friendliest place on earth.

She also liked the thought, if not the actual experience, of having traveled through several different states. Now, if Heather said something about, say, Iowa, April would be able to say, *Oh, yeah? Have you ever actually been there? No? Well, I have. And let me tell you . . .* Over some backstage phone call after his desperate and heartsick confession that he loved her and missed her, she would say to Keith Spinelli, *Listen—I've got to do the next set. You want to be with me? Do what I did. Break free.*

But as April studied the map, she started getting nervous. She was proud of the increasingly adult role she played in checking into roadside motels and using her grandfather's credit card to pay for gas and meals. She had no problem driving on the highway now and along the wide roads off the interstate. But what would happen when they reached San Francisco? It was a big city with hills and those strange cable car thingys in the middle of the road.

Whenever she asked her grandfather what they'd do when they got to San Francisco—where they'd stay, how she'd meet someone to introduce her to a band—he told her not to worry. He knew cities. *I didn't get to be an old man by being a rube,* he'd say.

Whatever that meant. She often got the feeling there was something he wasn't telling her. *A hidden agenda,* her mother would say. *Always a hidden agenda with him.*

"You by yourself?"

The man addressing her, a fat guy wearing a cowboy hat, boots, and butt-crack jeans, stared at her from the counter stool.

"No," April said. She returned to her map.

"Who you with?" the man asked.

Great, another pervert. She used her finger to follow I-80 from Green River to San Francisco.

"Miss?"

April couldn't ignore him any longer. "I'm with my grandfather," she said, not trying to disguise the contempt in her voice.

The man nodded amiably. "That him out there?" he asked, pointing to the window behind her. April turned and saw her grandfather walking toward the divided highway.

She bolted out of the diner. The parking lot was unpaved, and the wind kicked up a fine white dust in her face. She had to stop and rub her eyes. Her grandfather was getting closer to the highway. A semi roared past just as she grabbed him by the arm. He looked down at her. His eyes were unfocused. He was working his mouth slowly, as if trying to form words.

"I thought . . . I was trying," he began. Then his eyes sharpened suddenly. "Where in the holy hell have you been?" he demanded.

"I was waiting in the diner. We were going to have lunch. Don't you remember?"

"Of course I remember. You're always asking me if I remember. I remember everything—don't you worry."

"But where were you going, Grandpa?"

"Never mind. I'm here, aren't I?"

April looked at her grandfather. "That makes, like, no sense," she said.

"Maybe not to you. I can't account for your piss-poor education."

April tried to guide him back to the diner, but he shrugged her off whenever she took his elbow. When they got into the restaurant, the waitress and fat-assed cowboy gawked at them. April stared back defiantly until they went about their business. Her grandfather announced he wasn't hungry.

"But it's lunchtime, Grandpa. You said you were. Besides, *I'm* hungry."

"I thought you were in a big hurry to get to Seattle," he said.

"San Francisco."

"*Whatever,* like you're always saying. So what are we doing here? Let's go."

Her grandfather walked out of the diner. April paid for his untouched coffee and for her Coke. The waitress shoved a huge oatmeal raisin cookie at her. April almost cried.

"Tell me a story about Grandma Clare," she said a few minutes later, back on the highway, trying to get her grandfather focused. He was sharpest when he was telling his stories.

"I already told you my stories."

"Not about Grandma Clare," April said. "What did you like most about her?"

Bill squinted at her. "What kind of question is that? I liked everything about her."

"Well, then, what didn't you like about her?"

Bill looked at her again. "Now, that's a much better question," he said. He looked out the window. "But I'm not gonna answer it."

But he did—practically nonstop through Wyoming. None of the stories were bad, though, despite his promise. This was the thing she noticed about her grandma Clare. If all you had to go on were the stories that her grandfather and her mother told her, then Grandma Clare was right up there with the Blessed Virgin Mary, maybe higher. This seemed to April to be one of the good things about dying: A sort of amnesia sets in. People forget your faults, or at least they stop talking about them—unless you're a school shooter or a pedophile or a Hitler of some sort. Would her mother remember her grandfather this way? Would she stop calling him old man and Billy Boy and suddenly start talking about "my father" or "my dad" or even "Daddy"? April thought of her own father. Would her mother stop saying nasty things about him if he died? And what would she say about him? "Yeah, he walked out on us, but he was actually a really good guy. A really great dad. Really."

She shook her head, trying to ward off the bad karma that thinking about death—especially the death of people you know—is sure to bring on. Good topic for a song, though. She played with some lines while her grandfather talked.

Did you die to escape your lies?
Now that you're dead, it's an empty bed.
When you could breathe, you cheated with ease.
But now that you're gone, it's your touch that I . . . long?

She'd have to work on it later. Her grandfather was now distracting her, he was talking so much. He talked longer than April had ever heard him go on before. She started to get the feeling that she didn't even need to be there. But she knew it was good that she was, because if they weren't there together, driving to a place neither of them had been, he'd be telling the same stories, but he'd be telling them back in Ohio, sitting in his ratty brown chair in his dumpy little house, smoking his smelly pipe and picking at the gross gray hair in his ears, talking and laughing at the peeling wallpaper.

She felt her throat tighten and her eyes well. What was with the crying, April wondered as she gripped the steering wheel. They were getting close to San Francisco; she should be ecstatic. Why did a free cookie, or the thought of her grandfather alone, have such an effect on her? Sad stuff, she supposed, but enough to get all teary? She got emotional about being emotional. Ridiculous. She concentrated on her grandfather's stories.

"Graduation was her goal," her grandfather said.

April realized she'd lost the thread of whatever story her grandfather was telling her. "Grandma went back to school?"

"No . . . no . . . She wanted to see Nick, your uncle Nick, graduate from high school," he said. "She knew she'd never see Marcy graduate, but she tried to hold on for Nick."

Then, all of a sudden, he grew quiet. Another black-hole moment, and she tried to think of something to say that wouldn't sound stupid, a question to ask that wouldn't sound nosy. She saw a roadside memorial: a small white cross, a splash of color at its base.

"The doctors?" her grandfather said, as if answering someone else's questions. "They said she might hold on for quite a while, or there could be a sudden turn and she'd go quickly. They need a fancy degree to tell me that? And then she didn't even make it to Mike's graduation. She gave up."

April's head snapped up.

"What do you mean, she gave up?"

"It was too much for her. The cancer."

"Yeah, but you say it like—I don't know—like you blame her. She had *cancer*, Grandpa."

"I know what she had, believe you me." He said this quietly. He apparently wasn't in the mood to argue. "And I didn't mean anything by it. She was in incredible pain. Incredible." He paused. "Let's change the subject."

But for about thirty miles, there was no change of subject. In fact, there was no discussion at all.

Then he spoke up again as if he'd been talking all along. "Reminds me of the time Nick ran that touchdown," he said.

April tried not to get freaked out. "I thought it was a baseball game," she said. "You told me he hit a double in a baseball game."

Her grandfather frowned. "Am I repeating myself?" he asked.

"Only every story," April said, laughing.

Her grandfather laughed, too. A good sign.

"Whatever it was," he said, "I was relieved, I can tell you that."

"Relieved? Why?"

"I was worried Nick was a little . . ." He stopped. "What am I doing? Never mind."

"A little what?" April asked, trying to think of the word he had apparently forgotten.

After another pause, her grandfather said, "Well, in the marines we used to say that some guys spent a little too much time polishing their buttons."

April inhaled loudly. "Grandpa! You thought Uncle Nick was gay?"

"No!" her grandfather said quickly. "I mean, you never know for sure, right? Until they start going out with girls. Or they hit a home run or something."

"Grandpa, that is so Neanderthal! There are lots of sports people—"

"I know, I know, don't get all—whaddya call it—*PC* on me, okay? Remember, I'm talking about thirty years ago. Things were different back then. And it doesn't matter anyway. He married a beautiful girl. Poor thing."

Poor thing.

Those two words always seemed to come up whenever Aunt Marilyn's name was mentioned. April hadn't seen her all that often even though—unlike her other aunt in Chicago—she and Uncle Nick lived fairly close by. About the only times were on holidays, when they'd stop in on their way to one of Marilyn's relatives, but even on those short visits her aunt was always eager to find out what April was reading, what music she was listening to, and—here Aunt Marilyn would look around her and lean closer, secret-sharing style—did she have a crush on anyone? For her part, April liked her aunt but was always slightly intimidated by her. Aunt Marilyn was so tall, always so nicely dressed, with thick black hair swept up and back into elegant, complicated, fascinating styles. It wasn't that she was stuck-up or anything—it wasn't beyond her to get down on the floor with April, even in a nice holiday dress, to sit Indian-style during their "girl talk"—but April was afraid that any move she might make would somehow throw dirt or otherwise do damage to the perfection that was Aunt Marilyn.

But now that April thought about it, Aunt Marilyn seemed more eager during those visits to spend time with *her* than she did with her mom and dad. Which reminded April of a time Uncle Nick, who had been in the living room with her parents, came into the den to get Aunt Marilyn, who'd come in to listen to a CD with her. Uncle Nick, usually so serious, smiled at her aunt so broadly that, for a moment, April thought he was drunk. And she thought then—as she did now—that she had never seen her father look at her mother that way.

Uncle Nick, she thought. *Poor thing.*

The noise of the wind whistling through the slightly cracked driver's-side window was the only sound for miles. Her grandfather got talkative again just as April started watching the road signs for a motel. These stories were familiar to her: Korea, the family vacations, some of the characters he had met during his days in sales. And then, when April found a motel with the "Vacancy" portion of the "No Vacancy" sign lit, her grandfather talked again about how he had remained loyal to Clare (he had stopped calling Clare "your grandmother" somewhere in Illinois) while all his buddies were "sowing their oats."

April didn't want to hear it. There was something about it that bothered her.

"Am I supposed to admire you for that?" she finally asked.

Her grandfather stopped. "Admire me for what?"

"For not screwing other women when you promised Grandma you wouldn't."

Her grandfather glanced over. "You've got quite a mouth on you, don't you?"

"Well, that's what we're talking about, aren't we?" April didn't know why she was getting so angry. But she wanted to scream. She came close. "Being unfaithful. Screwing around. Fucking other women. Like my father did?"

"Enough!" her grandfather shouted. "I don't like that kind of language," he said.

"You use it all the time," April said.

"I mean from you," he said. "You're too . . . too . . . what word am I looking for?"

"Young? Well, that's wrong, Grandpa. I'm not too young. You wouldn't believe what some of my friends do with their boyfriends. I'm not too young. I just don't do it yet. But when I meet someone who isn't a complete moron and loser, I'm gonna find out what all the fuss is about. Believe me!"

"Good!" her grandfather shouted.

"You want me to do it? Fine. Believe me, I will."

"No. I mean, 'good' is the word I was looking for," her grandfather shouted. Then he quieted. "You're too good for that," he said.

April pulled over, threw the car in park, and hugged the steering wheel, crying.

"I'm not too good," she cried. "In fact, I'm not good at all."

She could sense her grandfather's uneasiness in the silence around her, but then he reached over and started to rub her back.

"Not so, Marcy," he said. "Not so."

CHAPTER TWENTY-FOUR

All sorts of scenarios played themselves out in Marcy's head. *The Heroic Scenario:* April falls in with a bad element; Marcy bravely ignores all threats to her own safety—a gun thrust up against her temple? a heavily tattooed gangbanger?—and leads her daughter home. *The Righteous Indignation Scenario:* Marcy and April finally come face-to-face, despite April's every attempt to evade her; Marcy unleashes a torrent of facts—the worry and inconvenience April has caused; the loss of income realized not only by Marcy but by Nick and Mike—and April collapses in a tearful realization of how wrong she's been and how right her mother is. *The Deathbed Scenario:* In a variation of the Heroic Scenario, Marcy rescues April from great danger—a pimp? a pusher? a pedophile?—but in the process is mortally injured; April screams out in anguish and remorse when she sees her mother in the hospital bed amidst the tangle of tubes and the steady, ominous beeping of the equipment keeping her, barely, alive.

These were easier to think about than the one Marcy knew would eventually take place, the one where she'd try to get April to explain what was so horrible about her home, her mother, her *life,* that needed escaping. *What exactly was so awful? What horribly unreasonable demands were put on you? You were expected to be a good person and get good grades. Excuse me for insisting. Pardon me for doing my job as a mother. Do you have any idea what I went through at your age?*

She knew she would lose April's attention if she started comparing childhoods. She knew that, for April, her past would seem as distant and as irrelevant as her own father's had been when Marcy was April's age. But how else to make the point? How else to show that April should be grateful, should show some admiration instead of . . . *hate.*

Marcy shivered at the word. Of course it was a word that kids use a lot, especially when venting to a friend over a parent's latest unreasonable demand. It was a word she herself had used often when she was April's age: a word directed, more times than not, at her father, when he would suddenly appear before her—full whiskey glass in hand, ice tinkling, eyes watery, breath boozy, posture wobbly—and establish a curfew or demand she get off the phone and get some goddamned homework done. She'd hated him. She knew, just knew, that her mother—who was fast receding into shadowy obscurity—would not have been such a huge pain in the ass. But she also knew, somewhere past the rebellious hormones, that her father was trying. And now that she was older, a mother, she knew exactly how much he'd been dealing with.

And yet still he tried.

He tried.

He really tried.

So what in the holy hell, as he might say, was he trying now?

Marcy gritted her teeth. Yes, he had tried, but this game he was playing now was beyond understanding. After everything she had put up with—for years!—he pulls this kind of crap. It was, finally, too much. After she got April home safely, that would be the end of any contact with the old man for good. Let him sit in his chair. Let the newspapers and filth pile up around him. Let the mail go uncollected, the grass go unmowed, the gutters fill with leaves and sticks. Let the paint peel. Let the roof leak. Let the basement flood and the toilets clog and the dirty dishes pile to the ceiling—a tower of maggots and vermin.

Let him become a newspaper item: *Long-Dead Body Discovered by Neighbors.*

Marcy would not care. Once she had April home, she wouldn't care about anything else.

"Why is he doing this?" she asked. "Tells us to meet him in the middle of nowhere. Then ditch us."

"Who knows?" Nick said.

Marcy continued as if they had been talking all along and despite the feeling that she should keep her mouth shut. "How can he do this to me? I mean, no offense, but I'm the only one who checked in on him. I'm the only one who called him practically every week. Did anyone else go over there, ever, and clean his house? And don't feed me that line about wanting to sell it, the way you did during our lovely little lunch together at the diner."

There it was: the reason she should have kept quiet. But Nick didn't argue. He wasn't much of an arguer. He pushed the wiper lever to spray fluid on the windshield and clear it of dead bugs.

"I'm sorry I made that crack about your wanting to sell the house," he said, quietly. "I was kind of going through a tough time, relationship-wise."

"Aren't we all," Marcy said. She was quiet for a while. "We're quite a pair, aren't we? You're a nice guy who manages to hook up with, excuse me, a bitch. And I'm a bitch who can't seem to stay hooked up with a nice guy. What's wrong with us?"

Nick shrugged. "We're Warringtons," he said.

Marcy started laughing. She couldn't stop.

"You were right," she said, wiping her eyes. "About the house, I mean. Not at first. But the more I started getting into real estate, the more I kept wondering about how long the old man was going to hold on to the place. I don't want to admit that, even to myself. But it's true."

Nick didn't laugh, but he was smiling. A sad sort of smile, Marcy thought.

"If it'll make you feel any better, I can top that."

Nick was quiet for a while before he continued. Marcy got the feeling he was trying to make up his mind about something.

"After Marilyn died, I took some time off from work. I figured I needed a week or two. My boss was very understanding. Told me to take whatever time I needed. But after a month, she started asking when I'd be back. And then at six weeks—the six-week anniversary, to the day, as it turned out—she fired me. She had to do it. I understood."

Nick was quiet as he maneuvered onto a new highway.

"It turned out she did me a favor. I took the job with this travel magazine, mainly as a way to get out of my funk. Get away from the house, away from everything that reminded me of Marilyn. And it worked. I had to think about catching planes, checking out trains, visiting museums, eating in restaurants, meeting deadlines. Only problem is, when I first started there, they didn't pay squat. I had the same salary as a kid fresh out of journalism school. It was humiliating."

He shrugged again, and Marcy squelched the urge to yell at him to get on with it.

"I didn't wish Dad ill. I guess I was just hoping that if he was going to check out within a year or two, that he'd do it sooner than later. I guess I envisioned a secret inheritance or, at the least, a third of whatever we'd be able to get for the house."

"Oh, dear," Marcy said, laughing and crying at the same time again. "It's all coming out. We are truly evil."

She grabbed her pocketbook and retrieved her cell phone. She did it as if something Nick had said had persuaded her on the correctness of the course of action she'd been mulling over. She started dialing.

"Who are you calling?" Nick asked.

"Three guesses," Marcy replied.

She waited for April's message, then left her own: "April, I've talked to your father about what's going on. He wants to talk to you. But I won't give him your cell phone number, and I won't give you his, until you call me and we talk. You and me. So call me right away."

She flipped her phone off, tossed it in her bag, and exhaled loudly. Nick didn't say anything for a while.

"You don't approve," Marcy said.

Nick kept his eyes on the road, signaling and moving into the left lane to make room for a car merging in from an entrance ramp. "You do what you have to," he said.

A while later, she asked, "Why do you think he's doing this? What's the deal with these ridiculous messages where we have to call someone else to figure out what they mean? And why this insistence on all three of us being there when we figure out what he's talking about?"

Once again, Nick didn't say anything.

"He's dying, isn't he?"

"That'd be my guess."

"Well, this is certainly a dramatic way to go about it, but I can't keep going like this. We have to do something. I can't go back to Ohio and just sit there, waiting."

"I agree. That's why, in case you haven't noticed, I haven't been driving on I-80 for the last hour."

"Where the hell are we?"

"I didn't think it right that we drive by Chicago without stopping in to see our long-lost brother."

"You're proposing we just show up on his doorstep?"

"Why not? If we call ahead of time, he'll just figure out a way not to see us, as always."

"I don't know, he sounds different lately. Something's up with him."

"All the more reason. Maybe we can call Dad when the three of us are together. Ask him what he wants."

Her cell phone rang. It felt to Marcy like it was taking forever to dig it out of her bag. As she searched frantically, she reminded herself to stay calm. *Remember: You're the mother. Don't let her hook you. Pretend she's a client.*

She found her phone and flipped it open without bothering to check the caller ID. "That was fast," she said.

There was pause, and then, "What's his number?"

"I'm fine, April. How nice of you to even care about how I've been holding up during the unexplained disappearance of my daughter." Marcy thought she saw Nick grimace. He was right. This was not the way to start this particular conversation. She tried to regroup.

"You said you'd give me his number if I called you," April said. "I'm calling you."

"And I want to know where you are, right now. Your uncle Mike flew to Iowa for nothing, apparently, and your Uncle Nick and I have driven all the way from Ohio. You weren't where you said you'd be. Enough, April. Enough is enough."

"I don't know what you're talking about," April said. "I never said I'd be anywhere. Give me Daddy's number, like you promised."

"I didn't promise you a damn thing, young lady."

Nick made a motion with his hand: *Calm down.*

Marcy couldn't. "I want you to tell me where you are and to stay there until Uncle Nick and I come and get you. You have no idea how much trouble and inconvenience—"

"So you're not going to give me Daddy's number."

"Listen to me, April. I'm not finished."

"You don't *have* Daddy's number."

"Forget about your father for a second, April, and listen—"

"You'd like that, wouldn't you?"

Marcy concentrated. There was one of those hooks. She would ignore it.

"Tell me where you are."

"You lied about Uncle Mike flying to Iowa. I know that because I talked to him."

"April? I want to know, right now—"

"And you're lying about Dad. I know *that* because you're a liar."

"—exactly where you are."

"I'm hanging up."

"I want you to give your grandfather a message," Marcy said quickly. "This might be of interest to you, too."

April didn't say anything. There was some static, a rustling sound, but the connection hadn't been broken.

"Tell him that if he doesn't contact us and tell us where you are and let us come and get you, I'm calling the cops. Enough is enough. He'll spend the rest of his life in jail. Tell him that, April. Tell him he'll spend what little time he has on earth in a jail cell. He's going to die a lonely old man, disgraced and humiliated. No one, certainly not me, will ever visit him or see him again. Tell him that, April. You got that?"

There was a pause. And then her father's voice said, "Got it."

CHAPTER TWENTY-FIVE

Mike bolted upright. He thought it was noise from the television that woke him, but when he opened his eyes—lids heavy and scratchy—he saw that the set was off. He closed his eyes, thankful he didn't have to move. His head was pounding, his mouth dry, but things would only get worse if he got up for a glass of water. He needed to stay where he was, to remain perfectly still. Time was the answer.

He must have been dreaming. Or maybe, he thought, it was that jerking reaction to the falling sensation you sometimes have when you're just about to fall asleep. Colleen knew the name for it. She'd told him a million times. Hypnotic . . . no, hypnologic . . . no, hypnic jerk. There was a longer name for it. Scientific. He could never remember.

Other things, he remembered very well. He'd been spending a lot of time in that chair remembering things. He'd not been making progress with his plans for getting back together with Colleen, for being with his kids. Would Colleen relent? The answer required another drink. What did Clare think of her father now? Would she be at all interested in hearing his side of the story—and exactly what would that side of the story be? It was somehow easier to imagine explaining it to Ty, who was conveniently at that age of hormonal insomnia. He was probably as obsessed with girls as Mike had been at his age—so eager to get laid that he'd understand his father's . . . *indiscretion,* he'd call it. Or would Ty understand, after all? He was a bit of a mama's boy. He might not empathize with an indiscretion that had hurt his mother. But Mike would be ready. *You think that now,* he'd say. *But when you get older, when you get to be my age, if you ever find yourself in a situation remotely close to mine, you'll understand. In the meantime, don't be too quick to judge.*

Exactly what Colleen had said to Mike that first night they were together.

"Unless there's something you haven't told me, you don't know for sure what your father was doing," Colleen had said all those years ago, lying in Mike's arms, stroking his chest. "Maybe he accidentally counted out too many pills and was just putting the extra ones back."

Mike shook his head. "I saw it in his eyes," he said. "His Claus von Bülow eyes. He might have changed his mind that night. But I knew that, eventually, he did it. I even confronted him about it once. Couple of weeks after my mom died."

"What did he say?" Colleen asked.

"Not a word."

"So you still don't know for sure."

"I know," Mike said, staring at the ceiling. "For sure."

But as the years passed, Mike began to doubt his certainty, although he never expressed these doubts to Colleen. Every now and then, when a family event would remind Mike of his own childhood and send him into a funk, Colleen would urge him, for the sake of his own peace of mind, to fly to Ohio, sit down with his father, and have it out once and for all.

Maybe now, Mike thought, thanks to the circumstances that had brought him to this crappy hotel room, he finally knew his father's side of the story. Maybe he had known and understood it all along but could never admit it to himself: that he didn't have with Colleen, or with any woman, what his father had had with his mother. That he was incapable—physically, mentally—of having it. And that he didn't have the other thing his father had and needed—courage? selflessness? love?—to make what suddenly struck him now, in the terrible, antiseptic loneliness of an overpriced flophouse, as a truly selfless decision, no matter what the price.

He heard a woman call out.

"You in there?"

Three sharp knocks on his door, three hammer shots to a spot just between his eyebrows. Colleen? No. Couldn't be. Had to be the maid. But this wasn't one of the cleaning days. He'd been very clear with the front desk: maid service every other day. Why can't anyone get even the simplest things right?

"Not today," he called out.

The effort upset the precarious balance in his stomach and his head. Hot waves of stale booze churned, threatening to shoot clear up to the heavy block pushing against his eyeballs. If only he had an instrument of some sort, a special scraper that could clear away the crap that was cementing his brain to his skull. An invention like that could make millions. Colleen would beg him to let her back in his life. The kids could have bigger rooms, more space for still more electronics to keep them from even a semblance of socializing with their parents.

Three more knocks. Time to let them know of his displeasure. *Tear 'em a new one,* as his father might say. He stood slowly, determined not to puke. He tried to cough away the phlegm from his throat, but that only increased the pounding in his head, echoed now on the door.

"Mike?"

A male voice. Who in the hell could that be? A supervisor. Front-desk clerk. Someone who knew his name. The manager? What the hell did he want? He'd been paying his bill.

"One sec," Mike called out.

With his first step, he nearly tripped over the empty bottle by the chair. It rolled partway under the bed. *That's the last of it,* he told himself, just as he'd told himself the night before.

He made it to the door but had to balance himself against the jamb before he opened it. Nick and Marcy stood before him. Talk about your bad hangovers.

"You don't look so good, bro," Nick said.

Marcy just stared.

"How?" It was all Mike could manage.

"Colleen," Nick said.

Mike nodded. That was all it took. He bolted to the bathroom and puked until he thought his head would fall off. He hoped it would.

When Mike next opened his eyes, Marcy was standing over him holding the nearly empty fifth of Jack Daniels she'd obviously re-trieved from beneath the bed. Nosy little thing, he thought. *Good thing I'm not into cross-dressing.* He felt something cool, a bit clammy, on his forehead. A damp washcloth.

"Turn it down, Nick," she called as she examined the label.

"It's practically on mute," Mike heard his brother call back. "Be-lieve me—he won't hear a thing for a while."

Marcy nodded, still looking at the empty bottle. "Probably not," she said softly.

Mike saw her look down at him.

"Well, hello there," she said. "Riding the pink elephant, are we?"

"Time?" he asked. He wasn't sure the word made it past the burn-ing sensation in his throat.

"Seven thirty," Marcy replied. "Night, if you're not sure. You've been out a couple of hours. Got a bit of an early start, didn't you?"

Mike nodded. His eyeballs felt like dry snot.

"Well, I'll say this for you," Marcy said, turning the label toward him. "You picked a tried-and-true brand."

CHAPTER TWENTY-SIX

B ill decided he needed a reporter's notebook. Why hadn't he thought of this before? It was important to keep track of the details, and they were becoming more and more elusive, just as that dimwit doctor had predicted way back when. Bill couldn't remember the quack's name, couldn't remember what he looked like. But he remembered what the pompous ass had said: nothing to be done; the process might go fast or slow; there's medication that might help slow things down.

Be damned if I start popping pills.

"Let's stop at a stationer's," he said.

April glanced over at him. With her right hand at the top of the wheel, her left elbow jutting out the window—he'd relented and let her open it—she looked as if she'd been driving for years instead of . . . how long had it been?

"What's a stationer's?" she asked.

"Hell in a handbasket. You don't know what a stationery store is?"

"You mean like where they sell cards and stuff?"

"Yeah. Is there one around here?"

April laughed. "Look out the window, Grandpa. There's *nothing* around here."

Bill saw that it was true. Highway nothingness. So what had he been looking at while they were driving? What had he been doing? Sleeping? Daydreaming? What had he been thinking about?

Marcy.

The name popped into his head, even though he was pretty sure he hadn't been thinking about his daughter. Or maybe he had—but about what, exactly?

Yes. He'd spoken to her not long ago. And afterward he had immediately set about making plans. But somehow he'd stopped making those plans and had started thinking about other things. Clare. That was it. He wanted to go back to thinking about Clare. But first he had to think about the plan.

"What's the next big city?"

"You asked me that about ten minutes ago. And ten minutes before that."

Bill felt the familiar warm wave pass from the back of his head to the front. It didn't hurt. A surprising but pleasant tingle of sorts.

"I don't care if I asked you two seconds ago," he said. "What's the next big city?"

"Geez, take it easy, old man."

"Don't you dare call me old man!"

April had to jerk the steering wheel back to her right to stay on the highway.

"What have I done to you that you should treat me like this? Would it kill you to treat me with just a little bit of respect? Is it so much for you to call me Dad? I'm sick of old man and Billy Boy. It's not funny. It's . . . distrustful. I mean . . . the other word . . . dis—"

"Disrespectful," April said.

Bill stared out the window for a while, trying to restring his thoughts. Why was her voice wavering?

"I was just kidding, Grandpa," April said after a while. "But you're starting to scare me. You're getting me confused with all sorts of people. Like my mother. It's me, Grandpa. April. My name is April."

Her voice had evened out. Bill smiled. She was tough. He liked that.

"I know your name as well as my own," he said, forcing himself to sound cranky. "So tell me, my name is April, what is the next big city?"

"Salt Freaking Lake City," April yelled.

"Thank you!" Bill shouted back.

April shook her head. After a few minutes she said, quietly now, "I'm serious, Grandpa. You are starting to really scare me."

Bill guessed that this was one of the moments where he should reach over and pat her knee and say something that would make her feel better. But his hand felt heavy. Cement.

"Just get us there, April," he said, his voice a whisper. "Okay? Just drive. This is all going to work out."

The same words he had used with Clare when that other idiot doctor told them, in so many words, that it was definitely not going to work out.

The same words he had used with Mike and Nick and Marcy after all the guests had left and they were still in the clothes they had worn to the service and the three of them were sitting at the kitchen table, staring at nothing, the silence suffocating them.

Words. Useless words. Useless. Useless. Useless.

He closed his eyes. Clare was nearby. He could feel her. He tried to bring her features into focus. He remembered a news story about a debate when a stamp of Elvis Presley was going to be . . . what was the word . . . *minted*? The debate was between "Young Elvis" and "Old Elvis." Which one had won? The young one, Bill thought. That's the one he wanted. Young Clare. Young Clare with the smooth skin and bright eyes and thick, beautiful brown hair. But these were just words: young, smooth, bright, beautiful. He didn't see any of this, didn't feel any of it. He saw, instead, the old Clare, the sick Clare. The sallow skin, the sunken eyes, the limp hair.

"You're not looking at me anymore," Clare had said to him one day as he settled her back into bed after helping her in the bathroom.

"What do you mean, I'm not looking at you anymore," he asked, adjusting the sheet and blanket and then carefully lining up the prescription bottles on the nightstand, marines in formation. "That's ridiculous."

"Remember when you couldn't stop looking at me, when you first started coming around? You reminded me of Buster, waiting for a treat."

Bill grunted as he moved her cup of water away from the edge of the nightstand. "I hated that dog."

"He hated you," Clare said, laughing. "I think he knew that you were the one who was going to take me away."

"Turned out he was right," Bill said, looking just over his wife's head, at a design in the bed board. "Stupid dog."

"Look at me, Bill," his wife said. Bill tried to focus on her eyes, not on the pallid skin or beads of sweat or on the red veins lining the yellowish whites of her eyes. "You're going to have to do it again."

"Do what again?" he asked. He grabbed a tissue—*floof*—and reached for the small line of perspiration above her thin, colorless lips. She grabbed his hand. Her strength surprised him. Her eyes were wide, pleading.

"You're going to have to take me away."

The wind woke him. April had done what she always did when he dozed off: opened the window all the way, stuck her arm partway out, and grabbed the steering wheel in a way that he assumed she thought made her look "cool." But the noise the wind created in the car never failed to remind him of the cold wind blowing through his helmet as the rest of his body froze. That sound was worse than the whistle and moan of incoming mortar. Mortar wasn't playing with you. It was just trying to find you, kill you. The wind always knew where you were, and it never promised a quick death. It never promised anything. It just taunted. Death itself taunted. It taunted in Korea; it taunted in Woodlake.

"Close that damned window, will you?" Bill wiped a small fleck of spittle from his mouth with the back of his hand. He hadn't meant to sound angry.

April did as she was told without protest. A passing semi drowned out whatever she said.

"See? I can never hear you when that damned window is open. What did you say?"

"First I said I'm sorry," April said, making Bill feel ashamed, "and then I said we're getting close."

"Close to what?" Bill asked.

"Salt Lake, remember?" April answered after a glance. "You wanted me to tell you when we get close."

"Guess I kind of dozed off there."

"Only for, like, two hours," April said. "Do you need to stop?"

The nap had done him good. Things seemed sharp, in focus. He remembered why he wanted to stop here. That feeling alone energized him—the sensation of being connected to things, not grasping about for a hint, for a clue, for a word that would somehow click everything back into place. He remembered his conversation with Marcy. He knew what had to be done.

"Take one of the exits that say 'Downtown,'" he told April. "I don't care which."

April opted for the first one they encountered, easily switching lanes and slowing down smoothly to handle the sharp turn of the exit ramp. At the end was a list of gas stations and restaurants.

"You want the McDonald's?" she asked. "You said they've got the cleanest bathrooms."

"Just turn and drive a little bit."

"Which way? Left or right?"

"Doesn't matter."

April turned right. Bill was surprised at how quickly the highway had been replaced by broad avenues. He told April to make a few more turns, to drive toward the city center.

"How do I get there?"

"Just aim for those," Bill said, pointing at a cluster of buildings on their left.

"This is random," April muttered. "You want to give me a hint?"

Bill concentrated on the streets. People hurried along much as they do in any other city. Most were talking on their cell phones; even people walking in twos or threes were chattering away simultaneously. "Worst invention yet," he said.

"What is?"

Bill sat up. A woman was pushing a baby carriage down the street, window-shopping. She looked to be in her early thirties. At one point she stopped and raised her face to the sun. She smiled.

"Pull over," Bill said, rolling down his window. "Quickly."

April checked the lanes before pulling over.

"You're going to get us killed," she said.

"Excuse me, ma'am," Bill called out to the woman.

The woman looked over. She pulled the stroller closer to her. She was no longer smiling.

"Can you help us?" Bill asked. "We're trying to find the Greyhound station."

The woman seemed to relax a bit. She looked around her as if the station might be near and she'd be able to point to it. But then she shrugged apologetically and walked on.

"Why are we looking for the Greyhound station?" April asked.

"Sir!" Bill called out to another passerby. "Can you help us?"

The man, whom Bill had picked because he didn't have a cell phone attached to his ear or appear to be in a hurry to solve the world's problems, was well dressed and carrying what Bill realized, too late, was a Bible.

The man walked to the passenger window and, maintaining a respectful distance, leaned over. "Ohio plates," he said. "You've come a long way."

"We sure have," Bill said. "But it was worth it. You got yourself a beautiful city here."

The man smiled. "That's true, thank the Lord. How can I help you folks?"

"We're looking for the Greyhound bus station."

The man frowned. He stood and looked around, much as the woman with the baby stroller had.

"I'm not sure," he said. "I do know that Amtrak is over by Pioneer Park."

"That's what I meant, Amtrak," Bill said quickly. "Don't know why I was thinking of the bus. My granddaughter says I'm losing it."

The man smiled.

"Kids today," Bill said. He winked. "No respect. You know what I mean?"

The man leaned over and smiled in at April. "I'm sure your grand-daughter is a fine young lady," he said. Still talking to her, he said, "Just follow this street to Fourth and take a left. You'll see Pioneer Park on your right. Amtrak's there, too. Can't miss it."

"Thank you," Bill said. "God bless you."

"God bless *you!*" the man said. He waved as April pulled away from the curb.

"Goddamned Mormons," Bill said as he rolled up the window. "Trying to convert everyone. Did you get that? Go straight to Fourth and take a right."

"He said left," April said. "I got it. But why are we going there?"

"Car's been acting up," Bill said. "It's old and unpredictable. I don't want to get stuck in the middle of nowhere. A bus will be safer."

"What are you talking about? The car's running fine. And do you want to go to the bus station or the train station? What's going on, Grandpa?"

"I'll tell you later."

When they got to the station, Bill got a baggage cart and loaded April's backpack and his suitcase onto it.

"You've got my credit card, right?" he asked her.

"Since Chicago," she said.

"Good. Go inside and buy two tickets for the next train to Seattle. Then wait for me by the ticket booth so I'll know where to find you. I won't be long."

"Where are we going? And you mean San Francisco, don't you?"

"Just do as I say," Bill said. "Give me the keys."

April had been holding the keys by the key chain, but now she closed her hand around them. "You're going to drive?"

"Taught you, didn't I?"

Bill held his hand out. April hesitated.

"Don't start," Bill said. "You want to get to . . . where we're going?"

"See?" April said. "That's exactly why I don't think you should drive. You can't remember something I said two seconds ago. Grandpa, let me—"

"Give me the goddamned keys," Bill yelled. "I got you this far, didn't I?"

A few people unloading cars nearby looked over. Bill saw April glance at them.

"Everything okay over there?" one man called out from a minivan.

"Mind your own," Bill snapped back at him.

"It's okay," April said. "It's my grandfather. Everything's okay."

Resisting the urge to flip the guy off, Bill took the keys from April, got in the car, and drove off. He felt light, almost jubilant. He knew what he had to do. Everything was clicking today. He had a plan, he knew how to execute it, and now he was doing it.

"Not totally gone, Clare," he said out loud.

He drove a few blocks, looking for a crowded parking lot. Settling on a twenty-four-hour supermarket, he parked the car between two SUVs. His toolbox was in the trunk, as he knew it would be. Knowing it would be there, remembering that fact and finding it to be true, encouraged him. He was doing what needed to be done. Marcy had made it clear she'd call the cops. Ditching the Ohio plates might buy some time. He grabbed a screwdriver, checked to see if anyone was looking, and then removed the license plates from the car and put them in one of the plastic shopping bags April had left in the back-seat. There was a garbage can near the entrance to the supermarket, but he felt that wouldn't work. Instead, he'd get rid of them later—maybe even take them with him and dump them somewhere in . . . wherever the hell they were going. Yes, that was the right decision.

"Still thinking, Clare," he said. "Still using the old noggin."

He looked at his car. By far the best he'd ever had. He didn't know what the odometer said, but it had to be well over 120,000 miles. He tried to remember a trip or a vacation or anything that the car had played a part in. But those things—the vacations, the good times with the kids, the drives with Clare—had all happened in different cars, long before he'd bought this one. Still, there was something about this car. It had been there. Just there.

"So long, you hunk of crap," Bill said, turning away.

On the street, he asked a kid in a brown uniform of some sort for directions to the Greyhound station.

CHAPTER TWENTY-SEVEN

To keep from freaking out while she waited for her grandfather, April studied the route of the California Zephyr. The name alone was enough to get her pumped. Here, finally, was something tangible, something that had the name California on it, a sign that she was almost there, that it was really going to happen. She was more excited by the name of a train than she had been when she saw the Rocky Mountains for the first time.

After Utah, just three stops in Nevada—Elko, Winnemucca (she tried to imagine saying, *Hi! I'm from Winnemucca*), Reno—and they'd be in California. Then six in California: Truckee, Colfax, Roseville, Sacramento (she'd heard of that one), Davis, Martinez, and—final stop, end of the line—Emeryville.

"But I want to go to San Francisco," April had said to the clerk when she purchased the tickets.

The man, who was younger than her grandfather but getting up there, looked at her over his half-glasses. "That's where you're going," he said. "Eleven thirty-five. Track two." He looked back down at the newspaper he was reading.

"Then why doesn't it say San Francisco?"

"It's just the name of the station."

"Are you sure?"

April was surprised at her question—not because it was a stupid question, but because she had asked it at all. A few weeks ago, she would have accepted the man's answer without question. Even if she didn't really believe him, which she didn't, she wouldn't have— what's the phrase her mother always used?—*stood up* to him. A few weeks with her grandfather had cured her of *that*.

The clerk looked up from his newspaper. He removed his glasses professorially. April wondered how his wife felt about all the hair sprouting up on the top of his nose.

"Young lady, I've been selling tickets to San Francisco for more years than you've been alive. Not one person has asked for a refund because I sent 'em somewhere else."

"Just wanted to make sure, sir," she said, offering her sweetest phony smile. Her grandfather would approve of the "sir."

The man nodded curtly and returned to his newspaper.

"I'm *so* sorry I interrupted; you look *incredibly* busy," April said. She turned and walked away. She felt his eyes on her back but made her way to the waiting area without turning around. She sat in one of the plastic chairs. The waiting area wasn't nearly as skeevy as she thought it would be. She'd expected to smell urine and see a bunch of homeless people, bums, and perverts hanging out. But the station seemed almost new, with lots of open space and windows and clean, well-polished floors. And it wasn't very crowded, either: a man in a suit reading a newspaper; a young couple snuggling against each other, trying to get some sleep; a tired-looking mother sitting near a pile of suitcases while her two young boys—they looked like twins— ran around the waiting area, laughing and screaming. The mother made no attempt to slow or quiet them; she looked too exhausted to do much of anything.

April renewed her vow to never have children.

She pulled out her road map. Just as she suspected. The ticket agent was full of it. Emeryville wasn't in San Francisco. It was across the Bay. *That* kind of sucked. You'd think that if you were going to build a railroad across the country, you'd go all the way and end it in San Francisco. Whoever heard of Emeryville? And how would they get from there to San Francisco, now that they didn't have a car?

She'd worry about that later. In the meantime, it was important to keep her mind occupied, because she was starting to wonder why in holy hell her grandfather was taking so long. It had been nearly an hour.

She created an acrostic, a memory trick her fifth-grade teacher had taught her, to help remember the stops in California: Trucks Carrying Roses Should Drive Mighty . . . she had trouble with an "E." That damned Emeryville again. No problem now, though; she'd never forget Emeryville—although she would do everything in her power to do so once they got out of there.

Easily! Trucks Carrying Roses Should Drive Mighty Easily. Truckee, Colfax, Roseville, Sacramento, Davis, Martinez, Emeryville. She was still disappointed in Emeryville. A final destination should be a city, not a *ville.*

A half hour later, the kids had stopped running around the luggage, but they were now hanging on their mother, whining and crying.

Their agitation was contagious. April felt herself starting to panic. Where was the old man?

She studied the train route map again and considered memorizing the stops in the opposite direction. But there were too many of them: twenty-three between Salt Lake and the end of the line, Chicago. Why did it stop in Chicago? Shouldn't it go all the way to New York? It would be cool to take a train all the way across the entire country. It would be even cooler if, by some weird coincidence, Keith Spinelli was on the same train. What would stop them from spending all day together? All night? She seemed to remember some movie about a man sharing a train compartment with a woman, although the woman didn't know the man was a man because he was in drag. It was a stupid movie, but her mother couldn't stop laughing.

Her mother's laugh used to make her cringe. But now she smiled.

And now she stood. The worn-out mother looked up at her in surprise. April started to pace. It had been two hours. Something was wrong. Something was definitely wrong.

She replayed what had happened. Her grandfather had said he needed to sell the car—but why? It was running perfectly fine. She should know—she'd been driving it. He had never even hinted that there was something wrong until after he'd spoken with her mother. That was it! Her mother had said something, goddamn her. Maybe she had threatened to call the cops.

April wanted to kick herself for being so stupid. Grandpa was dumping the car so the cops couldn't find them. But why was it taking so long? Was he really trying to sell it? Who would he sell it to? A picture of a huge, heavily muscled and tattooed biker formed in her mind.

"Are you all right?"

April had wandered near the mother. The kids were all asleep now. One of them was asleep at her feet; the other sprawled out across her lap like that statue of Christ and his mother.

"I'm fine," April said. "Thanks."

"Waiting for someone?" the mother asked. She seemed eager for exactly what April was not: conversation. "Boyfriend?"

April looked at her. "A boyfriend? No."

The mother nodded. "Running away?"

Something about having kids, April thought, makes it impossible for women not to pry into everyone else's business.

"I did when I was your age," the mother said when April didn't answer. "The first time, anyway. I was a little older when we decided to run off to LA and become famous movie stars."

April looked at the mother closely, surprised to find herself talking to someone she might have seen in movies. How cool would that be? But the face wasn't familiar, and April saw now that the woman wasn't as old as she originally seemed; probably her midtwenties. Old but not that old.

"Is that where you're going now?" April asked, realizing immediately how stupid her question was. They were in Salt Lake City, after all. Duh!

The mother smiled. "No. Going to Reno. That's where I grew up."

April nodded. "I guess the movie star thing didn't work out?"

Now the mother laughed.

"I didn't mean anything," April said quickly.

"It's okay. And no, the movie star thing didn't work out. Not nearly. Oh, we made it to Los Angeles. But Randy—that's his name—met some guys who liked to hang out in Venice Beach and get high all the time. He stopped going to casting calls. Eventually stopped working at his busboy job. Got into crack. Only paid attention to me at certain times, if you know what I mean."

The woman nodded at her sleeping children.

April felt herself redden. "So why are you here, if you don't mind my asking?"

"Randy met these two other guys on that beach. They were different. They were wearing nice blue suits. Promised Randy he'd be much happier as a Mormon. I guess Randy had hit rock bottom. He wanted to get clean. I wanted him to get clean. So we all came out here to start our new lives. That was a year ago."

"Oh, so you're going to Reno to visit your parents."

The mother shook her head. "I'm going to *live* with them. Randy kicked drugs, but he developed a taste for prim-and-proper Mormon girls. A choir girl, can you believe it?"

April looked away. She didn't want to see the woman—girl, really—cry. "I'm sorry," she said.

"You're sweet," the mother said, successfully fighting off the tears. She fixed her eyes on April. "I'll bet your mother misses you."

April didn't want to think about her mother. She had to think about her grandfather.

"Do you mind if I give you some advice?" the mother asked. "I know you're all excited about wherever you're going. I know you probably think you'll get a job, that your boyfriend will take care of you, that everything's going to be so much better there than at home. But take it from me—it won't be easy, not at your age. I know you think I don't know what I'm talking about. But if I were in your shoes, if I could do it all over again, I'd get on the next train or bus home."

April tried to think of a response other than *You're right—you don't know what you're talking about.* "Thank you," she said. "Thank you so much."

The mother held her in her gaze as April gathered up her bag and her grandfather's. April considered asking her to watch their things for her while she retrieved her grandfather, but even though she knew the mother would probably agree and say she wouldn't mind at all, it felt wrong.

"Do you know where the lockers are?" she asked at the same moment she saw them. She ran over, stuffed the bags into one of the larger ones, and started searching her pockets for five quarters. She only had two, along with a crumpled dollar bill. She hadn't realized she was carrying so little cash.

The clerk, now working on a crossword puzzle, looked up smugly when she asked for change. "Machine," he said, pointing his pencil to the left of the lockers.

It wouldn't take April's bill. She kept smoothing the bill out, trying to feed it in, but the machine kept pushing the money back at her. After half a dozen tries, she ran back to the ticket window.

"It's not working," April said. "It won't give me change."

"It sometimes does that," the clerk said, not looking up. "Keep trying. It'll take it."

April turned and started toward the machine. But then she stopped, as if someone had stepped in front of her, blocking her way.

Her mother would not do this. No way would her mother allow someone to treat her this way.

April turned and walked back to the ticket window.

"I'm not asking you to *give* me money," she said. "I'm asking you to give me four quarters for a dollar. I need it, and I need it quickly because someone who needs my help is waiting. So I'd appreciate it if you'd give me the change now. If you don't, if you make me leave this station to get change somewhere else, I'm going to make sure that my father, who is a lawyer, gets you fired for working on a crossword puzzle instead of doing your job."

April slapped the dollar bill on the counter.

The clerk leaned back in his chair and removed his glasses.

"Well, aren't you something?"

April made sure to thank the man as he pushed four quarters across the counter. After she secured her luggage, she returned to the window.

"Excuse me, sir. Which way to the Greyhound station from here?"

Another look up over half-glasses. "You don't know?"

"No, sir." *Would I be asking if I did?*

The agent put his elbow on the counter and, with his crossword pencil, pointed at the station doors. "See those doors there? You go out, take a left. Keep walking. You'll come to a little curve in the road. That's West Third. Don't go straight. Keep to your right. You'll walk right into it."

"How long will it take?"

The man looked at his watch. "Let's see. If you leave right now, and you walk the whole way, I'd say you should get there in, oh . . . two minutes or so." He smiled.

April searched the man's eyes. "You promise this is for real," she asked, her voice shaky. "I mean, I know you don't like me, but the person I'm trying to find really, *really* needs my help. It's my grandfather. He's like you—well, older, probably. A little. But he gets a little confused and I think he may be at the bus station because when we got here he kept asking people for directions to the Greyhound so that's why I need to go there and if you're trying to trick me to get back at me or something—"

The man held up his hand to stop her.

"Scout's honor," he said. He pointed to the door. "Go get your grandpa."

April ran.

CHAPTER TWENTY-EIGHT

As she stood in the checkout line at Dominick's Finer Foods, Marcy wondered how men these days survived. From the looks of things back at his "residence" hotel, Mike was living on TV dinners, cookies, and of course, Jack Daniels. For all their talk, all their cocky posturing, all their condescending certainty, it took very little for men to fall apart.

Take Hank. Big, tough, top-selling Hank. Had to be the protector. But threatened with a little separation, he puddled. Marcy stared at the head of the woman in front of her. Or had he? Marcy had been purposely driving thoughts of Hank away, trying to focus on April. But he kept elbowing his way into her thoughts: his big shoulders, his smile, his habit of listening so goddamned carefully to her.

Take Nick. He *still* couldn't get it together. And it had been three frickin' years since Marilyn died.

Take her father. Oh my god, take her father. Thanks to him, Marcy was pretty sure she had done more grocery shopping in her lifetime than any other woman her age. Because after her mother died, her father was too busy drinking to do what was needed to keep the family going. This included shopping for food. Her brothers were content to eat fast food and any crap that her father happened to pick up while on a booze run. She had to beg Mike to drive her to the grocery store. She had to beg her father for the money. At the age of twelve, she had to start doing all the things her mother used to.

She had enjoyed going to the grocery store with her mother, who'd shopped as if she were the queen of the A&P. The stock boys all smiled when they saw her. The cashiers loved to chat with her. Marcy could still remember, as a toddler, wrapping her arms around her mother's leg in the checkout line and, when she was older, leaning against her as the cashier punched in prices. Oddly, Marcy felt closest to her mother then, even though the woman might have been chatting with the cashier or someone else from the neighborhood, not paying attention to her at all. This was her mother's world outside the home. Perhaps that's why Marcy always felt a strange tug when she saw women and their children in the store. It reminded her not of shopping with April—shopping with April was a goddamned nightmare—but of shopping with her mother.

Did April ever feel that comfortable, that secure, with me?

Marcy shifted her gaze to her groceries. Mike's groceries. Groceries for Mike, who would never admit that he was on the skids. *Got something in the works,* he'd probably say. *Not to worry.* He wouldn't want to talk about the obvious—and he certainly wouldn't want to talk about Colleen. Colleen, on the other hand, had had no problem talking about Mike. A few minutes after Marcy and Nick rang the doorbell of the "Warrington residence," as Mike and Colleen's kids had been taught to say when they answered the phone, Colleen was telling them, over coffee and in explicit detail, precisely why Mike could not be found at the residence. Marcy noticed that the kitchen— the entire house for that matter—was spotless. It would show well. Marcy imagined herself pointing out the bright and airy great room, the fireplace in the kitchen and living room, the granite counters.

Colleen herself was very much together, as always: just the right amount of makeup, shiny black hair pulled back tightly, clothes that looked designed especially for her. But the bags under her eyes and the worry lines that formed on her forehead as she spoke told a less perfect story. That was the difference, Marcy thought: Women wear their pain; men simply disperse it among the dirty socks and underwear and fast-food wrappers. And bottles.

Still, when Colleen told them where they could find Mike, Marcy couldn't help but feel a certain level of anger with Colleen. She supposed that if the situation had involved someone other than her brother, her oldest brother, her sympathies would lie with Colleen. But when Colleen shook her head when Nick asked if she wanted to relay any sort of message to Mike, Marcy wanted to slap her. *He may have been a philanderer, but at least he was here,* she wanted to scream.

Marcy took inventory of the items in her carriage. Apples, pears, bags of prepackaged romaine salad, whole grain bread, eggs, skim milk, yogurt. What would Mike's reaction be when she walked in carrying bags of wholesomeness?

"Ma'am?"

The cashier was waiting for Marcy to begin loading her groceries onto the belt. Marcy glanced back at the woman directly behind her, who offered a tight smile that said, *I don't know about you, but I happen to be in a hurry.*

Would Mike even thank her?

Would Mike ever admit to what he had done? To Colleen? To his kids?

And would April ever be able to understand how she felt right now, at this moment, trying to keep the worst-case scenarios at bay while she shopped—shopped!—for the brother who left her as soon as he possibly could?

"Ma'am? You ready or what?"

Now Marcy was aware of all the beeps around her as items in the aisles next to hers were scanned. She heard the murmur of conversation, the sudden call-outs in Spanish, the crying of a child. It was the crying child that got to her.

"Excuse me," Marcy said to the woman behind her as she started backing up, pulling the grocery carriage.

"What? What are you doing?"

"Excuse me, need to get by."

The woman frowned as if Marcy had just peed on her leg.

"Why not just go through?" the woman asked.

Good point, Marcy thought. But Marcy was determined.

"Don't worry, your plastic surgeon will wait," she said.

The woman inhaled sharply as Marcy all but pushed her out of the way. Marcy then walked the aisles of Dominick's, returning each item in her cart to the appropriate shelf or bin. By the time she had finished, the crying child was gone.

It wasn't until she was halfway back to the hotel that she realized she didn't have her cell phone. She stepped on the gas.

CHAPTER TWENTY-NINE

Even though by most measures it wasn't much of a scuffle, Bill Warrington judged it to be one of the more satisfying fights he'd ever been in. All right, it wasn't really a fight. It was a mugging. A near mugging, actually. But it *would* have been real mugging if he hadn't taken action, if he hadn't fought back. But fight back he did. Got in a good jab, too.

Maybe it was the mountains that surrounded the city that reminded Bill of Korea. Strange how one minute he remembered what he was trying to do and who he was trying to find and then, the next minute, the next second, not so sure. The mountains threw him off. Korea? Colorado? He had to admit he was confused. Like the incident that had started the fight in the first place. He had been crossing the street looking for Marcy . . . no, April . . . and there on the other side was Clare. He was sure of it, even as he knew it could not be true. The staggering possibility, however remote, had made it impossible for him to move. He was sure it was her. The way she had given her head a shake as she walked, moving the strands away from her face as her hair billowed out behind her—how could it be anyone else? He'd reached his hand out in front of him, as if to touch, caress, and he saw the dark spots and the swollen knuckles and he was jerked back to . . . Utah! Yes, Utah.

So it couldn't possibly be Clare, any more than those bent fingers and yellow nails were his. But they were his, so why couldn't it be Clare? Things were upside down in this goddamned crazy world. Maybe he was a young man having a nightmare instead of an old man reliving a dream.

That's when the gook had suddenly started talking to him, his breath foul enough to kill a horse. "You can't stand here, mister," he said. No trace of an accent, Bill noticed. Pretty goddamned smart. "Let me help you. You're gonna get yourself killed."

Bill heard car horns and a few shouted obscenities, but he was focused on the drunk gook. Or if he wasn't drunk, he had been drunk not too long ago. Maybe he was on his way to get drunk . . . or drunker. Maybe he needed money to get drunk. He wasn't about to fool Bill. Bill knew gooks. And Bill sure as hell knew drunks.

"Lemme help, lemme help," the man said, and *now* he was starting to sound more like he should. That's the thing: They'd nod and smile and say *yes yes yes* but all the while they are wondering how they can rip your heart out. He'd seen it. He knew. Some of his buddies fell for the smiling, the subservient posturing, the irresistible stuff they said they had for the GI to buy. Women to buy. *Cheap, velly cheap.* They'd draw the sailor or GI or marine or flyboy into an alley, promising porn or liquor or a young girl, and then kick the crap out of the fool, leaving him with little more than his boxers and his balls. Bill never fell for it. His buddies should have known better.

Bill started walking. One foot in front of the other. Just start walking. He made it to the sidewalk and stopped. He looked around him, searching for a familiar building or landmark.

"Where you going, man?"

The gook again. Flies on turds, these guys, trying to sound cool, sound American. Bill knew the game.

But the question still knocked him off track. Where *was* he try-ing to go? For a moment he was thinking, *Back to my unit, back to my barracks.* But that wasn't right, couldn't be right. He looked at his hands again.

He was nothing but an old man. But at least he wasn't like this guy behind him: drunk, homeless. Kicked around every day like the old dog he'd probably eaten yesterday for lunch.

Dog—that was it! Greyhound. That's where he was going.

Bill looked around him for the sign. The sign of the dog. The Greyhound dog: elongated, leaping. There it was: right above him. He was here.

"Are you lost, man? Whatcha lookin' for?"

Bill needed to get away from this guy. Clare was waiting.

"Wait, man, maybe I can help."

He'd turned and thrown the first punch only after he felt a hand on his shoulder, but he missed wide and nearly lost his balance. The gook broke his fall, holding on to his right arm with both hands. Bill knew the drill. First the arm, then the legs got kicked out from underneath you, next thing you knew you were on your back. Chink meat. No thinking needed here, just action. He cocked his left arm and let fly.

From the gook's yell of surprise, Bill knew he'd connected. So why was he on the ground? Must've slipped at that point and knocked his head. He was sitting, and he touched his finger to a spot on his forehead that suddenly seemed on fire. He brought his hand away and saw blood on his fingers.

As the ringing subsided, he heard people yelling, "Leave him alone" and "Get outta here." Bill thought at first they were yelling at him, but then he heard his assailant cry out, "I was trying to help him, motherfuckers!"

People were helping Bill to his feet.

"Where are you going?"

"Do you need help?"

"Is there someone we can call?"

Bill felt dizzy. All these questions, all these people. He needed to focus. "I'm fine," he muttered, even though he wasn't sure he would be able to keep his knees from buckling. "I'm fine."

Someone put something against his forehead. A handkerchief.

"You're bleeding. We should get you to a hospital. Let's get you to a hospital."

"Hospital, no," Bill said. "I'm okay. Just let me . . ."

Someone—several people—led him to a bus stop bench and helped him sit. Out of the noise of the traffic and the people talking to him, he heard a girl's voice cry out.

"Grandpa!"

He was looking in Clare's face—no, not Clare's . . . April's. She was crying and asking what happened and then she was talking to the strangers and one of the strangers said the bleeding had stopped and April was saying thank you and she thought everything would be okay and no it wasn't necessary to call the police or an ambulance. A man's voice asked if she was sure and she said she was sure and Bill had closed his eyes until he felt her in front of him.

"Grandpa, you absolutely scared the shit out of me," April said.

Bill wanted to laugh, but a flash of pain across his forehead made him wince.

"Where did you go?" April continued. "You dropped me at Amtrak but never showed up. I finally realized you might be here, but then I got here and you weren't. Then I walk out here to find you bleeding and everything. What is going on with you?"

Bill wondered if this would be his last coherent thought, this realization that he was sitting at a dirty bus stop; that he didn't even know the name of the city he was in; that he was not with Clare or with Mike or with Nick or with Marcy; that he was about to break yet another promise, this one to his granddaughter, who was now begging him to say something, to open his eyes.

Bill hadn't realized he'd closed them. A hot wave—an ocean of pins and tacks and broken bottles—scraped across his forehead, across his temples, and across the back of his head. The pain actually felt pretty good; cleansing, in a way. He waited to be lifted up, he *expected* to be lifted up so that he could look down on the scene: an old man, a young girl, indifferent life bustling about and around them. Up and up he would go, he knew, until their two figures became small and melted like snow as he rose higher and higher into white.

CHAPTER THIRTY

April guessed she'd been in the zone Keith Spinelli and his buddies talk about when they talk about sports. *He was in the zone, man,* one of them would say, as if some stupid athlete had walked on water. It used to bug her, listening to that crap as she took books out of her locker or sat in the lunchroom. *Get a life,* she'd think.

But now she would give just about anything to be listening to that drivel, to be watching Heather get all gaga over some stupid boy talking about the zone with Keith Spinelli, to be anywhere but the Salt Lake City Amtrak station.

The thing about being in the zone, April thought, is that you remember it all, but you don't remember actually doing it until it's all over: how she found her grandfather sitting on the sidewalk in front of the bus station, with people huddled around him while he held a blood-soaked handkerchief to his forehead and noisily refused all medical attention, practically wrestling the handkerchief away from him to make sure he wasn't still bleeding, walking him back to the Amtrak station, her grandfather babbling away, making no sense, no sense at all. And here they were, sitting side by side on the plastic chairs, waiting for the train that April knew, with growing certainty, they could not get on.

The businessman was gone. The mother and her kids were still there, though. The woman, arms around her sleeping maniacs, gave April a sympathetic smile. April smiled back but then turned away. She was afraid that if she opened her mouth, if she said a single word, she would never stop crying.

Her grandfather sat quietly, staring off into space. A zombie. She wanted him to talk to her, but she was afraid that he'd start jabbering, loudly, about nothing. Maybe he'd wake the kids; maybe the mother would feel compelled to offer advice again. Everyone, it seemed to April, felt it was their civic duty to tell a teenager how to live. And she noticed it was usually from the perspective of regret. As if messing up their own lives gave them the right to advise others on how to run theirs.

She decided that when she became an adult, she wasn't going to try to solve world hunger or join some lying politician's campaign or try to figure out how to make blacks and whites and Arabs and Jews—freaking men and women, for that matter—get along. No, she was going to do the world a favor and just mind her own damn business.

Kind of like the ticket guy. He didn't say anything, didn't ask anything, when April returned with her grandfather. A sweet job, when you think about it. People ask for tickets, you give them their tickets. No questions. The train is either full, or not. Nothing to think about. No decisions to make.

You want to go where? Fine. That'll be fifty dollars. Have a nice day.

She'd been too hard on the clerk, she decided. She'd been a smart-ass. The guy was just doing his job. Until he said, "Well, aren't you something?" That, April thought, was unnecessary.

And yet—*aren't you something?*

Yes, as a matter of fact, I *am* something, April thought now, sitting next to her near-comatose grandfather. I am clueless. I am an idiot. I am a moron. What else could I be, traveling across the country with someone I knew was losing it? A singer in a band? Who's kidding who? My voice belongs at the top of my TITS list.

Her grandfather's eyes were open but vacant. April wanted to wave her hands in front to see if he'd blink, but worried about drawing the attention of the mother. He was breathing heavily. The cut on his forehead was a scabby brownish red. He needed to brush his teeth.

She took the tickets out of her pocket. *California Zephyr.* "Don't move, Grandpa," she said. "Okay?"

The request was unnecessary. Her grandfather made no sign that he'd even heard her.

The clerk was reading the paper. April wondered if it was a different one or if he read the same news over and over until the end of his shift.

"I need to exchange tickets," she said. "Please," she added.

He lowered the paper and looked at her as if he hadn't noticed her until that very moment. He then folded the newspaper noisily, the crinkling reminding April of boots against snow, walking home. "Well, the young traveler returns. How nice to see you again. You say you need to exchange these tickets?"

"Yes. I need to exchange them for tickets to Ohio."

"Ohio?"

"Ohio."

"Wow. Instead of desperately needing to go to California—*Emeryville*—you now desperately need to get to Ohio?" He blew out his cheeks. "Talk about your U-turns."

"Can you please just exchange these tickets?"

"No, I can't just exchange these tickets."

"Why not?"

"It costs more to get to Ohio from here than it does to California. You do know where Ohio is, don't you?"

April reminded herself that the guy was just doing his job.

"I grew up there."

"You grew up there? So . . . you're all grown up, is that it?"

One more comment, April thought. Just one more comment and I'm going to grab this guy's collar, pull him close, and punch him in the face.

April pushed the tickets she had, along with her grandfather's credit card, to the clerk.

"Can you just exchange these for tickets to Cleveland? Put the difference on this card."

The clerk didn't look at her.

"Please," April said.

He swiped. Waited. Swiped again. He grunted as he squinted at the readout.

"Won't take it," he said.

"What do you mean?"

"Says 'declined.' "

"Why?"

"My guess is you exceeded the limit. Lots of people think they can just keep charging and charging, until this happens."

April felt a trickle of sweat slither down her right side. She'd never bothered asking her grandfather about limits. Never thought about it as she checked into hotels, paid for meals.

"Do you—or should I say your grandfather—have a different card?"

April felt hot. Her eyes stung. Why does everything out of this guy's mouth have to be a dig? What had she done to him? It wasn't her fault this loser was stuck in a loser job.

"Is there a problem here?"

Her grandfather's eyes were clear and they were focused on the ticket clerk. He was standing straight. Apart from the scab and bruise on his forehead—which, April noticed, seemed to be getting bigger and bluer by the second—her grandfather seemed perfectly fine. In charge.

"No, Grandpa," April said. "Please go back and sit down. I'm just—"

"What's the problem?" her grandfather asked, still looking at the clerk. April noticed the slight rise in volume. The clerk had better not try any smart-ass response: her grandfather might turn into GI Joe again.

"I'm trying to exchange your tickets, but your credit card got rejected."

"Exchange? What exchange?"

"The young lady wants to exchange the tickets for Ohio. I tried . . ."

April cringed as her grandfather turned to her. She tried to speak, but her throat went Sahara.

"You have the tickets to Seattle?" he asked April.

April nodded. She hoped the clerk wouldn't correct her grandfather. "Grandpa, I think we need—"

"No way," he said, his voice flat, final. "Who are you, Moses? Coming all this way but not going in, God be damned?"

April thought she heard the ticket seller gasp.

"No granddaughter of mine is going to be a quitter."

"Grandpa, this isn't about me. It's about—"

"It's about quitting, that's what it's about. And you're not going to quit, you hear me? I will not allow it."

April knew from his eyes that he wasn't talking to her. She didn't know which son, or maybe her mother, or which war buddy he was talking to, but it wasn't her.

"Okay, Grandpa. Okay."

He was talking nonstop all the way back to their seats. But at least he wasn't screaming. The woman with the children was watching. April ignored her.

"Can't go through life not doing what you know you should do. When I knew I'd be drafted, I knew I should enroll in officer school. But I didn't. Didn't think I had the stuff, even though I knew I did. So what happened? Froze my damn ass off in the trenches."

His language was getting worse and the mother was smiling, but it was making April uncomfortable. She needed to distract him.

"Grandpa, why is it so important that all three be there?" she asked, uncertain herself as to where the question came from. "You told me—and sometimes when you don't know you're talking—that you want all to be there. Where? And who? Are you talking about my mom and Uncle Mike and Uncle Nick?"

He seemed not to understand the question. But then he nodded.

"Why is that so important, Grandpa?"

It was a long time before he answered.

"You're not a kid anymore. You probably noticed that your mom and her brothers don't keep in touch much. I always thought it was their own damn fault. But then I started thinking that maybe it was me. A misunderstanding. About what they think I did to their mother."

"What did you do? Did you beat her?"

He looked at her.

"Did I beat her?"

April thought for sure she had made him angry enough for him to hit her. But he didn't move. He just got very loud.

"I wouldn't touch a hair on her head! I could never do anything to cause her pain. 'Course, that only ended up causing her *more* pain, because I didn't have the guts to do what she asked me to do. But I couldn't bear it. Either way, I couldn't bear it."

April didn't know what he was talking about but figured she'd better keep quiet. People might start poking their noses into their business.

"Oh, some thought they knew what happened. Some even had the . . . the . . . *balls* to accuse me. To my face! It was beyond belief. Beyond even answering! How anyone, especially . . . could think I was capable . . . would even think of . . ."

She'd never seen him so angry. It took a while for him to breathe normally. When he spoke, his voice was low. He sounded exhausted.

"I just wanted to remind them of the fun we used to have. The vacations we took. Kind of remind them of things. That I wasn't someone who could do what they thought I did."

"What do they think you did, Grandpa?"

His eyes welled. "I just wanted one chance to tell them, all three of them together . . . face-to-face. Before I . . . couldn't."

"What *did* happen, Grandpa? What are you talking about?"

It was another long time before he answered.

"That'll be for them to tell you."

They sat. April glanced at the clock. 9:30. The train for San Francisco—freakin' Emeryville—was supposed to leave at 11:54.

The next time she looked at the clock, it was 10:15.

Her grandfather started laughing.

"What's so funny?"

Her grandfather pointed at something outside the window.

"Those banana trees over there."

April looked at where he was pointing. Just a couple of telephone poles and a streetlamp.

"Grandpa, those aren't—"

"Why don't you climb up and get me one. I could go for a banana right now."

He went on about bananas for a while. April felt as though the room was gradually being sucked dry of oxygen. She wanted to run over to the woman, snuggle next to the maniacs.

Her grandfather gradually quieted. He closed his eyes.

April stood and moved as far away from him as possible without leaving the station and without losing sight of him.

She didn't question her decision.

She took out her cell phone and dialed.

CHAPTER THIRTY-ONE

Nick Warrington sat in the near dark, the television screen flashing before him. To fend off thoughts of the different kinds of people who had sat in this particular chair, in various states of dress, engaged in various solo and tandem activities, he thought about mistakes.

Like flashing plastic to Marcy and telling her that he was on a company expense account.

Like pretending the Peggy Gallagher fiasco hadn't hurt as much as it had, that she hadn't played him for the fool he was, that he wasn't much more than a needy puppy to just about any woman he met.

Like pretending that he truly believed the three of them—especially with Mike involved—could handle this situation with their father and April.

He'd have to tell Marcy when she got back: It was time to go. It was time to let the cops handle this. It was time to go home and wait.

It wasn't a matter of getting back to his office; his office, after all, was his dining room table. There was no staff floundering without his direction; no one even reported to him at this job. Ohio wasn't

New York. Woodlake was not New York City. Even when he'd had an office, it didn't look out over Fifth Avenue or the streets of SoHo or Greenwich Village. It looked out over a bus stop.

Peggy wasn't Marilyn.

No woman was Marilyn. There were no Marilyns out there anymore.

Even their hotshot older brother—the super salesman, the man who could sell smoothies to Eskimos and lighter fluid to the devil— was nothing more than a sham. The 4,000-square-foot home, the beautiful wife, the straight-A kids: all gone.

And more: The brother had turned into the father.

Nick stood, as if doing so would ward off the smug satisfaction he felt at Mike's misfortune, which was playing itself out, real time, in the bathroom. He turned up the television to drown out the sounds of the dry heaves. The combination of TV talk and gagging made him want to pace. His eyes fell on Mike's suitcase propped up on the hotel portable luggage rack as if he were going to check out. Positive thinker, Mike.

After a few moments, Nick heard the sound of the shower. He walked over to Mike's suitcase. It was closed but not locked or latched. Opening it would be easy. Nothing major. Just a quick peek. Just to see.

He turned toward the bathroom door. Water still running. He lifted the top half of the suitcase. What you might expect: dress shirts folded and bagged from the cleaners; rolled-up T-shirts and socks. Might be something interesting under the shirts. Nick reached in.

He didn't hear the sudden increase in volume of the shower or see the light from the bathroom hit the wall he was facing until it was too late. He turned. Mike was standing in the light, towel around his waist. He looked like he'd been keeping himself in pretty good shape. And he didn't appear at all distressed by the audible testimony of his vulnerability just a few moments before. "Wallet's on the dresser," he said. "Help yourself."

"What?" Nick replied. "I just . . ."

Mike didn't throw him a rope.

Hell with it. "You look better. How do you feel?"

"Fit as a fiddle," Mike said. Nick recognized but didn't acknowledge this corny line of their father's. "Where's Marcy?" he asked.

"Went to grab some groceries."

Mike looked around the room. "Where did you two sleep?"

"Marcy slept on the couch. I slept there." He nodded at the chair.

"Guess I wasn't a good host last night." An apology, Nick supposed.

Mike took off the towel and started drying himself, putting his right foot on the bed so that he could dry his leg, but also to . . . what? Display his genitals in some sort of alpha dog routine? Demonstrate complete disdain? Nick reddened.

"I take it you two geniuses haven't figured out how to get April back," Mike said.

Their eyes locked for the first time in years.

"And you have?" Nick asked.

Mike snapped the towel as he moved it to the other leg. He rubbed furiously, which Nick knew was meant to show him that, for real men, the world was their locker room. "As a famous man once said, I ain't got a dog in this fight."

"We're not talking dogs here, Mike. Why don't you cover yourself and tell me what you mean? We're talking about our niece. We're talking about Dad."

Mike laughed and shook his head as he rewrapped the towel around his waist.

"No, we're not, Nicky," he said. "We're talking about how you two brought this on yourself."

"What are you talking about?"

"Or is it yourselves? You tell me. You're the writer."

"Cut the crap and tell me what you're talking about!"

Mike put his hands on his hips. "All right. Fine. You two let him off the hook."

"Let who off the hook?" Nick asked, pissed that he'd taken the bait. Now he'd have to listen to this . . . this *drunk*. This drunk brother of his who—as Bobby Gallagher might put it, and put it accurately— blew it. He'd had the perfect family and he blew it. Did he realize how many people wanted what he had . . . and lost? Did he have any idea how badly Marilyn had wanted to have kids? And yet, there he stood, Caesar in a towel toga, about to share his omnipotent wisdom.

Mike took a step toward him. Nick clenched his fist. Mike saw it. "Whoa, big boy, just want to grab some clothes. That okay with you?"

It would have been so easy, Nick thought as Mike reached into his suitcase, the back of his head within striking distance, to grab the empty whiskey bottle.

Mike stepped back. "I'm going to have to drop the towel now, Nick. You might want to avert your sensitive eyes."

More bait. Nick didn't hesitate. "Let who off the hook?"

"Dad, of course," Mike said, in a tone as calm and measured as Nick's had been frantic.

"What are you talking about?"

"You two seemed content to give him a pass, let him off the hook. So you formed your own little team. Nick and Marcy. Poor Nick and Marcy. Saints Nick and Marcy, martyrs. Suffering and silent."

Nick shook his head. "I still don't know what in the hell you're talking about."

"I'm the only one who stood up to him. Wouldn't let him just ignore what he had done—and still won't." Mike pulled his slacks up and started running a belt through the loops. He stopped and looked at Nick. "Tell me you don't remember that night. I knew what he was up to. What he was doing with Mom's pills. And where were you and Marcy when I confronted him?"

Nick knew exactly what Mike was talking about, but pretended he didn't. "You tell me. You seem to have the photographic memory here," he said.

"Nowhere to be found, that's where."

"I thought you were kidding," Nick said, trying unsuccessfully to keep calm. "I thought you were crazy, thinking Dad could do something like that."

"And now? You still think I was crazy?"

"We're not talking about now," Nick said. "Now you're just a loser. Back then ... Marcy didn't know what you were thinking. Still doesn't, as far as I know. And we were just kids, for god's sake."

"So was I!" Mike yelled.

Someone pounded on the wall. A muffled voice shouted, "Keep it down in there, willya?"

Mike turned and walked toward the wall as if he might punch it. "Hey! I have to listen to *you* jerking off to the porn channel every night so shut the fuck up!"

Nick and Mike waited for the reply. When none came, Mike turned back to Nick and smiled. "I hope he's not a member of the clergy," he said.

"I hope he's not a member of the NRA," Nick replied.

This was enough of a tension-breaker for Nick to think they might be able to continue at a more civilized level.

Mike chuckled and resumed dressing. "Marcy? Okay. She was young, and she was a girl," he said, his voice calm again, controlled. "But you?" He snapped at the shirt as he pulled his arms through the sleeves. "I'm only two years older than you, Nick. I may have been a pain in the ass, but I always looked out for you. Stuck up for you." He buttoned his shirt slowly, deliberately. "You always took the old man's side. Never wanted to make waves. Even after he killed your mother."

"Jesus Christ, Mike. You still believe that?"

Mike stared at Nick, then shrugged. "Doesn't matter. You made your decision. Marcy made hers. Even tolerating the guy was wrong, as far as I was concerned. When you guys got older and could leave, you didn't. You seemed to forget what he'd done. Marcy even let her daughter get to know that asshole." He tucked in his shirt. "So . . . you brought this whole thing on yourselves as far as I'm concerned."

"Marcy told me you invited him to Chicago," Nick said, knowing how weak that sounded, how obvious an attempt to distract. "So don't pretend you haven't—"

"He thought he was calling someone else," Mike said. "I wasn't *inviting* him anywhere. I was calling his bluff. Just as I did the night I told Dad I knew what he did, while you hid in a closet, pissing your pants."

Nick felt dizzy. Had he actually hidden in a closet? Or was Mike being metaphoric? Was Mike even capable of being metaphoric? The possibility that he *had* hidden in a closet bothered him more than the accusation Mike was making about their father.

"And during all this time, while you guys have decided to ignore me and my family, I've tried to help out," Mike said. "I was at the airport, ready to fly to Des Moines. But then when you guys—some BS about missing your flight—"

"We didn't *miss* it. It was canceled because—"

"—I figured it was just more bullshit. But none of it matters anymore. Because this morning I've come to realize that, as you can see"—he spread his arms out to encompass the room—"I've got problems of my own I should be working on."

Nick had trouble thinking. Where to start? None of this was making sense. Mike had been the one who pulled away, not him. Not

Marcy. He would never turn his back on his brother. Mike was the one who left. For girls. For school. Forever. Nick heard a buzzing in his head. Literally, a buzzing.

"That yours?" Mike asked. He pointed at the desk. A cell phone jumped about, vibrating.

"Marcy's," Nick said tightly.

Mike nodded. "Impressive. Her daughter is AWOL and Marcy leaves her cell phone behind. Smart." Then, with a sigh, he walked to the desk, inches from Nick. He picked up the phone and looked at the screen.

"This ought to be interesting," he said, flipping open the phone. "April?"

April? Perfect, Nick thought. Timing is everything. Mike paced as he talked.

"Hank?" He raised his eyebrows at Nick. "No, this is your uncle Mike. How are you? . . . Not at the moment. Just me and your other uncle . . . Uncle Nick, yes, unless you have an uncle we don't know about . . . Yes, we're all here together . . . Yeah, your mom, too, although she's at the store at the . . . Naperville . . . Chicago, yes . . ."

There was pounding on the door. Mike put his finger in his other ear so he could continue his conversation with April.

"Did you get lost?" Nick asked when he saw that Marcy wasn't carrying any groceries.

Marcy moved past him and into the room. Mike was standing near the TV.

"Is that my phone?" she asked Nick.

Before he could respond, Marcy was already walking over to Mike, who ignored her when she extended her hand. When she tapped him on the shoulder, Mike walked into the bedroom portion of the suite and closed the door.

"He's talking to April, isn't he?"

Nick nodded.

"So she called me!" Marcy said. She went to open the bedroom door, but Mike had locked it.

"Let me talk with her!" Marcy yelled.

"Hold on, Marcy," Nick said. "Let's see what happens."

"Screw that."

For a moment, Nick thought she might wait. But it turned out she was just being quiet so she could listen. Even from where he stood, Nick could hear Mike reciting a series of numbers.

"He's giving her his credit card number," Marcy said. "Son of a bitch is helping her!"

Now she stared pounding.

"Open this goddamned door! Let me talk to her." Marcy felt her voice grow weak even as she tried to get louder. "Let me talk to my daughter!"

She was crying now as she called out for her little girl. Nick was trying to pull her away from the door, to try to calm her, when Mike opened it.

"What the hell are you doing?" Marcy screamed. "I'm trying to get my daughter back and you're buying them—what? Airline tickets to Cancun?"

Mike pushed his hand through his hair. Nick thought he looked tired, hungover, and for the first time ever, old.

"What have you done now?" Marcy asked. "Where is she?"

"Can't tell you," he said. "I promised."

"What?" Marcy picked out a spot on his chest. She clenched her fist.

"Listen to me, Marcy. I made a deal—"

"You made a deal?" Marcy laughed, her voice cracking. "You're one for making deals, aren't you? Who are you to be making deals with my daughter? How about the deal you made with your own god-damned kids? Maybe you should worry about those deals!"

Mike was looking at the floor. He kept looking at the floor as he spoke. "Think what you want," he said. "But if you want to see April in about forty-eight hours, you won't ask me any more questions." Then he looked up at Marcy. His eyes, Nick thought, were surprisingly clear. Focused. "And you won't say another word about my kids."

He took a step back, into the bedroom, and closed the door.

Marcy turned and looked at Nick.

Nick tried not to feel useless.

CHAPTER THIRTY-TWO

April almost wished they were back on the train, with its stale stink and busted air-conditioning, because at least there was shade. Out here, the sun beat down on them as if truly pissed at them for venturing onto the beach fully clothed, including shoes. Her grandfather was sweating like a horse and April started to worry that he'd keel over from heat exhaustion or a heart attack. She pulled her sticky shirt away from her body and tried to ventilate: bad luck to think things like that. She was glad she'd taken her uncle Mike's suggestion to "stow"—his word—their luggage in one of the lockers at the train station, even though it had taken her nearly an hour to score the eight quarters. *New list idea:* Things I Will Do When I Am An Adult That Adults Usually Don't Do. Like give money to beggars. Not all of them are drunks or drug addicts or just plain lazy. Some of them, like all of us, are just trying to get someplace.

"Where are we going?" her grandfather asked, stopping to pull a gross snot rag out of his pocket and mop it across his forehead. "You said you just wanted to see the water. There it is, for god's sake."

There it was, indeed. She was so glad she remembered the beach, the ocean-lake, and that Naperville was one of the stops on the California Zephyr. When her uncle Mike answered her mother's phone and said they were all there together in Naperville, April's plan fell into place as if it had been there all along.

"Just up ahead," April said to her grandfather now, looking to her right at the skyscrapers that hugged the shore. She was relieved to see the huge sign for the Drake Hotel. The plan was to pick a spot somewhere directly in front of it. She saw a bench near the edge of the sand. She wondered if her uncle Mike knew about that bench. Whatever. The good news was that a bench was there; the bad news was that it was occupied by two guys sitting with their legs splayed open to make sure no one else could fit. They were eighteen or nineteen, April guessed, dressed in street clothes but shirtless—the better, apparently, to display their gross tattoos and flabby bellies on the incredibly remote chance they'd attract the attention of one of the bikinis jiggling by. One guy had a shaved head; the other wore a crew cut with some sort of lightning design shaved into the left temple area. April saw another bench farther down, but it was past the Drake; besides, she was afraid her grandfather wouldn't make it.

"Excuse me," April said when they reached the bench. "Could you make room for my grandfather, please?"

The two weren't subtle about checking April out. Despite herself, April couldn't help but think how gross she must look. She hadn't combed her hair in days, her clothes were stained with tomato soup and coffee that her grandfather had spilled on her somewhere near Omaha, and her underwear was so sweaty and gross that she'd need surgical gloves to remove them.

"Don't know about the old man," the shaved head said, "but we could prolly make room for *you.*"

They laughed, opened their legs wider, and high-fived each other. April rolled her eyes. She felt her grandfather move closer and she waited for the explosion, but he just stood there, mopping the top of his head. April felt something rising up in herself. Was every encounter with men going to be like this: first, an inspection; second, a pass; third, condescension? April looked around her. It was the middle of the day. The beach was crowded. What could they do?

"I'll bet if you gave up the space you're using to show off your junk, space you don't need by the way, you could fit half the beach on this bench."

It took them a minute to get it. When they finally did, they looked at each other, hooted, and started laughing and slapping their knees as if they'd said it themselves.

"You a sassy little bitch, ain't you," the shaved one said, talking ghetto like some of the boys at her high school did when they were trying to be cool but only succeeded in being more annoying than usual. April knew he wasn't angry. In fact, he and his lightning bug homeboy stood and made elaborate gestures for April and her grandfather to sit. They demanded she high-five them. Fortunately, they didn't try the same with her grandfather. Then they walked away.

April double-checked that they were in front of the Drake as she and her grandfather settled on the bench. He was in another of his quiet funks, not having said a word during the entire encounter with the two losers. Now he was staring straight ahead—just as he had for hours at a time on the train.

It had been one of the longest trips of her life. She was afraid her grandfather would catch on that they were going in the wrong direction and would create a scene. She tensed for the inevitable question at every announcement of the next station stop, and it seemed that there were a gazillion of them. The first close call was a few minutes after the announcement for Fort Morgan. He straightened up, and April sensed that he was about to start talking. She was sure he was going to ask why they were back in Colorado. But instead he said, "For a long time, your mom and your uncles thought I was a drunk."

It was about eleven o'clock, the people around them were quiet, and her grandfather's voice seemed to fill the night.

"That was random," April replied. "And a little too loud, Grandpa."

"I guess today they call that a dependency problem of some sort," he continued, a little more quietly, but not much. "An addiction. Well, they were right that I drank too much. No doubt. But I wasn't addicted to alcohol."

He stopped. April knew he was in a chatty mood and that he'd stopped only so she could ask the question that would give him the excuse to ramble on and on.

"What were you addicted to, Grandpa?"

"You're a lot like her, you know."

April rolled her eyes. This was going to be one of those all-over-the-map conversations, impossible to follow. But she wasn't in the mood at that hour. And she was tired of his telling her how much like her mother she was. She wasn't anything like her mother. Hadn't he at least learned that by now?

"God! She was so beautiful."

Okay, April thought to herself. He was talking about her grandmother, not her mother. Next thing he'd say would probably be something about Korea, or one of his triumphant business deals. Could go anywhere from here.

"Are you listening to me?" her grandfather asked.

"I'm listening," April said. "So you're saying I'm beautiful?"

She blushed. Until she spoke the words, she hadn't made the connection between what he'd said.

"No, I'm not saying that. I'm saying she had a first-class bullshit detector. She could smell a phony a mile away. And she didn't suffer fools lightly. She knew how to keep people from riding too high in the saddle."

"Like you?" April asked, flush with anger now. She pretended not to notice that he was trying to look her in the eye.

"Like me," he said, quietly.

He turned and closed his eyes. April thought he had fallen asleep. She took out her pen and notepad. She listened to the rhythm of the tracks.

> *Riding riding riding*
> *riding the rails.*
> *Whatever happens*
> *I will not fail.*
> *Riding riding riding*
> *riding the rails.*
> *Listening to that lonely*
> *oh so lonely wail.*

She looked at the words, pencil poised to cross them all out. Another sucky song. Who was she kidding? She wasn't cut out to be a singer. She wasn't cut out to be a songwriter. She wasn't cut out to be anything but another stupid fan of people who actually got out there and did something with their lives.

Still, she didn't cross out the words. *Not yet,* she told herself.

"I feel sorry for the boys your age," her grandfather suddenly said, not asleep, after all.

She looked over, closing her notepad quickly. "Why's that, Grandpa?"

"Because, April, when you get to be a woman, you're going to be beautiful. And when you combine knockout looks with that built-in BS detector of yours . . . well, there's going to be an awful lot of disappointed young men."

He reached over and patted her hand.

Ten minutes later, he asked how long before they'd see his mother.

It wasn't until their second morning on the train, when he woke up and looked out the window, that April feared he'd caught on to her ruse.

"How come we're going east?" he asked. April pretended to be absorbed by the *Rolling Stone* she'd lifted from the newsstand in Osceola.

A few minutes later, he said, "I know I'm going daffy, but I truly don't believe that the earth has started spinning the other way." He jabbed April's shoulder and pointed out the window. "There's the sun. We're headed right at it. East."

April recognized the signs of his growing irritation. He hunched forward and started looking for someone or something as if his life depended on it. In this case, April was pretty sure he was trying to find a conductor so he could confirm his hunch.

"You don't always go directly west to get west, Grandpa," April said, flipping pages nonchalantly. "It's like sometimes when you're driving on the highway and you're coming to a big city and you want to avoid all the traffic. So you take another highway around it and you have to go in a different direction than the direction you're taking, and you have to take that direction for a while before you get back to your original direction. Sometimes you have to go west to get east, east to get west. That's all this is."

Her grandfather stared at her. Then he sat back and, outside of a please or thank-you when April gave him something to eat, he barely said a word the rest of the trip. He didn't even question all the Chicago signs in Union Station. April was ready with several explanations—this was where people heading *to* Chicago caught the train; those were *advertisements* for the Windy City—but lying was unnecessary. He'd followed her out of the station, down to Lake Shore Drive, and across the beach to this bench in front of the Drake Hotel. They'd been walking forever, it seemed. But she'd done it. They were here. Only one more thing to take care of before it was all over.

She checked her watch. It was time.

She stood and looked down at her grandfather. He looked very small on the bench, his shoulders slumped, sun beating down on the

top of his head as if trying to melt him into the bench like a dropped
ice cream cone. She removed the baseball cap she'd "found" in the
food car on the train and put it on his head to protect it.

"Grandpa," she said.

"So that's it, huh?"

April's heart stopped. Had he sensed this? How could he possibly
have known?

"What's it?" she asked.

He jutted his chin out toward the water. "The Pacific Ocean," her
grandfather said.

April nodded, her heart pounding in relief.

"Yeah. The Pacific."

April looked around to make sure she wasn't taking too long. She
needed to get going.

"Remember our deal?" her grandfather said.

"What deal?"

"Back in Woodlake? The one where we're always straight with
each other?"

Now April's heart threatened to punch its way up and out of her
throat.

"I'm being straight with you, Grandpa."

"Yeah?" Her grandfather looked at her. "You sure? Well, I got
news for you, smarty-pants. That's not the Pacific."

Great. Of all the times to be lucid. April tried to think of how she
was going to respond to this one. *Actually, Grandpa, they relocated
the Sears Tower. You didn't know that?*

"Grandpa—"

"THAT," he shouted, pointing ahead, "is Puget Bay!" He broke
into laughter.

Some people sunning themselves nearby looked over, and April
veered between laughing and crying out in relief.

She looked at her watch. She kneeled in front of her grandfather. "Grandpa, I gotta go to the bathroom. You stay here, okay?"

"Most people don't know that it's a bay. The ocean stops at the whatchamacallit bridge. Golden Gate. Did I say Puget? I meant—whatever . . ."

April waited. But her grandfather's eyes started to get that filmy look.

"Grandpa, you have to stay here, okay? You can't move. I won't be gone long." Her voice caught as she realized that when she saw him again, even if in just a few minutes, everything would be changed.

"We had fun, didn't we, Grandpa? You know, getting here. All the way from Ohio. It was cool, wasn't it?"

Her grandfather didn't respond.

"Grandpa?"

"I should have kicked him in the balls," he said. "That would have taken care of everything."

April stared at him for a moment. It occurred to her that this was one of the few times she'd looked directly into his eyes, into the very center of them. But she could tell that he wasn't seeing her. She smiled and kissed him on the cheek. "I'll be right back."

"Smack dab in the scrotum," he answered.

April walked to a sidewalk kiosk renting Rollerblades and bicycles. Just as her uncle Mike had told her, she could still see her grandfather, but she would also be able to see the three of them approaching, which he'd promised would be from the opposite direction. She had insisted on keeping her grandfather in sight. And she told him that she'd disappear if all three of them weren't there.

"It's what he wants," she told Uncle Mike, even if as she said it she realized her grandfather probably didn't even know that anymore.

"I notice that you've made all these preconditions *after* you obtained my credit card number," Uncle Mike had said. Then he laughed. "My father's been in good hands," he said. "Thank you, April."

Those words, and the way he'd said her name—*bothered* to say her name—stuck with her on the train. She kept chewing them, digesting them. No matter what kind of person this uncle of hers was or turned out to be, April would always consider him an all-right kind of guy.

And suddenly, they were there. A bit far off, but April recognized her mother's walk, and then the way her hair bounced off her shoulders stiffly. She almost ran out then and there, but remembered the plan. She recognized Uncle Nick's easy gait. She had no real memory of her uncle Mike but was surprised for some reason to see that he was taller than Nick, more solid. Not fat, but not as skinny as Nick. April was holding her breath. She had to grab the side of the kiosk to keep herself from running out.

It was her mother who started running. At first, April thought she was running toward her. But she had spotted her father on the bench. April watched as she ran to him, leaned over, and embraced him. But as she did so, she was looking around. Finally, she let go of him and crouched down to look him in the eye. April knew exactly what was happening. In fact, she could practically hear her mother saying, *Where's April? Where's April?*

Suddenly, her mother turned and faced Uncle Mike. April guessed that this was the part where Mike delivered on his promise to April that he'd tell her mother, after all three were with her grandfather, that she—April—was nearby. April didn't want her mom going psycho. But she didn't want to show herself immediately. She wanted her grandfather to have time with his three children. It's what he had wanted.

Nick had taken a seat next to his father and was talking to him—or trying to. Her grandfather was looking at Nick, and while April was too far away to see it, she was sure her grandfather had that quietly desperate look on his face, as if trying to remember where he'd left his keys or his glasses. His head moved; he was looking away from Nick and at the other two. Did he recognize them? April fought off tears and resisted the urge to help her grandfather by shouting out their names. *They're here, Grandpa! Mike, Marcy, Nick. All three are here!* But her cries would only confuse him. All she could do was hope that, even if for only a second, her grandfather understood.

Meanwhile—and of course—her mother wasn't cooperating with the plan. April was sure she could hear snatches of her mother's voice punching their way through the sounds of collapsing waves and shrieking children. She was standing close to Mike now, arms akimbo. April smiled. She recognized her mother's ready-to-pounce stance.

And so she started walking toward them, quickly now, knowing that if she didn't make herself visible to them pretty soon, like in another second or two, her mother would start beating the crap out of Uncle Mike.

CHAPTER THIRTY-THREE

Everyone needs a break every now and then, so Bill decided—after a rare and unusually loud argument with Clare—that he'd sit in the backseat for a while. Close his eyes. Let someone else help with the driving.

They'd been at the beach for hours. He could feel the sand in his shoes—why hadn't he taken them off at the beach? He loved the feel of sand between his toes. But not in his shoes, not in his socks. What had they been doing on the beach fully clothed? Why hadn't they been in the water? Mike and Nick clawing at him, trying to knock the old man down, squealing with delight and frustration when they couldn't budge him. And flinging Marcy high in the air. Her nervous screams and giggles. The way she'd wrap her arms around his neck so tightly, her little wet body shivering fiercely.

The kids were growing faster than he realized. There wasn't much room in the backseat, what with the boys next to him, Nick in the middle, Mike next to the window. They'd probably fought about that one. *I call window,* Nick would have shouted. Didn't matter to Mike. He'd take the seat he wanted. Nick would appeal to his mother, but Bill would tell the two of them to work it out themselves, which meant Mike got the window. Might makes right. Law of the land. Nick would have to learn that sooner or later.

Clare was in the front seat, yelling at Marcy. Something was definitely wrong with Clare. Very unusual for Clare to yell. He'd stay out of this, though, just as he always did. Mother-daughter relationships were minefields. With the boys, sometimes all it took to end an argument was a look or a whack on the back of the head. Much, much easier.

But Clare was really laying into Marcy, and while he tried to concentrate on other things, he couldn't help but overhear. *What were you thinking? Do you know how much worry you caused me? Caused us all?* Marcy must have gone out too far in the water. So who could blame Clare for being so angry?

But Clare wouldn't let up. And Marcy, uncharacteristically, was staying quiet. Every now and then she'd pipe up: *I was never in any real danger. It wasn't like that. I needed the money to help get Grandpa home.*

Grandpa?

The next beat of his heart shot blood up to his eyelids to open them. He saw a young girl's profile. April's profile.

April.

Funny how in one moment there is nothing and in the next there is something. A moment ago it was as if April was not there, never was, had never even existed. And suddenly she is there. She *is*. And in that same instant, Clare is gone and it was a dream, her presence so fleetingly real that he wanted to go back to sleep and never wake.

But he couldn't close his eyes. He could barely breathe, for that matter. The blood still pounding in his ears drowned out all sound for a few minutes. His children were grown. April was in the front seat. His granddaughter, a bunch of pictures of her, a collage, all at once. She was singing. She was mouthing off. She was reading him something she'd written after he'd insisted. Something about hairy ears. Bill closed his eyes. He remembered her trying to convince him about how sometimes you have to go north to go west, or some such nonsense. *April April April.* He loved that name. He laughed.

You think this is funny, old man? Do you have any idea what you've done?

Leave him alone, Mom. Can't you see? Can't you tell?

Now you're some sort of expert? You have no idea what your grandfather is capable of.

Hey, Marcy . . . would you mind keeping your eyes on the road? Maybe I should drive.

If I don't drive, I'm likely to strangle the two of 'em. Maybe the two of you should do something instead of sitting in the back like a couple of turds.

No, it definitely wasn't Clare. But it was music nonetheless. Bill tried to figure out how it was possible that he'd forgotten the sound of his children's voices, the give and take, the sudden burst of anger . . . or laughter. How was it possible to miss it? They were right there. His kids. They, of course, didn't appreciate what was happening. But eventually they would: crammed together in a crowded car, sniping at each other, wondering how many more miles to go before they got . . . where? No matter. It'd come in a second. But they'd appreciate it, he knew it. They'd look back on it and laugh when they grew up.

Bill opened his eyes. They were passing a semi. The person sitting next to him was a grown man. They've all grown up. Of course. But where in the hell were they?

He leaned forward and looked to his left. Strong-looking, good-looking men. Grown.

"You okay, Dad?" the man sitting next to him asked. Nick. That's who it was. He saw in Nick—had he noticed it before?—Clare's eyes, maybe a little of his chin.

"Beautiful," he said.

He saw Nick's brow crease. How could he explain? He looked at

Mike, sitting next to Nick. Was it really Mike? Something seemed off. He looked . . . old. Tired.

Mike, or whoever it was, looked at him. He wasn't smiling. But he didn't look angry. Just . . . uninterested. Like he was there. Mostly just there.

Eternity gave Bill a headache. Father Somebody-or-other was trying to explain it to the class. Think of a planet. Size of the earth. But instead of oceans and continents and trees and mountains, it is a solid ball of metal. And imagine that every thousand years, a small bird from deep space flies to the planet and pecks at it. A single peck. Once every thousand years. Makes a tiny little nick, and a sliver of the planet, small as an atom, flies off into space. How many billions and trillions of years would it be before the planet was gone? Now, children: Those billions and trillions of years are just a small nick of time in eternity. And so, children, think: Where do you want to spend eternity?

McDonald's.

Bill is surprised to see a cheeseburger on a yellow piece of paper in front of him. Fries spilling out of a red cardboard box onto the paper. A small red puddle of ketchup. Someone had been talking to him. One of his children.

You have to eat something.

April says you always eat at McDonald's.

Do you want one of my onions?

"No!" April said loudly. Bill and everyone else looked at her. "He definitely does not want an extra onion."

One of the men addressed her. "April, if he wants—"

"Trust me," April said, cutting him off, not timid at all. *Go, April!* "You don't want to be in a car with him after he's had an onion."

Music again. The laughter. He picked up his cheeseburger and started eating. He concentrated on the taste of the pickle. Couldn't describe it. But he was here with his grown children, something he knew he had wanted but wasn't quite sure why. Didn't matter. They were talking, laughing. Bill felt the washing sensation come over him from the top of his head, sending a vaguely familiar and wonderfully warm feeling everywhere. He remembered the beach. He remembered Clare swimming up to him. Her smile. The way she wrapped her arms around his neck and the feel of her swimsuit breasts against his chest.

He saw Nick looking at him. "You want to say something, Dad?"

"Yeah," Bill said. They all looked at him, holding a fry midair or a soda in hand or looking over the sandwich about to be bitten into. But he didn't say a word. He just smiled.

Bill's eyes snapped open. It was like all those moments he'd woken up and realized that it's Saturday morning, after all, that he wasn't out in a crowd wearing only his boxers, that he hadn't moved out of his house, and that he wasn't back in a foxhole missing a hand or a foot. He knew exactly where he was: in a car, with his family, and they were all heading home. His kids were talking to each other. Bill couldn't hear much of what was being said, but it didn't matter. Nobody was yelling. They were talking. They were together.

He felt the weight of his granddaughter next to him. He felt it was safe enough now to close his eyes again.

And then, suddenly, he was standing outside of a hotel of some sort. People were taking turns hugging someone, calling him Mike. But when Mike stood before Bill, Bill saw that it wasn't Mike at all. He recognized this person—the name would come to him in a moment—but it definitely was not Mike.

"I'll be in touch," the man said. "And you press that button on your speed dial every now and then, okay?"

Manny! Of course it was Manny. Bill never did buy that malarkey about Manny killing himself with his service revolver. Not the

Manny he knew, the Manny he shared a foxhole with, shared a winter with, shared a lifetime with. But now Manny was leaving.

"I never said this to you, and I wish I had," Bill said, surprising himself, not sure where the words were coming from but knowing they were as true as anything he'd ever said in his life. "You stayed strong through some tough times with me. Makes me proud whenever I think of you."

And then he turned and got in the car quickly, because from the look on Manny's face, Bill was afraid Manny might start weeping or, god forbid, try to give him a hug.

CHAPTER THIRTY-FOUR

The automatic doors whooshed open barely in time for April. She had gotten used to the slightly antiseptic smell months ago, but she was so excited to get started with what she had planned that she wouldn't have noticed it in any event.

She turned left and hurried down the wide, carpeted hallways. This was one of the first things she liked about the place, one of the reasons she had argued so hard for it: the light beige carpeting, the spacious halls with paintings in frames, the large dining room to the left with cushioned wood chairs and actual tablecloths on the tables, and the activity room to the right, where people could sit in armchairs near a huge fireplace or around card tables playing cards or board games or whatever.

"Still a nursing home, no matter what you call it," her mother replied when April said that the place felt more like a hotel than an assisted-living facility. "Carpet's not going to help him live longer."

April resisted the urge to say, *I'll remember that when it comes time for me to stick you in one of these places.* She had been resisting the urge to say a lot of things these days, now that her mother seemed finally able to get through a day without some subtle reminder of the pain and agony—*Yes, that's the word I mean, young lady,* agony—April had "caused" her last summer. April had argued about it with her at first, insisting it hadn't been that big a deal, that she hadn't been gone long enough to cause anyone enough stress to raise a zit, much less *agony*. But one morning she looked up from her cereal and caught her mother, elbows on the table as she sipped her coffee, staring at her. Her mother quickly shifted her eyes and pretended to be looking out the kitchen window. But in that moment, through the wisps of steam that rose up to the lines of her mother's forehead, April saw something more than agony. She saw a quiet sort of terror.

When April went upstairs, she typed "getting old" at the top of her TITS list. It was the last entry April made on any of her lists. She hardly even thought of them now. When she did, it was usually by accident. She might come across one as she searched for a file or folder on her computer. She might click it open and read it as if she'd come across a picture of her and Heather in seventh grade, mugging for the flashing light in one of those instant photo booths.

Maybe it was that terror that had prevented her mother from punishing her. April assumed she'd be grounded for the rest of high school, but her mother had worked the silent treatment for about a month, never attempting to strike up a casual conversation—a tactic that April had always believed, before the trip, was a guilt-trip tactic her mother used to eventually pry information out of her. But as the first few weeks passed and the only times her mother talked to her was to check on homework or to announce that she was leaving to show a house, April knew that her mother wasn't just using some ploy. She was probably quiet because she was afraid that if she brought up the subject of the trip, she'd relive feelings she never wanted to experience again. It was kind of like the time April woke up one morning—Nebraska? Wyoming?—and discovered that her grandfather had gotten up, left the room, and taken the car keys with him. He had started the motor and was sitting there, with his hand on the gear shift, as if trying to remember if he'd forgotten anything before driving away. April had talked and waited for her grandfather to remember who he was and who she was. For a few terrifying seconds before she found him she was convinced he'd never come back, as if he'd actually driven off and was now lost in the vast expanse of nothingness that surrounded them. She understood that, sometimes, the greatest fear you can have has nothing to do with your own safety.

And so when, about six weeks after the return to Woodlake, her mother had asked her, after another silent dinner, if April was at all interested in going to see a movie with her, April burst into tears and asked—no, begged—her mother to forgive her. Her mother stood, came around the table, and cradled April's head against her stomach until April was quiet. They didn't go to the movies. They sat at the table and talked about what to do with Grandpa.

This is how April knew that the whole process of finding a place for Grandpa to live was so difficult for her mother, even though she sometimes acted—especially when she was on the phone with her brothers, reporting on one or more places she and April had inspected that day—that the whole process was nothing more than another nuisance manufactured by Bill Warrington merely to disrupt everyone's life.

Clifton House was a perfect, unpretentious name, as far as April was concerned. And the community room really was a community room, the dining room really was a place human beings could eat in without contracting some disease eradicated centuries ago, and it was close enough for April to get to on her bike.

April had insisted on being a part of the call with her uncles once they'd settled on the place. Her mother had purchased and installed, with the help of Hank Johnson, a new "home office" phone line with three-way conferencing capabilities. She and her mother sat next to each other at the makeshift desk in the old sewing room, talking into the phone's speaker.

"Sounds expensive," Nick said after Marcy had finished her description of Clifton House. Marcy nodded. No one said anything

"They can't hear you nod, Mom," April said, finally. Then, to the speakerphone: "My mom's nodding, which means she agrees that it's expensive but she also think it's worth every penny, especially considering the other dumps we've checked out. So she's just going to have to sell another house or two. Uncle Nick, you're going to have to write more articles, and Uncle Mike . . . you're just going to have to get a job."

For a moment, there was only the hum of the line through the phone speaker.

"Quickly," April added.

A staticky laugh came through the speaker.

"Just like your mother," a voice said. April knew it was Uncle Mike, but for a moment she thought someone else had joined the call. And then she remembered hearing those exact words before: the first time she visited her grandfather, and he stood at the front door of his house, holding the door open for her. She had a picture in her mind that he was smiling, but chances were he hadn't been.

"I'm in," Uncle Nick said.

"Me, too," said Uncle Mike.

After a pause and a look at April, Marcy said, "So are we."

There were more conference calls as her mother and Uncle Nick made the arrangements to move their father—who put up surprisingly little resistance—and sell the house. April often didn't understand what they were talking about, but she felt it was her duty to be there, just as it was her duty to visit him at least once a week now that he was settled at the home. She usually visited twice, often to share with him a new song she had written for her group, Hidden Agenda. The band—mostly friends of Keith Spinelli's, who for no reason that April could put her finger on went from hot to not in her estimation—wasn't very good. And it wasn't actually *her* band, but they liked her songs.

She'd been so busy with rehearsals and with the surprise she'd been putting together for her grandfather that she hadn't found a chance to get to Clifton House for a little over two weeks.

She found him sitting in front of one of the three floor-to-ceiling shelving units that represented the library collection. He had apparently dragged a folding chair from one of the long tables and placed it where he sat, hands folded in his lap, out in the open. He looked like a schoolboy serving detention.

"That you, Clare?" he called out.

April groaned. There were more and more Clare Days these days. It might take her a while to remind him who she was and where they were. She hoped that today, of all days, he wouldn't be beyond her reach. She knew the day was coming when she'd never get him back.

But, please, god, not today.

"It's me, Grandpa, April," she said, walking to him. "Why are you sitting out here in the middle of the room?"

She leaned over and kissed his cheek. She was surprised at its smoothness. And was that aftershave she smelled? She straightened and smiled as she remembered he was expecting someone. Her grandfather did not smile back.

"Who the hell are you?" he asked. "Where's Clare?"

"Come on, Grandpa. Let's go sit at the table. I've got something to show you."

She reached for his arm. He recoiled.

"Get the hell away from me," he said.

April stared at him, her arm still extended to help him stand. This was a first, a rejection of some sort that April couldn't absorb. She knew this was an off moment for him, that he couldn't help himself.

But after all they'd been through together, after everything she'd done to make sure he ended up in a better place, a place like this, she couldn't help feeling that he was being intentionally cruel. She forced herself to do what she had seen her mother do: just keep talking as if nothing were different, nothing had changed.

"Two surprises for you today, Grandpa," she said, her voice quivering at first. "First, check this out." She dug into her pocket, retrieved her new acquisition, and held it out to him. He looked at it as if he wasn't sure she wanted him to take it. He eventually did, though, his hands looking to April skinnier, more veined, and shakier than even just a few weeks ago.

"What's this?" he asked.

"My driver's license! See? That's me." She pointed to the picture, which had actually turned out pretty well, she thought. She didn't look like a hillbilly or an alien.

"I got it yesterday," she said as her grandfather silently examined it. "The guy who graded me said it was like I'd been driving for years." She waited for a response. "I almost said, uh, yeah—like, practically across the country and back. But I didn't know if there was some sort of statute of limitations on that sort of thing."

Her grandfather continued to stare at the license, although April had a feeling he wasn't even trying to figure out what it was. It was like he wasn't even looking at it.

"Remember when you first started teaching me? And then the accident and the hospital and everything? How you caught hell from Mom?" April waited, growing impatient. "Your daughter, Grandpa. Marcy?"

Her grandfather looked up. April thought she had finally gotten through.

"Where's Clare?" he asked.

April sighed. She had wanted him in one of his sharper moods. And not just so that he could appreciate her getting her driver's li-

cense, but also because Uncle Mike would be there. If he wasn't with
it for Uncle Mike, why would Uncle Mike bother coming to visit
again? She could almost hear her uncle asking that very question.
She had gotten to know him much better, through e-mails and text
messages, as she planned her grandfather's eightieth birthday party.
When she left a voice mail message on his cell phone about coming
to Woodlake, he texted back, asking what a girl about her age would
want as a surprise gift. April thought it was cool that he could text,
but he was obviously confused about whose party he was being invited to.

GPs bday, not mine, she'd texted in reply.

My dgtr, not u, he texted back.

They started exchanging texts and e-mails as the day drew closer,
and April learned that he'd gotten a job somewhere in Chicago selling stuff over the phone—something to do with money was all
April understood. While he never came right out and said it, April
realized through his questions—What bands are popular with boys
today? What kind of store would a girl your age want a gift certificate
from?—that her uncle was trying to win his family back. It didn't
sound like it was going too well.

May b just some face-2-face? she suggested.

Cuz AC will rip it off, he replied. Deservedly so.

The "deservedly so" is what made April like her uncle, even after
she found out from her mother exactly why Aunt Colleen would want
to do him bodily harm.

"Where is she?" her grandfather asked—loudly now. "She's supposed to be here."

The library doors opened. A man entered with his back toward
April and her grandfather as he pulled a wheelchair in. When he
wheeled the chair around, April saw that he was an older man,
dressed impeccably in a tie and tweed jacket, with a white handkerchief peeking up out of the front breast pocket of his jacket.

"Well, look here," he said, his voice deep and friendly. "Bill has a pretty young visitor."

The woman he began pushing forward was apparently too busy scowling to have heard him. She stared off to her left. She, too, was nicely dressed. April had a feeling the man was responsible for that, although he wasn't dressed like the other orderlies. Maybe he was a volunteer.

"Hello, young lady."

April squeaked out a "Hi" as the man wheeled the woman past her. When he reached her grandfather, the gentleman—which was how April was already starting to think of him—turned the chair so that the woman and April's grandfather were sitting side by side.

"Here we are," he said, his voice a gentle roll of thunder, like after a storm.

April lost her breath when she saw her grandfather reach over, take the woman's hand, and hold it between his own.

"Where have you been, Clare?" he asked, in a voice April had never heard. "I've been waiting so long."

The woman's scowl disappeared. She relaxed visibly, as if shedding a winter coat. She smiled. April thought she was watching some sort of miracle cure, proof of something she might hear on television or the radio, a quick medical tip: The simple act of holding hands can add years to your life, turn sour frowns into glowing smiles, release tension from your back and shoulders, help you feel human again.

April realized that she herself had been transformed for a moment. The gentleman was watching her, a small smile on his lips. He offered a small bow.

"My name is Mitchell," he said.

She was caught in one of those strange adult situations where she knew she was supposed to say something simple, like—duh!— "I'm April." But she also knew she was supposed to call the man by his name, but he was too old to call him by his first name. Or was Mitchell his last name? Adults did that, too, sometimes.

Unable to do anything else, she extended her hand. The man smiled, walked to her, and shook it. "Pleased to meet you," he said.

"Keep your goddamn hands off my granddaughter."

April saw that her grandfather was still holding hands with the woman. But he was looking at Mitchell as if he might jump out of the wheelchair and attempt a kung fu kick or something.

"Grandpa!"

Mitchell lifted a hand, his index finger slightly extended, as if to calm her. Or maybe he meant to calm her grandfather. In any case, he addressed him. "Just getting acquainted," he said. "I see you've taught your granddaughter her manners."

"Damn straight," Bill said, glancing sideways at the woman, as if to make sure she'd heard the compliment. She was still smiling at something off in the distance. April thought she saw a squeeze of the hand.

Mitchell smiled and, with a gentle wave of his own hand, motioned for April to follow him. He pulled back a chair for her near a table by a stack of books. As they settled, April whispered, "I'm sorry. He's not like that at all."

"I'm sure he's not, April," he said. "Don't worry."

April looked up.

"How did you know my name?"

The man smiled. He had perfect white teeth to go along with his perfect clothes and perfect manners. "Your grandfather talks a lot about his children. I imagine one of those children is your mother or father?"

April nodded. "Marcy."

Mitchell nodded back knowingly. "But his favorite stories seem to be about his granddaughter. Oh, you should hear him: *April this* and *April that.* I figured you were her. You sound like quite a young lady. I'm so pleased to meet you."

"Same here," April said, wishing she were more polite and polished. "Same here" sounded like she was also pleased to make her own acquaintance. How would she ever get comfortable with this stuff?

"Is it true you told a state trooper to go to hell?" Mitchell asked.

He laughed when April could only shake her head.

"He likes his stories, doesn't he?"

"Tell me about it," April said.

"Oh, I enjoy them," Mitchell said. "Of course, he's not telling them to me. After a while, if I just sit here quietly, he'll start talking. It seems to calm him. More importantly, if you'll forgive me for being selfish . . . they calm my wife."

His wife? April looked at the woman holding her grandfather's hand. What was God trying to do to her? She had come in, fully in control of the day, and now it's just one thing after another knocking her off track. Next thing you knew, Mitchell would reveal that he's her great-uncle.

April couldn't think of a thing to say. Her grandfather was whispering to the woman. The woman was smiling, nodding, staring off. April wondered if she understood the words or if she was just responding to something in her grandfather's voice, something that reminded her of a moment half a century ago or more.

Finally, she spoke up.

"It doesn't bother you? The two of them . . . you know . . . holding hands?"

Mitchell smiled. "As I said, it seems to calm her. At this point, that's all that matters."

April wondered if there was anything she could ever do—would ever do—to match the generosity of this man's willingness to sit and watch his wife of fifty years holding hands with another man, all but unaware that her real husband was in the room, unaware, perhaps, that he had ever even been her husband. Who could bear it?

"I'm never getting married," April muttered. She blushed when she realized how that might sound to Mitchell.

But Mitchell only chuckled. "I suppose I felt the same way when I was your age," he said. "Then I met Clare."

April took this in calmly.

"Her name is Clare? I thought my grandpa was just confused. I mean, sometimes he even calls me Clare."

Mitchell smiled and nodded. "I've been taking Clare to as many of the group events as possible. I kept hoping that being around other people might bring her back out of her . . . distance. So we went to this crossword party they have each week. Your grandfather heard me say her name. After that, there was no silencing him. He had to be with her." Mitchell grew quiet for a few moments. "I knew he was confused, but I have to admit that I was ready to punch him in the nose. But then I noticed that Clare was looking up. She was smiling at your grandfather, just the way she's smiling now."

April looked over to see that Mitchell was right. Clare was smiling like a girl on a first date. Her grandfather was smiling, too. He had stopped whispering, although April was listening so carefully to Mitchell that she had no idea what story her grandfather might be telling now. Mitchell took the perfectly positioned handkerchief from the pocket of his jacket and dabbed at his forehead. He put the handkerchief back carefully, and folded his large hands together on the table.

"I'm grateful to him," he said, simply.

April looked at his hands. It was another of those situations where she knew what to do but there simply wasn't any way to do it without feeling like a doofus. She knew she should reach over and place her hand on top of his, maybe give it a squeeze, and say something profound. If her mother was here—where was she, anyway?—that's what she would do. Mitchell's hands themselves seemed to invite this kind of reaction, folded as they were so calmly and peacefully, even though the knobby knuckles and twisted digits and veins embossed against his dark skin warned that the story wasn't that simple.

They both turned when they heard the doors behind them open. Nick, Mike, April's mother, and Hank Johnson. Hank was carrying the cake; her mother and uncles each held a box covered in bright happy-birthday wrap.

"What in holy hell?" her mother called out. April saw the line, like a laser, from her mother's eyeballs to her grandfather's hand. And Clare's.

April looked at Mitchell. Mitchell gave her a tight, knowing smile.

"We're grateful to him, too," she said.

ACKNOWLEDGMENTS

I am extremely grateful to Penguin Group USA and Amazon for helping make this writer's lifelong dream come true. Special thanks to Tim McCall, Stephanie Sorenson, Jeffrey Belle, Aaron Martin, Kyle Sparks, and Amanda Wilson.

I hit the jackpot a second time when my book landed in the incredibly capable editorial hands of Liz Van Hoose and Molly Stern. Liz, thank you for all those fields of green. I'm also fortunate to have a wonderful literary agent, Rebecca Gradinger, looking out for me.

Much of the book was written while I was enrolled in the Masters of Writing program at Manhattanville College. I benefitted greatly from the insights of both professors and fellow students. Special thanks to John Herman, whose course on novels was the springboard for this one.

I am blessed to have family and friends whose encouragement and support also made this possible. Huge thanks to Sheila O'Brien, John Kennedy, Tom Bingle, Joe Corcoran, and Liz Corcoran.

To Bob King—brother, mentor, friend—here 'tis. Thanks for everything.

Finally, my thanks and love to my first readers: My daughter Katie and son Daniel, both of whom read several drafts of the novel and provided oft-needed reality slaps whenever my prose veered toward the corny or unlikely; and my wife Joanne who, through all the earlier attempts and rejections, never once so much as hinted that maybe it was time to pick a different dream.